William Francis Shaw

Liber Estriae

Or Memorials of the Royal Ville and Parish of Eastry, in the County of Kent

William Francis Shaw

Liber Estriae
Or Memorials of the Royal Ville and Parish of Eastry, in the County of Kent

ISBN/EAN: 9783337039219

Printed in Europe, USA, Canada, Australia, Japan

Cover: Foto ©Andreas Hilbeck / pixelio.de

More available books at **www.hansebooks.com**

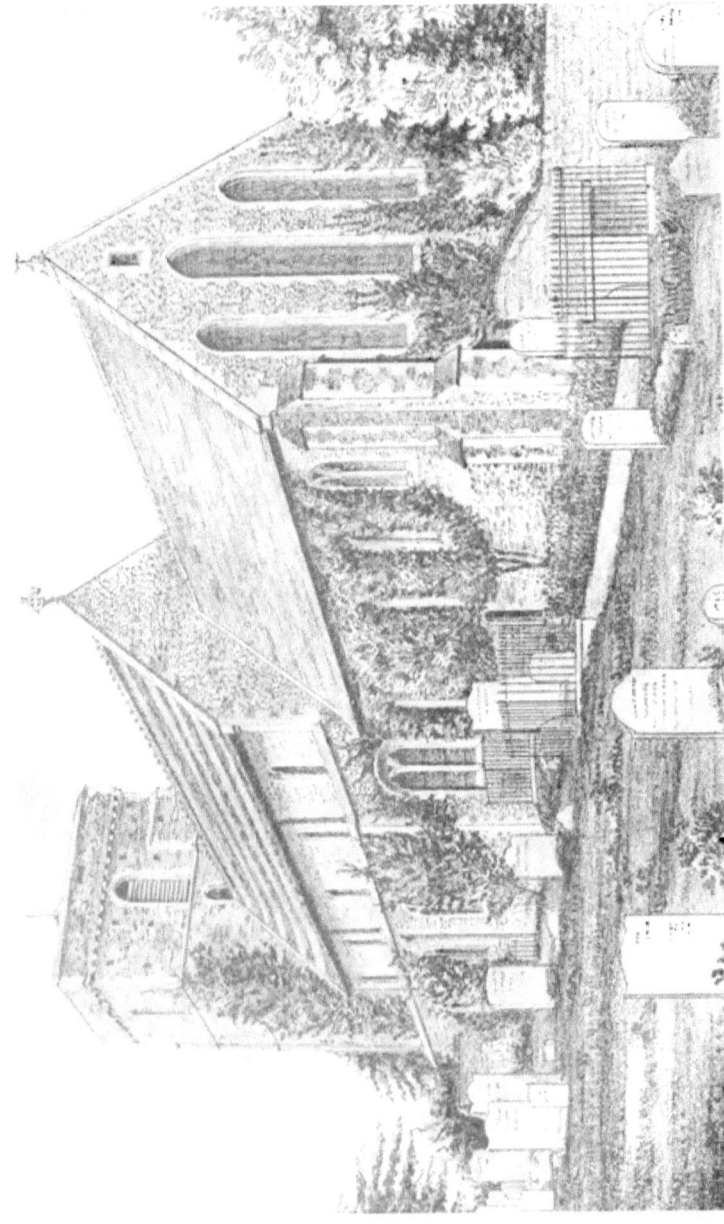

Liber Estriae;

OR

MEMORIALS OF THE ROYAL VILLE

AND PARISH OF EASTRY,

IN THE COUNTY OF KENT.

BY

WILLIAM FRANCIS SHAW, M.A.,

Gonville and Caius College, Cambridge,
Vicar of Eastry.

*" Walk about Sion and go round about her : tell the Towers thereof.
Mark ye well her Bulwarks, consider her Palaces : that ye may tell it to
the generation following."*—PSA. xlviii. 12, 13.

LONDON:

JOHN RUSSELL SMITH, 36, SOHO SQUARE.

MDCCCLXX.

TO

HIS GRACE

THE RIGHT HONOURABLE AND MOST REVEREND

ARCHIBALD CAMPBELL,

LORD ARCHBISHOP OF CANTERBURY,

PATRON OF THE VICARAGE OF EASTRY,

This Volume

IS

(BY HIS GRACE'S KIND PERMISSION)

MOST RESPECTFULLY

DEDICATED.

Preface.

THE following pages, commenced for my own information, shortly after coming to Eaſtry, and continued as the occupation of leiſure hours, were not originally intended for publication. But the indulgent approval of my friends, and the ſtrongly expreſſed wiſh of ſome of them, that the information thus collected ſhould be made more readily acceſſible, and rendered more permanent than it was poſſible for it to be in MS., have induced me to place it in the hands of the printer.

I may briefly ſay then that, in the enſuing chapters, I have endeavoured to gather together ſuch particulars relating to the Pariſh of Eaſtry, as are of general intereſt, or as may be uſeful for reference in time to come. And, in ſo doing, I have largely availed myſelf of the MS. collections of William Boteler, Eſqre., the contemporary of Haſted, the Kentiſh hiſtorian, who derived a large portion of his information about Eaſtry, from the ſame ſource. Theſe collections, contained in three volumes diſtinguiſhed by the letters A, B, C, have been moſt kindly placed at my diſpoſal by the Miſſes Boteler, of Brook Street; to whom my beſt thanks are due both for this act of kindneſs and alſo for much other valuable aſſiſtance, rendered to me in the progreſs of the work. Mr. Boteler's information has been brought down to our own times, and has been ſupplemented in not a few particulars, as for example, in the deſcriptions of the Freſcoes, and of the Dominical Circle, which are taken from two papers on theſe ſubjects by Weſton Styleman Walford, Eſqre., F.S.A.; to whom I am much indebted for his kind and ready permiſſion to inſert them.   To William White, Eſqre., F.S.A., I offer my warm thanks for having read through the chapter on " *The Church*," and given me ſeveral valuable ſuggeſtions ; as alſo to Lieut.-Col. Rae, of Walton Houſe, for information concerning the Bells and Bellfounders.

Chapter VI. on " *The Rectors, Vicars, Chaplains, and Curates*," gives the reſult of a diligent ſearch amongſt the Regiſters in the Archiepiſcopal Library at Lambeth Palace ; where I have experienced great kindneſs and courteſy from all the officials, eſpecially from S. W. Kerſhaw, Eſqre., M.A., the Librarian, to whom I return my moſt ſincere acknowledgments.   To the ſkilful pencil of Miſs Grimaldi, of Hernden Houſe, I am indebted for the very accurate delineation of the Roman and Saxon remains ; to Arthur Baker, Eſqre., for his drawing of the interior of the Church ; to my friend and nameſake, the Rev. William Stokes Shaw, M.A., for the Chronological Table of Events, &c. ; and to other friends, for information and aſſiſtance, hints and ſuggeſtions, without which these " Memorials " would have been more incomplete than they are.   In an undertaking of this kind, carried on from time to time, amidſt many interruptions and the neceſſary preſſure of parochial engagements, it would be hardly poſſible that ſome miſtakes ſhould not have crept in, or ſome omiſſions have been overlooked.   For theſe I crave a kindly indulgence.

Such, however, as it is, I now ſend forth this volume in the words of Geoffry Whitney :—

" *Peruſe with heede, then frendlic iudge and blaming raſhe refraine*
So maiſt thou reade vnto thy good and ſhalt requite my paine."

W. F. S.

Eaſtry Vicarage, 19 Aug., 1870.

The Contents.

List of Illustrations.

List of Subscribers.

Alford, The Very Reverend Henry, D.D. ; *The Deanery, Canterbury.*
Bateman, The Reverend Canon, M.A.,R.D. ; *The Vicarage, Margate.*
Bellamy, The Reverend J. W., B.D. ; *Sellindge Vicarage, Hythe.*
Bliſs, The Reverend J. W., B.A. ; *Betteſhanger Rectory, Sandwich.*
Boteler, Captain J. H., R.N. ; *Cranford, Hounſlow.*
Boteler, Miſs C. G. ; *Eaſtry.*
Boteler, Miſs Catherine ; *Eaſtry.*
Boteler, The Miſſes ; *Dover.*
Bradnack, S. W., Eſq. ; *Sutherland Houſe, Surbiton.*
Brooke, Miſs ; *Walmer.*
Brooke, F. C., Eſq. ; *Ufford, Suffolk.*
Campbell-Colquhoun, A. C., Eſq., J.P. ; *Chartwell, Weſterham.*
Camden, William, Eſq. ; *Anderida, Midhurſt.*   2 Copies.
Catberd-Boteler, W. J., Eſq.; *Taplow, Co. Bucks.*
Caſtle, Robert, Eſq. ; *Eaſtry.*
Chicheſter, The Rev. A. Manners, B.A. ; *St. Mary's Vicarage, Sand-wich.*
Coleman, George, Eſq. ; *Eaſtry.*
Croaſdill, Mrs. ; *Weſtgate Houſe, Canterbury.*
Deane, J. Parker, Eſq., D.C.L. ; *Weſtbourne Terrace, London.*
Deviſon, Mr. R. ; *Eaſtry.*
Drew, The Rev. Profeſſor, M.A. ; *King's College, London.*
Fitzwalter, Lord ; *Goodneſtone Park.*
Furley, Robert, Eſq., *Aſhford.*
Gardner, George, Eſq. ; *Eaſtry Court.*   2 Copies.
Gloſſop, Miſs ; *Iſleworth.*
Grimaldi, Mrs. ; *Hernden Houſe, Eaſtry.*
Harnett, John, Gent. ; *Eaſtry.*
Harvey, John James, Eſq., J.P. ; *Eaſtry.*
Harvey, R. Springett, Eſq. ; *25, Nottingham Place, London.*
Hatfeild, Charles, Eſq. ; *Hartſdown, near Margate.*

Hilton, S. Musgrave, Esq., late High Sheriff; *Bramling Wingham.*
Hoile, Mr. Valentine; *St. Bartholomew's, Sandwich.*
Holmes, The Rev. J. R., M.A.; *Blo Norton Rectory, Co. Norfolk.*
Hughes, William, Esq.; *Margate.*
Iggulden, J., Esq.; *Deal.*
James, Sir Walter C., Bart; *Betteshanger.*
Jenkyns, The Rev. Charles, B.A.; *Tuckingmill, Cornwall.*
Jenkyns, Francis, Esq.; *Sidmouth, Devon.*
Kemplay, Mifs; *Leeds, Co. York.*
King, Mifs; *Gower Street, London.*
Knocker, Edward, Esq.; *Dover.*
Lake, Benj. G., Esq.; *Taywell, Goudhurst.*
Latham, Mrs. A. P.; *Richmond, Co. Surrey.*
Leggatt, R. S., Esq., M.R.C.S.; *Eastry.*
Mann, Mifs; *Eastry.*
Maugham, The Rev. H. M., M.A.; *West Farleigh.*
Morley, James H., Esq.; *Blackheath.*
Musgrave, The Venerable Archdeacon, D.D.; *Halifax, Co. York.*
Parkes, Mrs.; *Sydney Cottage, near Southampton.*
Pearce, Mifs; *Eastry.*
Rae, Lieut.-Col. James A.; *Eastry.*   3 Copies.
Reid, James, Esq.; *Bridge Street, Canterbury.*
Rice, Edward, Esq., J.P.; *Dane Court, Sandwich.*
Sayer, Commander G., R.N., J.P.: *Eastry.*
Shaw, William Flamank, Esq.; *Bodmin, Cornwall.*   2 Copies.
Shaw, The Rev. William S., M.A.; *Beechen Cliff Villa, Bath.*
Shaw, The Rev. John, M.A.; *St. Margaret's, Westminster.*
Smallfield, Mr. J. S.; *Little Queen Street, Holborn.*
Smith, The Rev. Sydney, M.A.; *Worth Vicarage.*
Solly, Edward, Esq.; *Sandecotes, Co. Dorfet.*
Spong, Mifs; *Rochester.*
Taylor, Mrs. Jackfon; *The Grove, Garlinge, near Margate.*
Toker, Mifs; *Eastry.*   2 Copies.
Turner, Mrs. Charles, *Eastry.*   2 Copies.
Vickers, The Rev. V. S.; *Debtling.*
Weft, F. G., Esq.; *Horham Hall, Thaxted, Effex.*
Winn, Charles, Esq.; *Noftel Priory, Wakefield.*

The Early History of Eastry.

CHAP. I.

" If man be cut off from the knowledge of the paft, he becomes indifferent to the future, and thenceforward finks into the rudenefs and ferocity of the fenfual life.—
ISAAC TAYLOR.

E ASTRY is the name of a parifh in the hundred of Eaftry, and Lathe of S. Auguftine, in the county of Kent.

Speaking ecclefiaftically it is in the rural deanery of Sandwich, and in the archdeaconry and diocefe of Canterbury.

The name *Eaftry*—which has been varioufly fpelled Eftre, Eftree, Eftrei, Eftrey, Eftry, Eftrye, Eaftrie, Eaftire, Eafterige, Eaftereye, Eafterye, Eaftrye—was originally given, fo Lambarde tells us, to our town and parifh, in order to diftinguifh them from *Weftrye*, commonly called *Rye*, near Winchelfea, in Suffex. But others derive the word from the Saxon, and interpret it as meaning *below the side water*.

The village, which is fituated on rifing ground, two and a half miles from the ancient town and port of Sandwich, five from Deal, nine from Dover, and twelve from Canterbury—was, in olden time, a place of confiderable importance and repute.

Long before the coming of the Saxons, the Danes, or the Normans,

B

into Britain; when Thanet was ſtill an iſland, and ſhips and galleys coming from France ſailed paſt Sandwich and Reculver into the Thames and thence to London ; when the country was moſtly covered with denſe foreſts, which afforded ſhelter to bears, wolves, wild cats, and foxes, and amid whoſe leafy glades the red deer and the wild ox roamed at will; when the beacon light ſtill burnt in the Roman pharos at Dover (DUBRIS) ; already was there at Eaſtry a "clearing" amidſt the foreſt, where had ſprung up a little ſettlement of huts, through which ran, ſtraight as an arrow, that Roman road, which may even now be traced, almoſt uninterruptedly from Woodneſborough well nigh to the caſtle at Dover.

Whether the early inhabitants of this place were attracted hither by the medicinal properties and healing virtues of that mineral ſpring, in after days dedicated to S. Ivo, which cannot now be traced, and of which the tradition has alone come down to us in books, it is impoſſible to ſay. At all events, whatever value the Britons and the Romano-Britiſh inhabitants may have ſet upon this S. Ivo's well, the Romans muſt have been well acquainted with the woody eminences and pure invigorating air of Eaſtry. And we may well ſuppoſe that the officers of the legions ſtationed at the camp at Richborough (RUTUPIÆ) often came hither to ſpend a day away from the noiſe and buſtle of the camp, or ſtopped here to refreſh themſelves as they travelled down along the paved military road to Dover.

But, be this as it may, the fact of there having been a Roman ſettlement here is proved by the Roman graves, containing human bones, weapons, and ornaments, which have been diſcovered, from time to time, in that triangle of ground, in the pariſh, which is formed by the Lynch, " the Five Bells," and Buttſole Pond. The firſt recorded diſcovery of theſe remains took place A.D. 1792, and the account of it will be beſt given in Mr. Boteler's own words : " In March laſt (1792), in digging a cellar in the garden of a cottage belonging to me, eaſtward of the highway leading from Eaſtry Croſs to Butſole, I diſcovered the ancient burying ground of this neighbourhood. I cauſed ſeveral graves to be opened, and found, with the ſkeletons, fibulæ, beads, knives, umbones of ſhields, &c., in one an elegant glaſs veſſel. From other ſkeletons that have been dug up in the gardens nearer the Croſs, I am of opinion that they extended on this ſide the road up to the Croſs, now covered pretty much with houſes. I mean at a future time to purſue the diſcovery. The tumuli that formerly covered them have long ſince been levelled by the plough. The graves were very thick, in rows parallel to each other, in a direction from eaſt to weſt " (*Botel. MSS., vol. C. p.* 164).

Since Mr. Boteler's day other ſimilar remains have been brought to light at different times ; and, about the year 1860 or 1861, in the making of some alterations in and around *Southbank,* ſkeletons were diſcovered lying in clay in the bed of chalk.

Several of the objects diſcovered by Mr. Boteler, in A.D. 1792, as well as other ſimilar remains—Roman and Saxon—found on the ſame property, and near the ſame ſpot, are repreſented in the accompanying plates. They may be deſcribed as follows :

Nos. 1 and 2. Coarſe brown earthen pots with more or leſs of narrow moulding about them.

Nos. 3, 4 and 5. Portions of *ſeveral* Saxon veſſels made of thin glaſs of greeniſh colour : each veſſel or vaſe having apparently had ſeveral handles, which are twiſted. Vaſes ſimilar to the above are figured in the *Archæologia Cantiana,* vol. vi.

No. 6. A bronze fibula or brooch—full ſize.

No. 7. A ſmaller bronze fibula—full ſize.

No. 8. A fibula of filver gilt, with inlays of red and blue enamel—full fize.

No. 9. A ftring of beads of various kinds.

No. 10. A ftring of amber beads—much worn.

No. 11. A ftring of pearls and bugles.

No. 12. A large glafs bead of conical fhape, with internal pattern of twifted glafs.

" Almoft all the beads, particularly the larger ones of amber, &c., and the fmall ones, bugles, &c., round the neck, found in a grave, the bones full large for a woman, though probably one."[*]

There were alfo knives, umbones of fhields, circular pieces of brafs, and fome other fragments difcovered—fome of which I have been unable to identify, whilft others, though capable of being identified, are nevertchelefs in fuch a decayed and crumbling condition as to be beyond the reach of the limner's art.

In Anglo-Saxon times Eaftry would appear to have been a place of fome fize and much importance. Indeed, the fact that the kings of Kent had a palace, and held their court here, would naturally caufe a confiderable population to affemble in the neighbourhood of the court, and increafe the profperity of the town.

During the reign of Ethelbert the 5th King of Kent, Chriftianity, which had been driven into the remote wilds and faftneffes of Wales and Cornwall, was revived by the miffion of S. Auguftine, the monk.

In A.D. 664 Egbert, the fon of Erconbyrht, feventh king of Kent, fucceeded to his father's kingdom, and took up his refidence at the royal palace at Eaftry. This palace was probably fituated on much the fame fpot as that now occupied by *Eaftry Court.*

---

[*] A memorandum in Mr. Boteler's handwriting.

ANTIQUITIES FOUND AT EASTRY.

full size

full size

5 inches

5½ in by 3 in

3¼ in by 3 in

5 in by 5¼ in

5⅞ in by

ANTIQUITIES FOUND AT EASTRY.

half the size of the Originals.

At this place, and at this time, there lived two young noblemen, named Ethelbert and Etheldred, coufins of the king, who lived in the palace, ate at his table, and were brought up with him. Thefe noble youths were adorned with many virtues, and became noted for their learning, their feats of activity and ftrength, and their court-like manners, " fo that they gave to all well-difpofed perfons and louers of vertue, great expectation that they would become at the length worthie of much eftimation and honour : and, on the other fide, they drew vpon them the feare, mifliking and bitter hatred of the naughtie, wicked and malicious fort."* Now, there was among the royal houfehold "a certain man of fin and fon of perdition, a limb of Satan and of the houfe of the devil,"† who moved by that envy which the wicked ever feel towards the good, fought occafion againft them, and ceafed not to accufe them untruly to the king, as alfo of other matters, fo efpecially of ambitious defigns upon his throne and kingdom. One day Thunner, for fuch was his name, fuggefted to the king that he fhould either banifh the young princes from his dominions, or be content to wink at the matter, fhould any of his friends make away with them. The king, though in *words* he repudiated the idea, feems, neverthelefs, by his *manner*, to have been not wholly averfe to the fuggeftion. At all events, Thunner [or Thunur, as Simeon of Durham has it, and which he explains to mean " Thunder] watched his opportunity, flew the young men, "and buried their bodies in the king's hal vnder the cloth of his eftate."‡ But " murder will out," and this was not long concealed, " for in the dead of night there appeared

---

* Lambarde's *Perambulation of Kent*, ed. 1596 : *Eaftrie.*

† Simeon of Durham : in Stevenfon's *Church Hiftorians of England*, vol. iii. part 2.

‡ Lambarde.

.   .   .   .   .   . a glittering pillar of light fhining over the hall of the king's palace."* The ftrange illumination firft aroufed the houfehold, and then affrighted them. The fhrieks of the fervants awakened the king, who, as foon as he faw the myfterious light, " was touched with the confcience of the murther, whereunto hee had a little before in hart confented."† Calling in hafte for Thunner, he ftraightly examined him as to what had become of the royal youths Ethelbert and Etheldred, and on learning the fad truth, he became moft forrowful, charging himfelf with the whole crime of their death. Forthwith he fent for Deodatus, the good archbifhop, that he might learn from him how he might expiate his guilt. The archbifhop advifed him to incoffin the bodies and fend them to be buried in Chrift Church, Canterbury ; but, when they attempted to go thither, no force availed to move the hearfe. They next bethought them of S. Auguftine's, but ftill the hearfe could not be moved. But when, at laft they agreed to lead it to the monaftry of Watrine, then it moved as lightly as if nothing at all had been within it.

Philipott, in his *Villare Cantianum*, p. 148, fays, " there was an ancient tradition that that altar-tomb, which was placed at the eaft end of the little chappel, which belonged to *Eaftry Court*, was the fepulchre wherein the reliques of the two princes (mentioned before, to have been mur- dered) were enfhrined : nay, it went farther, and did affirm that there was a light hovered conftantly about that tomb, as if the clearneffe of the innocence of thofe who flumbered under that repofitory could not have been manifefted better then [*fic*] by the beams of fuch a perpetuated irradiation."

To thofe who wifh for a detailed account of the murder of Ethelbert and Etheldred I would recommend the chronicle of *Simeon of Durham,*

---

* Simeon of Durham : in Stevenfon.　　　† Lambarde.

and *Lambarde*, who profeffes to quote *William of Malmsbury* and *Matthew of Westminster*. After much fearch I have, however, been unable to verify his references, and think that he may allude to *Simeon of Durham*.

My apology for having dwelt at fuch length upon this event is, that in many writers, e.g., Lambarde, the whole hiftory of our parifh is fummed up in the narration of this fingular occurrence. It fhows, at leaft, what a ftrong hold the ftory had upon the popular mind.

The profperity, and confequent importance of Eaftry, would feem to have reached their zenith in the early Anglo-Saxon times, when the kings of Kent refided here. For after the confolidation of the feveral independent kingdoms into one monarchy under Egbert, in A.D. 827, Eaftry gradually ceafed to be the refidence of royalty until, in A.D. 979, the reigning fovereign beftowed his palace at Eaftry, and the manor pertaining to it, upon the monks of Chrift Church. And fo it came to pafs, that the court being no longer held here, and the town being lefs reforted to than formerly, its population diminifhed, and its profperity and renown decreafed.

The Archbifhops of Canterbury would appear to have become poffeffed of Eaftry in very early times, for, in A.D. 811, we find Archbifhop Wilfrid exchanging the ville of Eaftria for Burne or Bourne, fince called Bifhopfbourne, from this circumftance.[*]

Again, in A.D. 844, in the time of Archbifhop Ceolnoth, Duke Ofwolf gave fome lands in Eaftrie to the prior and convent of Chrift Church, Canterbury;[†] but thefe lands may have been in the hundred of Eaftry, and not in the ville or parifh.

In A.D. 979 King Ethelred increafed the church's eftates here by giving

[*] Dugdale, *Monaft. Angl.*, vol. i., p. 96.

[†] Dugdale, *Monaft. Angl.*, vol. i., p. 89.

Sandwich for the clothing of the monks ("ad veftitum monachorum ")
and Eftrey "ad cibum monachorum ;" that is fay, for the maintenance of
the kitchen.   The following is the charter by which the king confirmed
his gift :

"Anno dominice incarnationis dcccclxxix Ego Ægelredus rex gratia dei
totius britannie monarcha pro falute anime mee concedo ecclefie chrifti in
dorobernia terras juris mei s. sandwich et eftree ad opus monachorum
in eadem ecclefia deo fervientium, liberas ab omni feculari fervitio et
fifcali tributo, exceptis expeditione, pontium et caftrorum conftructione.
Quisquis hanc meam largifluam munificentiam violare prefumpferit cum
reprobis in die judicii a finiftris chrifti collocatus accipiat fententiam
dampnationis cum diabolo et angelis ejus."[*]

Tranflation of the foregoing :

"In the year of our Lord's incarnation 979, I, Ethelred, King,
Monarch of all Britain, for the fafety of my foul, give to Chrift's
Church, Canterbury, the Lands of my Right, to wit, in Sandwich and Eftree
to the ufe of the monks ferving God in the fame church free from all fecular
fervice and fifcal tribute ; [military] expeditions, and the conftruction of
bridges and camps, only excepted.   Whoever fhall prefume to violate this
my bountiful munificence let him be placed with the wicked at the Day
of Judgment at the left hand of Chrift, and receive the fentence of dam-
nation with the Devil and his angels."

Concerning the original of the foregoing charter of King Ethelred,
(*Botel. MSS., vol. A., p. 44*) remarks : "This very curious deed is preferved
in the archives of the library of the College of S. John the Baptift, at the
beginning of a collection of very ancient manufcripts in Latin (fhelf 2, No.

---

[*] The above, although given in Dugdale, *Monaft. Angl.*, vol. i. p. 111, is, neverthelefs here extracted from Mr. Boteler's MSS., as being apparently more accurate.

40): it is written in two columns, the Latin on one fide and a Saxon verfion on the other, with the figure of King Ægelred prefixed.

A facfimile engraving was made of it, 1754, at the expenfe of Richard Rawlinfon, LL.D., F.R.S., and A.S."

We now come to Norman times.

Philipott, in his *Villare Cantianum* (p. 148) fays: " In the time of Edward the Confeffor this mannor was held by the monks of *Chrift-Church* under the Notion of Seven Plough-Lands, nor was it reprefented under a leffe Bulke in the reign of *William* the Conquerour, and was rated in the Whole in *Doomfday Book*, at Thirty-Eight pounds Ten fhillings and Threepence."

Neverthelefs, Doomfday Book expreffly ftates that the *archbifhop himfelf held* Eftrei : but this would appear to refer to the *Rectory*, and not to the *Manor*.

But before proceeding to give the extract, which relates to our own parifh, it may not be wholly uninterefting to fome of my readers to have a fhort account of that very ancient, remarkable, and valuable record—the Doomfday Book.   It contains the refults of a furvey made by order of King William, the Norman, about the year A.D. 1086. For the execution of this furvey, the king's jufticiaries were to go into every county and " enquire into the name of the place, who held it in the time of King Edward, who was the prefent poffeffor, how many hides in the manor, how many carrucates in demefne, how many homagers, how many villans, how many cotarii, how many fervi, what free men, how many tenants in focage, what quantity of wood, how much meadow and pafture, what mills and fifhponds, how much added or taken away, what the grofs value in King Edward's time, what the prefent value, and how much each free man or foch man had or has.   All this was to be triply

c

eftimated : firſt as the eſtate was held in the time of the Confeſſor ; then as it was beſtowed by King William ; and thirdly, as its valuation ſtood at the formation of the ſurvey."

The following deſcription of Eaſtry occurs in Doomſday Book under the general heading " Terra Monachm̄ Archiepi," i.e., " The Land of the Monks of the Archbiſhop."

(i) In Latin : with the original contractions.

" In Leſt de Eſtreia. In Eſtrei Hvnd. Ipſe archieps. ten. Eſtrei. P. vii. folins ſe detd. Tra. ē. . . . . . . In dn̄io ſunt. iii. car. et lxxii uitti cū .xxii. bord. hn̄t. xxiiii. car. Ibi .i. molin̄ et dimid de xxx folid, et .iii. ſalinæ de .iiii. folid. et xviii. ac̄ pti Silua .x. porc."*

(ii) Tranſlation of the above.

" In the Lathe of Eaſtry. In Eaſtry Hundred. The archbiſhop himſelf holds Eaſtry. It was taxed at 7 fulings.† The [arable] land is . . . . . In the demeſne there are 3 carucates ‡ and 72 villeins with 22 borderers§ having 24 carucates. There is one mill and a half of 30 ſhillings, and 3 ſalt pits of 4 ſhillings and 18 acres of meadow. Wood for [the pannage of] 10 hogs."

---

* See Domeſday Book of Kent—photozincographic facſimile, p. ix. : alſo Haſted, vol. iv.

† Concerning the word *ſuling* or *ſwollyng*, Du Cange ſtates that it was a Kentiſh term for *carruca*, a carucate or plough land.

‡ Dr. Deering, in his *Hiſtorical Account of Nottingham* (Introd. p. 8, note *b*), thus explains the term carucate : " Carucat with the Normans is the ſame as family manſe or hide of the Saxons, it is at a medium computed 100 acres, ſix ſcore to the 100, of arable land, together with paſture and meadow, with barns, ſtables, and dwellings for ſuch a number of men and beaſts as were neceſſary to manage ſo much land. But as ſome ſoil is lighter and ſome ſtiffer, ſo the quantity may be more or leſs, and therefore by it is generally underſtood, as much land as, with one plough and beaſts ſufficient, could be tilled in one year."

§ Borderers or borders, our modern " boarders," were bondſmen, whoſe food was provided for them by their lord : hence the term.

From the above ſtatement we may make a rough gueſs at the population of Eaſtry in the thoſe days. For taking the number of villeins and borders; and multiplying by 3 (inſtead of 5, in order to allow of ſome being unmarried) to arrive at the groſs population, i.e., men, women, and children, we have the following reſult, viz. :

Villani or villeins	=	72
Bordarii or borders	=	22
		—
Male population	=	94

And 94 × 3 = 282; or, *in round numbers*, 300, which we ſhall not be far wrong in accepting as the number of our population in or about the year A.D. 1086. For further and more recent particulars reſpecting the population of our pariſh, ſee under " *The Bounds.*"

A hundred years later, viz., in the time of *Thomas a Becket* (A.D. 1162-1174) Eaſtry again comes into notice; for the Court Lodge belonging to the prior and convent of Chriſt Church was a very favourite reſort of that bold and unflinching Archbiſhop of the Church, and martyr in her cauſe. Hither he came in his flight from Northampton, in A.D. 1164, and here he remained concealed for eight days, until, on the 10th November, he embarked in a fiſhing boat at Sandwich, and landed the ſame evening at Gravelines.* In this houſe, now called *Eaſtry Court*, tradition affirms that there was a ſmall ſecret chamber, communicating with the pariſh church, in ſuch a way that the archbiſhop was able to attend the celebration of the Holy Euchariſt, and to give the final benediction at

---

* " At Lincoln he took the diſguiſe of a monk, dropped down the Witham to a hermitage in the fens belonging to the Ciſtercians of Sempringham ; thence by croſs roads and chiefly by night, he found his way to Eſtrey about five miles from Deal, a Manor belonging to Chriſt Church in Canterbury. He remained there a week. On All Souls' Day he went on board a boat juſt before morning, and by the evening he reached the coaſt of Flanders." (*Milman's Lat. Chriſtianity*, vol. v., p. 64).

the conclusion of the liturgy, unknown to the congregation, or at leaft unrecognifed by them.

On his return to England, in A.D. 1170, he landed at Sandwich, where the common people of the neighbourhood, including doubtlefs many of the inhabitants of our own parifh, received him with great joy.

About the year A.D. 1180 the parfonage of Eaftry was given to the monks of *Chrift Church*, for the ufe and maintenance of the Almonry, by Archbifhop Richard (A.D. 1174-1185); but was taken away from them by his fucceffor Baldwin (A.D. 1185-1193) in a very few years after. For 165 years the parfonage, thus unjuftly wrefted from the prior and convent, continued in the poffeffion of the archbifhops until A.D. 1365, when Archbifhop Simon Iflip (A.D. 1349-1366) reftored it to the monks on receiving from them the advowfons of three churches, viz., S. Dunftans, S. Pancras, and All Saints, in Bread Street, London; but he dying the very next year the arrangement of the whole was finally fettled by Archbifhop Simon Langham (A.D. 1366-1368), in A.D. 1367. For this Inftitution and Endowment of the Vicarage, see *Appendix.*

In A.D. 1275 *Ofwald de Eaftria*, whom we may fuppofe from his name to have been a native of our parifh, was appointed abbot of the monaftery of Faverfham by the Archbifhop of Canterbury (Kilwardby, A.D. 1273-1279).*

In A.D. 1285 *Henry de Eaftria*, a native of this our parifh, was elected to the high office of prior of the convent of *Chrift Church, Canterbury*, and proved himfelf in every way fitted for that arduous and refponfible pofition.

He was a man of fingular prudence, well learned in Holy Scripture, and moft diligent in the management of the affairs of the Church, to which

* Taken from the Regifters or other MSS. at Lambeth, though there is no reference to the exact paffage in my note book.

he was a confiderable benefactor. He difcharged the convent of a debt of 3000 marks = £2000: a fum much larger in thofe days than in our own. He alfo caufed all, or nearly all, the domeftic chapels on the manors belonging to the prior and convent to be rebuilt, as alfo the butteries. The remains of the domeftic chapel at *Eaftry Court* may ftill be feen. But its ufe has long fince been changed from things fpiritual to things temporal, for it is now a part of the kitchen !

At Canterbury, Henry de Eaftria fpent nearly £900 in repairing the choir and chapter houfe (*Dugdale, Monaft. Anglican.*, vol. i., p. 112). He alfo built or repaired many parts of the priory. He caufed an exact account to be taken of the lands, income, treafures, veftments, plate and ornaments of the church, and was himfelf a very great benefactor to it in plate, jewels, veftments, and books. To thofe who are curious in fuch matters, and wifh for further information refpecting our prior, I may mention two MSS., one in the Britifh Mufeum (Cottonian Library, Galba E. 4), and the other in the library at Lambeth Palace (MS. No. 582, art. 157), which relate to Henry of Eaftry, but are fomewhat beyond the limit of thefe pages. This good man at length fell afleep in Chrift, at the time of the celebration of the Holy Eucharift, being of the advanced age of 92 years.

Some time before A.D. 1290, another native of this parifh, viz., Sir *Robert de Eftre* was rector of the parifh of Henley-upon-Thames. And it was during his incumbency that " Edmund Earl of Cornwall gave to God, the bleffed Mary, and to the church of Henley, and to Sir Robt. de Eftre, the rector, two acres of land at Henley Park, and two acres near the river" (*Burn's Hift. of Henley*, pp. 132, 134). He feems to have refigned the rectory of Henley in A.D. 1290, but I have not been able to difcover anything refpecting his fubfequent hiftory.

In A.D. 1289 a furvey was made by a bailiff and 12 lawful men appointed by the commiffioners of fewers of all the lands in the Hundreds of Eaftry and Cornilo lying in peril of the fea, in order that an affeffment might be raifed to repair the banks, &c., of thofe lands. The following were the lands particularifed in the Hundred of Eaftry :—

	acres.
The prior and convent of Chrift Church, Canterbury	cccciii
The tenants of Halklyng	lx
The tenants of Worth	xc
Likewife towards Henelyng	iii
The field called Herynglond	x
The field adjoining to Herynglond on the north	xv
In one marfh called Gareftoft	xxv
In the marfh called Stapynberghe	cviii
In the marfh called Preftmed*	xv
In the marfh from Hamme Bridge to the curtilage of Jⁿᵒ· Feyking	l
Sir Bertram Frauncrey and his tenants	lviii
John Fitz Bernard	xl
Nicholas de Sandwyche	lxxxix
The heirs of Simon de Ercheflo	l
Thos. Edwards and his partners at Sanddowne	cxxxiv
The heirs of Henry de Schenebroke	vi
Total number of acres	mclvi
Total of the affeffment	xxivˡ. jˢ. viijᵈ.†

In A.D. 1317 the prior of *Chrift Church* obtained a grant of "free warren" in all his demefne lands in the manor of Eaftry.

In the xviii year of King Edward, the Third after the Conqueft, (A.D. 1343-4), a deed‡ granting 10s. to the Almonry of *Chrift Church* from lands in Eaftry, executed by *Joanna Jofep* is witneffed by "Thom. Taylor . . . . Prykke— Nich. Sompe—Ed. Holkebon—Will. Godwyn—Hen. Goodwyne— Joh. atte Wood—Joh. Baily—Tho. Peke—Sam. Holkebon —and others," who would feem to have been inhabitants of this parifh.

---

* Prefumed apparently = Prieft's Mead.   † *Botel. MSS. A. p.* 57.

‡ From the *Chartæ Mifcellan.* at Lambeth ; vol. v. No. 28.

Some of the above names flourished in this neighbourhood for many centuries, and some of them are borne even to this day.

In A.D. 1356, a dispute having arisen between *William de Cusynton*, rector of this parish, and Richard de Monyngham, vicar of *S. Mary's, Sandwich*, the bounds and limits of our parish were carefully sought out and ascertained by Richard Cook, Thomas Wade, Adam Prikke, William Godewyn, William Goft, John Clerk, and Thomas Rulbone. A translation of the document, which sets forth the bounds of the parish of *Eastry* is given hereafter under " *The Bounds*."

In a valuation of the spiritualities and temporalities of the priory of *Christ Church, Canterbury* made about A.D. 1384, we find the church of *Eastry*—i.e., the rectorial portion of it—appropriated to the alms of the said priory and valued at £53 6s. 8d.[*]

On the xxi December, A.D. 1392, (in the time of Archbishop Courtney) a general ordination was celebrated in the parish church of Croydon when we find,[†] amongst the list of subdeacons, the name of a native of this parish, viz. :—

Thomas Gerard de pochia de Eastry Cantuariẽ dioc̄ ad titulum prioris et conventu de lewes[‡] ledes ordinis sancti Augustini Cant. dioc.

Again, on the xxvi of March, A.D. 1393, Thomas Gerard was ordained deacon in the parish church of Croydon, on the title of the Prior and Convent of Ledes Priory. And on the xxxi May, A.D. 1393, in the parish church of " Maydeston," the same Thomas Gerard was advanced to the holy order of priesthood.

In A.D. 1400, amongst other temporalities of the prior and convent of

---

[*] Dugdale, *Monast. Angl.*, vol. i., p. 89.   [†] Reg. Courtney, f. 181.

[‡] This word *lewes* is underlined with a dotted line, in the original, by a later hand.

Chriſt Church, we find a valuation of "The Manor of Eſtrey with the appurtenances* £65. 03s. 00d."

The following rental of the manor of Eaſtry, extracted from records in Chriſt Church, Canterbury, is taken from the Boteler MSS., *vol. A. p.* 159; and is intereſting as giving us the names of ſome of the inhabitants of Eaſtry, and the neighbourhood, in and about the year A.D. 1445.

Rentale dominii de Eaſtry anno dom. 1445.

Rentale de Eaſtry.

Imprimis de Willo Stevedey vĉt. pz [videlicet pretio?]	lxjˢ iij^d q.
de Willo Byllyngton modo Joh. Boteler	ijˢ x^d
de hered Robti hey	ijˢ viij^d
de Thoma Tomlyn Bocher	xiij^d q.
de hered Johis Bartelot pro j acra terre	v^d
de Robto Bartelot	xij^d
de Johe Odle senʳ	vj' j gallin.
Thoma att Welle	j^d ob.
Johanna Barfeld	iiijˢ v^d ob. q.
Henrico Bakar Smyth	viij^d
Rico att Worde	ijˢ
Johe Swayne	iiijˢ v^d j gallin.
hered Laurencii Cundy	viijˢ vij^d
Thoma Benet	j^d
Johe Bokelonde	vˢ ob.
Willo Dykes	xvjˢ j gallin.
Rico Pyfyng	iiij^d q.
Johe Wolwych	v^d
xvˢ x^d ob. q. Johe ffrenne	
xxix^ ix^d ob. q. Rogo^d ffrenne	
Thoma Palmer	xixˢ vij^d ob. q.
De Willo ffurner	xvj^d ob.
hered Carpintarii	xx^d ob. q.
Colyn frenthman	vj^d
Thoma Lorchon	vj^d

* Dugd., *Monaſt. Angl.*, vol. i p. 88.

Thoma Godyn	iiij^s q.
viij^d Matylda Thachar	nil.
Jacobo Holkebon	iiij^s x^d
Johe Dene	iiij^s vj^d iij gallin.
he^r. Whytpeſe	j^d ob.
Stepho Dene	ij^d
Thoma Chyrche	ix^d
Johe Boteler de Sandwico pro terris Garwynton	xvij^s ij^d
Willo. Dene	ij^d
Rico Byrcholte	ij^s
Walto. Langle pro terris juxta Northcourte	vij^s iiij^d
xij^s eodem Walto.	
Johe Whytſton	iiij^s j^d
Robto Dene	vj^d
Tho. Tomly	xiij^d q.

Summa — ix lib. vj^s x^d ob. q.

Summ. gallin. vj, prec. —xviij^d

FELDYRLAND.

De Edwardo Setvans pro terris ſuis	xxxiij^s
De Ric. Coke de Sandewyco pro terris nuper Thome Kempe	ij^s vj^d
eodem pro terris propriis	vj^s xj^d
Willo Symnet de Sandewico	vj^s vij^d
Johe Dunmowe de Sandewico	xxiij^d
Thoma Boye de Sandewico	vij^d ob. ix^d q. di. q^r.
Willo Bryan pro terris ſuis apud Statyngbergh	(nil.)
Willo Fenell draper de Sandewico	vj^s iij^d
Rico Symnet Folſthawe de Sandewico	viij^d ob.
Simone Ruddock de Sandewico	iiij^s
Thoma Leueryk de Sandewico	xxj^d
Thoma Weſtclyve de Sandewico	iij^s ij^d
Robto Whyte de Sandewico	ij^s vj^d
Thoma Langle de Sandewico Taylor	iiij^s ix^d ob.
Valentina Hepys de Sandewico	ij^s v^d
Willo Edwards de Sandewico brewer	vj^d

D

Henrico Broke bocher de Sandewico	ix^d
Henrico Baker de Sandewico	vj^d
Johe Terry de Sandewico bocher	v^d
Witto Grygory de Sandewico grocer	ij^s vj^d
Witto Chylton de Cantuar	xv^d
Johe Cartar de Sandewico brewer	x^d
Cecilia Sanders de Sa. m°. Synnet	vj^d ob.
Hofpitale Sci Barthi juxta Sandewic	xvj^s
Thoma Broke de Sandew. draper	ij^s ix^d ob. q.
under p°. vj acr. & j virgat. terre	ij^s vij^d q.
p°. hered. Nichi Dene de Sandewico	xv^d
Johe Grene de Sandewico marchant	xxxix^s ij^d
Robto Dyer de Sandewico (nil)	
Johe Gerard de Sandewico bocher	xxj^d ob.
Joh. Gyffard de Sa. fpicer	j^d
Joh. Plmar de Sa. draper	vij^s iiij^d ob. q.
Thoma Bolle de Sa. brewer	iij^s iiij^d
Robto Dreylond pro terris fuis juxta	
Sand. m°. Ric Cok	viij^s
Rogo Clytherowe armigero	xxij^s

Summa   viij^{lib}—xvij^s—iiij^d q. di. q.

Ultra x^s refolut. Clytherowe ad cur. s. de Poldre pro Monketon keye Sandewic.

GORE.

De Will Baxe	x^d	De Rob. Dane	vj^d q.
Thoma Roger pro terra Elwyn xiiij^d ob. q.			
Henr. Walter pro terris Joh. Bafele	v^d	Summa	iij^s

Worth—de Cantaria Thoma Elys lxvij^s iij^d Summa vj^{lib} xix^s ob. di. q.

Opdowne   Summa viij^s ij^d ob. gallin ij prec. vj ovor. xxv. j ob.

    ✻   *   *   *   *

Henry the VI, in the 28th year of his reign (A.D. 1450) confirmed to
the prior the right of " free warren " in the lands of his manor at Eaftry,

and alſo granted a market to be held at Eaſtry weekly on a Tueſday, and likewiſe an annual fair to be held on the Feaſt of S. Matthew the Apoſtle and Evangeliſt. The weekly market has fallen into diſuſe, for how long time I cannot ſay; but the fair is ſtill held on old S. Matthew's day (Oct. 2nd), in the field oppoſite *Southbank*, and called *the Fair Field*, from ancient date. This is now-a-days chiefly a cattle fair, and is *very far* from being ſuch an advantage as it was when the right was originally granted.

In A.D. 1488 (*Reg. Morton*, f. 49 b) we find under the heading of the " Tenths of the Prior and Chapter of *Chriſt Church, Canterbury*," the following returns relating to our pariſh :—

> " Ecclia de Eaſtry in decanam de Sandwich tax   xliij^s. vj^s. viij^d."

And a little further on in the ſame regiſter (f. 56 b) a return for the Deanery of Sandwich, which ſeems to relate to a ſubſidy granted to the king, and which I extract in ſo far as it relates to Eaſtry :—

> " Vicār de Eaſtry   x^{li}
> Decima   xl^s."

From *Stevens' Monaſticon* (vol. i. p. 345) we find that, in the year A.D. 1494, another native of our pariſh named_ *Robert Eſtrie* was appointed Cuſtos or guardian of Canterbury College, Oxford.

In the records of a *Viſitation* of the clergy and people of the deanery of Sandwich, held in the great chancel of S. Peter's, Sandwich, on the 17th September, A.D. 1511, by the moſt Reverend Father in Chriſt his Grace William, by Divine permiſſion Archbiſhop of Canterbury, we find the following particulars relating to our pariſh, under the two headings of (i) " The Chapel of Worth," and (ii) " The Church of Eaſter "—i.e., Eaſtry.

" Capella de Worth.   Comptū [i.e., compertum] eſt, That Richard

Broke w'holdeth from the churche xls for a chaleis that was bequethed by oon John Burton.

" Itm̃ that oon Thomas Aleyn of feint Barthilmewes w'drawith A cowe that was bequethed to the Churche by oon H. Patryke the piffhe preeft.

" Itm̃ that oon patryke fforft and Thomas Aldon w'drawith from the fame churche A cowe that was geven to A lampe afore the Roode ꝑpetually." (*Reg. Warham*, f. xlviii.)

(ii.) " Ecclefia de Eafter [i.e., Eaftry].   Compertum eft, That the Roodeloft lakketh great repacõn.

" Itm the churche nedith greate reparacions.

" Itm̃ that they lak books and fpially of the new fefts, as the Tranffiguracion of oʳ lord, as of the name of Ihu.

" Itm̃ that oon William Gilham, otherwife callid William Breten, kepith evill and very fufpect Rule with diũfe women and fpially wᵗ oon Marian Johnfon.

" Itm̃ that Robert ffrende and oon Julyan his wife are openly talked of that they arʾ not lawfully conioyned togid in matrymony for a certeyn goftly caufe." (*Reg. Warham*, fol. xlviii., b.)

Again, on the 12th Jany., 1512, in the Cathedral Church, at Canterbury, before Mafter Robert Woodward, Lord Commiffary, "appeared Rich. Broke, of Sandwich, and denied the fubtraction of any legacy of John Burton.   .   .   .   .   .   And fo the Lord Commiffary difmiffed the aforefaid Richard Broke.   Alfo at the aforefaid day and place appeared Thomas Aleyn, brother of the Hofpital of Saint Bartholomew near Sandwich, and faith that he hath not withheld a cow bequeathed to the faid Chapel.   And forthwith the Churchwardens [*Iconomi*] of the faid Chapel took upon themfelves to prove it; and the Lord Commiffary appointed the viii day of the month of May next [for the hearing of the cauſe.] And coming on the viii day of May, the aforeſaid Church-wardens, in the preſence of the aforeſaid Thomas Aleyn produced Henry Adam in witneſs, and Alice Callwell, who having been ſworn and examined, and their depoſitions having been examined, the Lord Commiſ-ſary adjudges and pronounces that Thomas Aleyn do deliver to the Churchwardens of the aforeſaid Chapel one cow or the value thereof before the Feaſt of the Nativity of S. John Baptiſt next enſuing under penalty of excommunication. Alſo the aforeſaid Churchwardens ſay that patrick froſte and Thomas Adam have compounded with them." (*Reg. War-ham*, fol. lxvi.)

" On the xvii day of the month of January the aforeſaid year (viz., 1512) appeared the Churchwardens of Eſtry, and they were ordered by the Lord Commiſſary to repair the Roodelofte there before the Feaſt of the Nativity of our Lord next enſuing under penalty of excommunication. It is alſo notified to the ſaid Churchwardens that they ſufficiently repair the Nave of the ſaid Church before the Feaſt of the Aſſumption of the B. Virgin Mary next (Auguſt 15th), under penalty of excommunication.

" It is alſo notified to the aforeſaid Churchwardens that they provide books for the new Feſtivals before the feaſt of the Nativity of Saint John Baptiſt next under penalty of excommunication.

" Alſo the ſaid Churchwardens ſay that William Gylhm̅ alſ Breten hath departed beyond ſea, and doth not intend to return.

" Alſo at the ſaid place and day appeared Robert frenne [notice the corruption of the word Friend] and confeſſes that he and Juliana his wife are within the degrees of conſanguinity. And the Lord Commiſſary divorced them." (*Reg. Warch.*, f. lxvij.)

In a liſt of the *Procurations* of the monaſteries and other religious

places, and of the Deaneries within the diocefe of Canterbury, made about
this time (1512) occur the following, under the heading DECANATUS
SANDWICI, which I infert as relating to our fubject:

Ecclia de Eftry	xxi^s viij^d
Vicaria eiufdem	v^s

From a return made in the 26th year of Hen. VIII (A.D. 1535) of the
value of all Manors, Lands, Revenues, Penfions, and other Emoluments of
Chrift Church, Canterbury, we gather that the Rectory and Manor of
Eaftry were refpectively valued as under:

Eftrye Rectoria	£89. 8. 10$\frac{1}{2}$
Eftrye Manerium	69. 16. 11" di. q.

(Dugdale Monaft. Angl., vol. i., p. 119).

In a valuation of benefices in the Deanery of Sandwich, made the fame
year (1535), is the following entry refpecting our parifh:

Ecclia de Eaftry cum capella de Worthe eidem ecclie annex' appro-
priat' priori ecclie X̄p̄i Cantuar.'

ESTRY.

Richard Champney vycar there receyveth yerely of the pryour of Cryftchurche in Caunterbury	v£ vj^s viiij^d	S̄m̄a
In tythes p'dyall and parfonall oblacons and other fp̄ruall p̄fetts yerely	xviij v j	xix£ xj^s ix^d
	In p x^a —£ xxxix^s ij ob.	
Thereof to be allowed of the forfeid pencyon and paied to the clerke yerely	—£ xl^s —^{d}	

(Valor Ecclefiafticus.)

On the diffolution of Chrift Church, Canterbury, in 31st Hen. VIII, the Manor of Eaſtry came into the poſſeſſion of the king, who, however, did not long retain it; but in the 33rd year of his reign gave it to his newly-created Dean and Chapter of Canterbury, in whoſe poſſeſſion it ſtill remains. (See *Patent Rolls*, Hen. viii., No. xxxiii., ſkin 20, at Record Office.)

The advowſon of the Vicarage, though granted to the Dean and Chapter at the ſame time as the Rectory and Manor, appears to have paſſed ſhortly after to the Archbiſhops of Canterbury, the preſent patrons of the benefice.

In the year 1650 a ſurvey was made by order of Parliament of all the property belonging to the Rectory of Eaſtry. The ſeveral particulars of this inquiry I give below from the *Parliamentary Surveys*, vol. xix., p. 30, at Lambeth.

Rectoria de Eastry.

Sʳ Tho. Smith
Sʳ Jo : Scott
Sʳ Rich : Smith
knight

At the Parſonage or Rectory of Eaſtrey in the county of Kent, conſiſtinge of a ffaire parſonage houſe conteyneinge a Hall twoe parlours a Kitchen a Buttery a Milkhowſe a Lawther [Larder] a Brewhouſe A maulthouſe with Eight Chambers ouer them Three Barnes two Stables with a Granary over them three Sellers one pidgeon loft three pudder [fodder ?] howſes with other howſes One Garden, One Orchard, One little bowlinge Greene, one Courte yarde and one greate yard   ——xˡˢ : ▬ : ▬

Together with the Tythes of Corne and other profitts to the ſaid Parſonage belonginge wee Eſtimate to be worth Omnibus Annis :   ccccˡˢ : ▬ : ▬

Memorandum the late Deane and Chapter of the Cathedrall and Metropoliticall Church of Chriſt Canterbury by their Indenture dated the Twentyeth day of January 1615 have Demiſed unto Sʳ. Thomas Smith Sʳ John Scott and Sʳ Richard Smith, All that the Rectory or Parſonage of Eaſtry in the County of Kent with all howſes Barnes Stables, and buildinges Gleabe lands Tythes Oblācons, Obvencons, Emoluments, Profitts and Comodityes whatſoeuer with all and ſingular their Appurtennces to the ſaid Rectory belonginge ſcituate lyeinge and beeinge in Eaſtry and Tilmanſtone aforeſaid together with Authorityc to keepe Courts there, and to receiue the profitts of the said Courts, Except and referued all Tymber, Woods and vnderwoods growinge vpon the pmisses. To haue & to hold from the makeinge of the said Indenture for and dureinge the Tearme of the Naturall liues of Sr Richard Sonds of Leeds Courte in the Countye of Kent Knight, George Sonds Esqre oldest Sonne of Sr Richard Sonds, and Anthony Sonds his third Sonne, and for and during the life of the longest liuer of them, paying therefor yearly to the said Deane and Chapter lxxxix^{ld}: and v^s att Christmas and Midsomer by even porcons or within viii days next after the said ffeasts and alsoe payinge euery Seauenth yeare ouer and aboue the said rent the sume of 200^{ld} in the Treasury howse of the Said Church att the said ffeasts by euen and equall porcons, But are worth vpon Improuement ouer and aboue the said Rent referued per ann. ccclix^{ld}: xiiij^s: iiij^d

Redd: lxxxix$^£$: v^s and euery seauenth yeare —200^{ld} ffor entertainment 4^{ld} y^r the last 7th yeere I suppose this yeare 1650 to be a 7th yeare.

The Lessees in all thinges to repayre maynetaine and vpholde the Howses and buildinges demised togeather with the Chauncells of the parrishe Church of Eastry and word and all the ffences and Inclosures belonginge to the Gleabe landes and in the end of the Tearme soe to leaue the same.

There is only Sr George Sands aliue and in beeinge.

The present Rent of lxxxix^{ld}: v^s: Is thus apporconed viz:

To bee Sould with the Lands	09^{ld}: 15^s: 00^d
To remayne vpon the Tythes	79: 10: 00
In toto	89: 05: 00

I conceiue this beinge a 7th yeare the share of the Lands in the 200^{ld} now due will bee about xxv^{ld}. And there beinge One life in beeinge in the said Lease I judge the Commonwealths Interest in the Lands proporcon may be valt in grosse at: l^{ld}.

Grosse Vall: L^{ld}: /

And then there will remayne to be payde this yeare for the Tythes proporcon of the said 200^{ld}: 175^{ld}: and soe every 7th year 175^{ld} duringe the life in beeinge. q^y: whether last euery 200^{ld} were paid 7 yeares agoe

Novemb^r. 16th 1650 Will: Webb.

And now to recapitulate somewhat. From even a very cursory glance at the foregoing extracts, we cannot fail to be struck with the number of men whom our parish gave to the service of the Church at the close of the xiii century, some of whom rose even to confiderable eminence; thus, in A.D. 1275 there is Ofwald de Eaſtria, Abbot of the Monaſtery of Faverſham, in 1284 Anfelm de Eaſtria, Rector of our own parish, in 1285 Henry de Eaſtria, Prior of Chriſt Church, Canterbury, and in 1290 Robert de Eaſtria, Rector of Henley-upon-Thames. The value of *the Manor* would appear to have increaſed as follows : in A.D. 1086 it was worth £38. 10. 3 per annum; in A.D. 1400 it had rifen in value to £65. 03. 00; and in 1535 it was eſtimated at £69. 16. 11. *The Rectory*, in A.D. 1384, was worth £53. 6. 8 per annum; in A.D. 1535 it had rifen to £89. 1. 10½; whilſt in A.D. 1650, little more than 100 years after, it had increaſed ſo much as to be eſtimated at £410 a-year.

The Vicarage, in A.D. 1535, was valued at £19. 11. 9 in the King's Book. Camden, in A.D. 1586, gives £17. 11. 9 as its value; but probably this would be a ſlip of the pen for £19. 11. 9, i.e., the eſtimated worth of the benefice, in the year 1535, as taken from the King's Book. For Haſted ſays that, in A.D. 1588, it was worth £60, and in A.D. 1640 £100, a-year; alſo that at both periods there were 335 communicants in the pariſh.

The *Boteler MSS.* contain an extract from "*Sʳ George Sondes, his plain narrative to the World of all paſſages upon the Death of his two Sonnes. London : Printed in the year* 1655. This is given below, and may ſerve as an example of the hard dealing of the Cromwellian Parliament :—

Fol. 27. "The laſt year 1654 upon ſuit of the Truſtees in the Exchequer for arrears of Rent due to the Church, I was there denied the Benefit of the general Pardon, which as I conſeived took off theſe

E

arrears. And it was likewife decreed that I fhould pay for them 105£s as Rent for the Parfonage of Eaftry, for that year 1643, when the Parliament farmed it out for 410£s, and received all the money for it: I had not one Penny Benefit by it, they had it all, and yet I muft pay that rent."

Hafted mentions a Sir Michael Sondes, then of Eaftry, Kent, who afterwards refided at Throwley, and died A.D. 1617.

> " *The old order changeth, yielding place to new,*
> *And God fulfils Himfelf in many ways,*
> *Left one good cuftom fhould corrupt the world.*"
>
> MORTE D'ARTHUR.

The Bounds; or, a Perambulation of the Parish.

CHAP. II.

" Remove not the ancient landmark which thy fathers have set."—PROV. xxii. 28.

THE prefent divifion of our country into parifhes had its origin in the time of Archbifhop *Theodore* (A.D. 668—690), when wealthy perfons were encouraged to build churches on their eftates, by the promife of the patronage of their own foundations, and other advantages. Thus originally *parifhes* were frequently *co-extenfive with the eftates* of the founders of their refpective churches. And this may account for the fact that many parifhes have feparate and detached portions, lying far away from the main body, in the midft of other parifhes. In this way *Ticknefe* (properly *Tickenhurft*) is detached from Northbourne, and numerous other examples will readily fuggeft themfelves to my readers.

It feems fomewhat uncertain, however, whether, in the cafe of our own parifh, the foundation of the church and the boundaries of the parifh were thus clofely connected the one with the other.

The earlieft notice of the *Bounds* of the parifh of *Eaftry* which I have yet met with, is taken from a MS. amongft the Court Rolls of the

Almery or Priory Manor of Eaftry, formerly in the poffeffion of Mrs. Rammell. The account there given is as follows:

"This bowndes and Lymites of the piſhe of Eaſtrye that be here reherſed weare fought out by Rychard Cok Adam Pricke Thomas Ward William Goſt William Goodwyne John Clarke Thomas Rulbone growen before Mr. John Generli Dene of my Lord Symon Iſplyp audyens at the tyme beinge Archbiſhoppe of Canterburye the xth Daye of Jullye the yeare of our Lord m ccc lvj for a plee Revyſed by one Richard vicar of S. Marye Chourche in Sandwiche for tythes of a place in the faid piſhe of Eſtrye in the $_w^{ch}$ plee the vicar was caſt/ in witnes thereof the fayd Archbiſhopp hath put thereto Sealle of Offyce as it appeareth one the fame plee. . . . . . . This Boundes begyn in a place called the Standward the $_w^{ch}$ is in pte of the Northeweſt of the piſhe of Eaſterye and fro the place foreſayde extende the boundes and Lymites of the fayd piſhe of Eaſterye by a broode wey called weines wey extendinge toward the Sowthe to a place called weines Devidinge the pyſhe of Eaſterye one the eaſt part froo the weye of woodinſboroughte toward the weſte. And froo the weye foreſayde called wenis extende the boundes and Lymmites of the piſhe of Eaſterye by a wey called lyſte toward the eaſte goinge forthe to a place called the Bellet devidinge the pyſhe of Eaſterye one the northe ſyde froo the pyſhe of woodneſborough toward the Sought, and froo the fayd place called the Belet extende the boundes and lymmites by the fame weye toward the ſouthweſt, So goinge forthe to a place called Bocklond devidinge the pariſhe of Eaſtery one the fouth eſte fro the pyſhe of Woodneſboroughte on the northe weſte pte fro the fayd place called Bockelond[*] extende the boundes and limmites by the

* Now Buckland.

Kingfwey toward the wefte foe goinge forthe to a place called grenehedgger* devidinge the pyfhe of Eafterye one the fouthe fyde froo the
pyfhe of woodnefborought toward the north and froo the fyde way called
grenehedgger extende the Boundes and Limmites by a ftreet or way †
toward the fouth, fo goinge forthe to a croffe called mathewes croffe‡
devidinge the pyfhe of Eafterye toward the eaft froo the pyfhe of Woodnefboroughte toward the weft and froo the fayd mathewes croffe extende
the boundes and Limmites of the fayd pyfhe of Eafterye by a way or a
ftreet called Broodeftreete§ toward the wefte fo goinge forthe to the hedd
of a hegge northe called Deneheggeǁ devidinge the pyfhe of Eafterye
one the fouth fyde froo the pyfhe of Woodnefboroughte one the northe
fyde and froo the forefayde northe hedd of the fayd denhedgge extende
the bounds & limmites of the pyfhe of Eafterye by the fame hegge
againfte the fouthe-wefte foe the hegge makeing ane end by a grene waye
devided or a landfchare unto a place called Redis¶ devidinge the pyfhe
of Eafterye one the foutheaft from the pyfhe of woodnefborought and
knowlton toward the northweft and foorthe to a place called Redis
extende the bounds & .limmites of the pyfhe of Eaftery by a way called
Pilholt toward the Eaft fo goenge fourth to a place called hoddyngef-

---

* Part of this green hedge has been grubbed up, but a confiderable portion ftill remains.

† This is the road to Woodnesborough Church from Poifon Crofs, and the boundary line is in the middle of the road.

‡ Now Poifon Crofs.

§ Part of the Canterbury road.

ǁ Moft of this hedge has now difappeared—it runs from the Canterbury road towards Harnden Hill.

¶ Redis = Ridges, a term not uncommonly ufed. The Redis or Ridges here mentioned muft be near the Cottages on Harnden Hill.

downe* devydinge the piſhe of Eſtry one the north part from the piſhe of Nonington toward the Sowth ptie, And fro the ſeid place called hoddingeſdowne extend the bownds and lymytts of the piſhe of Eſtry to another greene waye towards the eaſt, ſo goenge fourth to a hill called Gavliteſdowne ſo devydinge the piſhe of Eſtry on the Northſyde from the piſhe of Nonington and Tylmanſtone towards the Sowthſyde, and fro the ſeid Gaveletiſdowne extend the bownds and lymytts of the piſhe of Eſtry by a greene footewaye agaynſt the North, ſo goenge fourth to a corner one the Northſyde of a feilde called danefeild†devydinge the piſhe of Eſtry one the weſt ſyde from the piſhe of Tylmanſton one the eaſt ſyde, And from the ſeid Sowth corner of the ſeid Daneſſeild extend the bowndes and lymyttes by a devyded greene waye toward the head eaſt devydinge the piſhe of Eſtry toward the Northſyd from the piſhe of Tylmanſtone toward the Sowth, And the ſame waye making an ende the bowndes and Lymytts by an other greene waye from the hedd eaſt, toward the Northeaſt So goenge fourth to a myll called Betteſhanger Myll,‡ And the ſeid greene waye endinge by a highwaye§ be half the hamlett or the villadge called updowne unto the highway that leadeth fro Eſtry unto Northborne devydinge the piſhe of Eſtry one the Northweſt part, fro the piſhe of Betteſhanger toward the Sowtheaſt, And fro the ſeid waye that leadeth fro Eſtry toward Northborne extend the bownds and Lymytts

---

* The down oppoſite Shingleton Down.

† A field not far from Dane Court.

‡ Betteſhanger Mill was ſtill in exiſtence in the laſt century : but has now for many years diſappeared. It ſtood in much the ſame place as the preſent *Lodge* at Betteſhanger.

§ This "highwaye" is the road which leads from near Buttfole to Northbourne, and paſſes the lodge gates of Updown Houſe.

by a greene* way towards the north, So goenge fourth to a place called the
Parſonyſſeild† of hame devydinge the piſhe of Eſtry one the weſt
parte fro the piſhe of Bettiſhanger and hamme towards the eaſt, And
from the ſeid Parſoniſſeild of hamme extend the bownds and Lymytts
by a broad waye‡ towards the North, So goenge fourth to a place
called hamebridge§ devydinge the piſhe of Eſtry toward the weſt
from the piſhe of hamme towards the Eaſt, And fro the ſeid hamme
bridge‖ extend the bowndes and lymytts by a great water towardes
the eaſt, So goenge fourth to a place called hawkelinge devydinge
the parryſhe of Eſtry towards the North from the parryſhe of hame
towards the Sowth, And from the place called hawklinge extend the
bowndes and lymytts of Eſtry lynially towards the Eaſt, unto a place called
Spruckelham, And fro the ſeid place called Spruckelham ſo rightfourth to a
place callyd langhauke, And fro the ſeid place called langhauke unto the
coaſt of the Sea devydinge the piſhe of Eſtry towards the north fro the
piſhes of hamme and Northborne toward the Sowthſyde, And from the ſeid
coaſt of the Sea, extend the bownds and lymytts of the piſhe of Eſtry by
the ſame coaſt of the Sea toward the northweſt, So goenge fourth and
ſhettinge in the parryſhe of Eſtry toward the Sowth weſt unto a place
called the naſe, And from the ſeid place called the Naſe extend the
bownds and lymytts towards the Sowtheaſt, ſo goenge fourth by

---

* This "green way" is ſtill in exiſtence, though it is in great danger of being
obliterated owing to the conſtant encroachments of the plough.

† There is a field here which ſtill belongs to the Rector of Ham.

‡ This is the road that runs from the corner of Fred. George Terry's garden
paſt the back of Ham Houſe and Ham Church.

§ The further bridge next Word Mill.

‖ From this point the bounds, as here deſcribed, are thoſe of Word, and *not* the
bounds of the *preſent pariſh* of Eaſtry.

a ftreame callyd Geftlinge unto a place callyd the Sclufe fhettinge in the pifhe of Eftry toward the north eaft fro the pifhe of S'. Clements in Sandwich toward the Sowthweft parte, And fro the feid Sclufe extend the bowndes and Lymyttes towards the Sowth So goenge fourth by a Dyke called Erchiflodick devydinge the pifhe of Eftry toward the Eaft from the feid pifhe of S'. Clements one the weft fyde unto a place called hovelinge, And fro the feid place called hovelinge extend the bownds and lymytts toward the northweft, So goenge fourth by a dyke called the delfe devydinge the pifhe of Eaftry toward the Sowthweft from the pifhe of S. Clements toward the northweft unto the Sowth corner of the Hofpitall of S'. Bartholomewe, And from the feid Sowth corner of the feid hofpitall extend the bownds and lymytts of the pifhe of Eftry toward the North, So goenge fourth by a runninge water called the delph unto a place callyd the Stonebridge devydinge the pifhe of Eftry toward the weft from the pifhe of S'. Clements towards the eaft parte, And fro the feid Stonebridge extend the bowndes and lymytts toward the Sowth weft, So goenge fourth by the kinges highwaie to the Sowth hedd of a lyttle dyke or a vorowe lyenge of length $\frac{th}{w}$ the lands of John Terrey toward the eaft parte of the feid lands devydinge and fhettinge in the pifhe of Eftry toward the Sowtheaft fro the pifhe of S'. Maries in Sandwich one the north weft parte, And fro the feid Sowth hedd of the feid Dyke or vorowe extend the bowndes and lymytts by the fame dyke or vorowe toward the north, So goenge fourth to a corner of a feild called Polder land* towards the northeaft fhettinge in the pifhe of Eftry toward the Eaft, And from the feid corner that ys north-eaft of the feid Polder lande extend the bownds and lymytts toward the weft parte, So goenge right fourth by a lyttle dyke or a vorowe lyenge of

* Now "Felderland," but commonly pronounced "Fenderland."

length $\frac{th}{w}$ the north of the ſeid feild called Polderfield unto the *highwaye that leadeth from Sandwich toward Canterbury and by the weſt hed of the ſeid dyke or vorowe extend the bowndes and lymytts by the ſeid highway toward the Sowth, So goenge fourth a cloſeinge in the piſhe of Eſtry one the eaſt ſyde from the piſhe of woodneſborowe toward the weſt to a place callyd the Standard.

23° Julii 1585."

[*Botel. MS. A.*, pp. 104, 105, 106.]

Thus much as to the bounds of our pariſh in A.D. 1356. Since that time, however, the pariſh of *Worth* or *Word* has been cut off from the mother pariſh of Eaſtry, ſo that Eaſtry is now ſmaller in extent than in the time of Archbiſhop Iſlip. In his time, at the time when the vicarage of Eaſtry was endowed, and for many generations afterwards, the church at Word (dedicated to S. Peter and S. Paul) was merely a chapelry attached to the mother Church at Eaſtry, in the ſame manner as Shrinkling, or Shingleton; but with this difference, that whereas, the vicar of Eaſtry was to "find one Chaplain in the Chapel of Worth depending upon the ſaid Church of Eaſtry to celebrate divine Service every day, at leaſt as far as it may be done with convenience," and there to "officiate in divine Things according to uſual Cuſtom;" the prior and convent of Chriſt Church, Canterbury, were held and bound to the "maintenance of one Chaplain in the Chapel of Shrynglynges depending upon the ſaid Church, provided the Rectors were held in times paſt to the ſame" (ſee *Endowment of the Vicarage*).

In courſe of time the Church of Word acquired certain parochial

---

* "The Sandwich Road," as Eaſtry folk call it.

rights; but whether it ever actually became a *separate parish* until it was legally feparated from Eaftry in A.D. 1854, feems very doubtful. From certain memoranda that I have come acrofs in one of the parifh books, the queftion feems to have been raifed fometime between A.D. 1686, and A.D. 1688, as to whether at that time Word was or was not a feparate parifh: fome perfons—apparently the inhabitants of *Word*—afferting that it was fuch, and " Charles Bargrave, Churchwarden, and Sollomon Harvey and Thomas Adams, Overfeers of the Poor," of our parifh, maintaining as ftrenuoufly that it *was not*, and giving as their reafon " that the Inftrument of Inftitution and Induction gives [*sic*] to the Minifter or Clerk of Eaftry runns only to Eaftry Cum Capella de Woorth and he is Inducted only into Eaftry." The parifh of *Worth* was conftituted *Vicarage* by an Order in Council which appeared in the London Gazette of December 6th, 1867.

But to return to the perambulation of the parifh. The ancient and proper time for the perambulation of parifhes—or " beating of the bounds," as it is often called, from the cuftom in former days of beating boys at certain points, in order to imprefs the boundaries, marks, and limits of the parifh the better on their memories—is fome day in Rogation week, i.e., the week in which Afcenfion Day or Holy Thurfday falls. For when, at the Reformation, all other religious proceffions were abolifhed, the perambulation of parifhes in this week was ftill retained.

The following extracts from the oldeft[*] account book of the churchwardens, which is now extant, furnifh us with a complete lift, as far as it goes, of the dates at which our parifh has been perambulated :—

---

[*] Mr. Boteler fpeaks of the tradition that there had once been two other and more ancient books. Thefe however, had difappeared even in his time.

		£	s.	d.
" 1689 P^d upon the perambulacōn		o.	5.	o"
" 1690 Spent at the perambulacōn		o.	7.	11"
" 1692 Spent when wee went the Boundes of the parish		o.	11.	4"
" 1696 p^d to goody Samson mony spent for going ye bounds of ye parish		1.	o.	o"
" 1703 May 5th p^d att Goodman Sampsons when we went ye bounds	o.	9.	o"	
" 1719 Spent att the five Bells when went the Bounds of the parish	1.	2.	6"	
" 1719 p^d John Cock more w^h which was spent when we went the Bounds of the Parish		o.	15.	o"
" 1722 Spent when we went the Bounds of the Parish		o.	13.	o"
" 1743 May 12 Spent going the Bounds of the Parish		o.	16.	10"
" 1747 May 29 Spent going the Bounds of the Parish		o.	16.	6"
" 1762 May 20 Spent at the Five Bells going the Bounds of the Parish		1.	19.	o"
" 1782 May 15 Paid at the Bull going the Bounds of the Parish		2.	16.	o"
" 1801 Expences at the Five Bells (28th May) going the Boundary of the Parish		3.	2.	10½"
" 1814 June 11 paid Eastes Bill for Dinners, &c., for going bounds of parish*		9.	14.	2½"

1833 May 14. This day & year the bounds were walked by the Vicar, Churchwardens & others.

1856 Mar. 31. This day & year the Vicar, Curate, Churchwardens, Parish Clerk and others walked the bounds of the Parish beginning at Hay Hill.

1868, Sept. 24. At nine o'clock in the morning of this day and year, there met, at the boundary stone on Hay Hill, near the Crofs Roads, a number of the parishioners, including the Vicar, Lieut.-Col. Rae, Mr. G. Turner (The Lynch and New Coll., Oxon), Mr. Churchwarden Terry, Mr. William Wilson (Guardian, Shingleton Farm), Mr. James Cobus (Overseer), and Messrs. Joseph Bowman (Parish Clerk), R. Moat, Junr., J. Bushell (Kent C^y Const^y), G. Foord (of "Five Bells"), J. May-

---

* In this year Mrs. Pettman gave £2 2s. towards the expenses of the Perambulation.

nard (Kent Cʸ Conſtᵇ), E. Dunn, and W. Deveſon, Jos. Manſer, E. Pay, G. Dungey, Chas. Dungey, E. Culver, E. Moat, W. Thompſon, J. Fitz-gerald, J. Foord, S. Hopper, A. Soames, G. Lawrence, John Manſer, and J. Spickett. At 9.15 they ſtarted, Bowman—who had " beaten the bounds " on two previous occaſions (viz., in 1833 and 1856), and who had been round ſtill more recently with the Ordnance Survey—taking the lead, and the reſt following; Lieut.-Col. Rae, Meſſrs. Terry and Wilſon, and the Vicar, being mounted, the others being on foot.   On the borders of the pariſh of Betteſhanger the Eaſtry party were met by Walter James, Eſqr., and the Rector of Betteſhanger (Rev. J. W. Bliſs), who accompanied them as far their own bounds extended.   Arrived at Shingleton Down the Old Hundredth Pſalm was ſung, according to a cuſtom obſerved on previous occaſions.   Thence proceeding onwards they were met by the repreſentatives of Nonnington, the only other pariſh beſides Betteſhanger, which ſent its officers to the boundaries in time to meet the Eaſtry party. On Harnden Hill a halt was made, juſt outſide the cottages of Cox and Friend, for luncheon—which, conſiſting of bread and cheeſe and bitter beer, was partaken of by all preſent, and thoroughly appreciated.   After a reſt of half an hour the party again ſtarted, and in due time came into the Canterbury Road.   Going on from thence *Poiſon Croſs* (anciently *Matthews' Croſſe*) was reached, and the party proceeded halfway up the hill which leads to Woodneſborough Church.   Then turning to the right acroſs the fields, under a high-banked hedge, and following the various turns and windings of the boundary line, after ſome time the Sandwich road was croſſed.   Next the brooks, ſeparating Eaſtry from Ham, were reached and jumped by ſome, though more jumped in ! the foothold being very bad for leaping on either bank.   Henceforward the bounds kept to the road, and fo going on the markftone on Hay Hill was reached about 3 o'clock, after a very pleafant, but fomewhat tiring, walk of more than 14 miles.

The parifh of Eaftry, confifting of the borough of Eaftry, the borough of Heronden and part of the borough of Felderland, is about two and a half miles from north to south, and not more than one and a half mile from eaft to weft.

It contains, according to the Tythe Commutation Deed, 2664 ftatute acres, by far the greater portion of which is arable land, the extent of meadow or pafture being but fmall, and of hop gardens very much lefs.

The greater portion of the land in the parifh is claimed over by the Manors of Eaftry, Adifham, the Almonry, Dane Court, North Court, and South Court. Of thefe the principal are the Manors of Eaftry and Adifham, which are divided, the one from the other, by the high road leading from Woodnefborough by Gore to Elham.

The population of Eaftry has, of courfe, varied in different ages; but there is good reafon for fuppofing that during the time of the Roman occupation, in the Romano-Britifh period, and afterwards in Anglo-Saxon times, prior to the year A.D. 900, the ville of Eaftry had more inhabitants than at the time of the Norman invafion.

From the information given in Doomfday Book (fee p. 11) we may gather that the population of Eaftry, in or about the year A.D. 1086 was 300

In A.D. 1774 the population was 656

  " " 1801 " " (including workhoufe) was 852

  " " 1811 " " . . 909

  " " 1821 " " . 1062

  " " 1831 " " . . 1245

In A.D. 1841 the population of Eaftry (with the Union) was   1629

„ „ 1851   „   „   „   „   „   „   „   1697

„ „ 1861   „   „   „   „   „   „   „   1505

[In this year the population of the parifh proper was 1175, and of the Union Workhoufe 330].

In A.D. 1871

Since the beginning of this century about 90 new houfes have been built in Eaftry.

The *foil* of Eaftry, northward of the ftreet, is very good, fouthward it is poorer land, being in places very near the chalk. Upon the whole it may average about 30s. an acre; which fhows a confiderable improvement in the land fince Mr. Boteler's time (1774), when on the average it was worth only 15s. an acre.

The rents as affeffed to the poor amount to £7994. 6s. 6d.

And now, having perambulated the parifh, afcertained its boundaries and markftones, meafured its broad acres, examined its foil, numbered its people, and fummed up its rental, let us enter it by the road from Sandwich, and view its different localities fomewhat more in detail.

The firft object that meets our view, as we begin to approach Eaftry by the Sandwich Road, is an ancient Yew-tree ftanding at the corner of the road, that leads off on the left to Felderland. It has probably feen the travellers of many centuries. Bifhops and abbots and plain parifh priefts, barons and knights and fquires, merchants and burghers and artizans, country maidens and ladies of high degree, all in their day and generation have paffed by the old *Palm tree*, for fo is the Yew-tree called in this neighbourhood.

Paffing onwards through the turnpike, we come on the right to a large and handfome houfe, called *Statenborough*, the refidence

of Commander George Sayer, R.N., J.P., to whom the ancient eftate of
Stapenberghe, now Statenborough, belongs. This is at prefent the principal eftate in the parifh, including Gore, the lands of which are laid to
it: the whole confifting of about 141 acres. The land is in general good.

"From the title deeds it appears, in 1391, a fmall piece of land was
conveyed to Wm. Cook of Stapynberghe, and part of the premifes at this
day is called Cookfborough. In 1419 a part belonged to the family of
Atte Halle. In 1437 John Frynne & Thos. Terrey of Eaftry convey 16
acres feparate, at or near Stapenbergh, which they had of Ingram Atte
Halle fon & heir of J^no. Atte Halle of Dovorre, to W^m. Bryan of Canterbury who, from divers other conveyances, feems at this time to have been
in poffeffion of a confiderable part of the eftate. To whom or at what time
Mr. Bryan's property was alienated, does not appear: but, in 1484, the
whole belonged to J^no. Kennett of Canterbury, Gent. In 1534 Thos. Kennett of Canterbury Priest (capellanus) fon of the above J^no. conveyed his
whole property here—the quantity not fpecified—to Chrift^n. Hales Efq^r,
the King's Attorney-General, afterwards Sir Chriftian, Knight; whofe
daughter Margaret, the wife of Ralph Dodmore of Lincoln's Inn, Gent.,
jointly with her Hufband in 1557 conveyed the Eftate, fpecified in the
Deed as containing 120 acres, under the general name of Statynborough
to Saffrey Paramor of Eaftry Yeoman. In this Family it continued in
lineal fucceffion from Father to Son, and was the place of refidence of
each, till Jofhua·Paramor jointly with his mother Mary fold it in 1713,
fadly encumbered with mortgages to his Coufin Capt. J^no. Paramor of
Sandwich, who rebuilt the Houfe and refided here. Capt. Paramor died
1737 and bequeathed it to his only fon Jn°. Paramor Efq^r. who dying
1751 without iffue, bequeathed this, amongft other eftates, to Mary eldeft
daughter of his fifter Mary deceafed, the wife of Thos. Fuller of Sand-

wich Efq'.; but fhe dying fingle and under age, the whole fell after the
death of Mr. Paramor's widow in 1759 to his 3 nieces Jane, then Jane
Hawker widow, afterwards the wife of John Dilnot Esq'., the daughter
of his fifter Jane Hayward deceafed; and Jane & Sarah Fuller two other
daughters of his fifter Mary before mentioned. On a divifion of the
feveral eftates in 1761 this was allotted to Jane and Sarah Fuller, & on
a further divifion betwixt the two fifters in 1774, this with Gore formed
a part of the fhare that fell to Jane then the wife of W. Boys of Sandwich Efq⟨s⟩,"*—author of " *Collections for a Hiftory of Sandwich.*"

Mrs. Boys eventually fold the eftate of Statenborough to Mr. George,
who in his turn difpofed of it to Mr. Moulding, after whofe deceafe it
was fold by his widow to Mr. Greville, from whom it defcended to his
grandfon Col. Fulke Greville (now Lord Greville). In 1846 Commander George Sayer, R.N., purchafed the eftate of Col. Greville.

Captain Sayer is in the commiffion of the peace, and bears for his
arms :—

Proceeding onwards we come to *Little Statenborough,* or Statenborough
Cottage, likewife the property of Capt. Sayer, who, about the year 1847,
purchafed the houfe and a few acres of land adjoining it of Col. Greville,
whofe grandfather, Mr. Greville, had acquired it of Mr. Upton. G.
Coleman, Efq., is the prefent occupier. Statenborough is claimed over by
the Manors of Dane Court, North Court, and South Court, Tilmanftone.

Great Walton, fituated on the Sandwich Road between Statenborough
and Eaftry Street, next meets us. It is a nice old-fafhioned houfe, with
trimly-kept greenfward, pond, gardens, and outhoufes adjoining, and about
70 acres of land—30 being in Eaftry, and 40 in Woodnefborough; the

* *Botel. MSS.*

land and houfe in Eaftry are affeffed at £84 in all. This farm was formerly much larger than it is at prefent, and was for fome generations in the family of Geering,* by one of whom it was divided towards the latter part of the feventeenth century. After the divifion Great Walton became the property of Mr. Wm. Sharp who, in 1694, conveyed it to Jofeph Neame of Word, yeoman, from whofe defcendant, Mrs. Elizth. Neame, the eftate was conveyed, in 1773, to Mr. John Nelfon and wife of Sandwich. Mr. Nelfon died in 1789, and by his laft will bequeathed it to the children of Mr. Wm. Caftle of Sandwich (the fon of his wife by a former hufband), whofe fon, Mr. Thos. Caftle, fold fome of the lands belonging to it. His fon, Robert Caftle, Efqre., is the prefent owner of the eftate, the lands belonging to which he lets, but occupies the houfe. He bears for his arms:

Little Walton, lying betwixt Great Walton and Eaftry Street, is a farm confifting of about 100 acres, 49 of which lie in Eaftry, the reft in Wood-nefborough. The lands, which are very ftraggling, were for many generations the property of a family of the name of Nutt. John Nutt, of Putney, Gent., was the owner in 1716 *(Botel. MSS.).* In 1733 Wm. Nutt was in poffeffion of the eftate, and in 1740 James Amey, but whether in right of himfelf or his wife, feems doubtful. The eftate was afterwards in litigation. In 1749 two females claimed poffeffion by law of the name of Wollaftone: and on a divifion between them, this amongft other eftates became the property of the one who was married to Taylor White, of Hertfordfhire, Efqre. In 1824 James White, Efqre., fold the property to Bargrave Wyborn, Efqre., in whofe family it ftill remains.

Walton Houfe, fituated between Great Walton and Eaftry Street, and

* The whole farm was in the poffeffion of the Geerings in A.D. 1623.

G

opposite Little Walton, is a large houſe, with about eight acres of land attached to it, originally built by Mr. George about the year 1805. In 1807 the property was purchaſed by Mr. White, who, in 1821, ſold it to Henry Warrell, Eſqre. In Nov., 1830, Mr. Warrell granted a leaſe of the houſe and land to James Rae, Eſqre., who eventually purchaſed the ſame in Sept., 1834, and in whoſe family it ſtill remains, being the reſidence of James A. Rae, Eſqre., Lieut.-Col. of the Cinque Ports' Volunteer Artillery. They bear for their arms : *Vert—three flags in pale courant, argent.* For a creſt : *a ſtag at gaze proper.*

A little further on there are two good houſes on oppoſite ſides of the Sandwich Road. The one on the right hand, a modern houſe, running back to the Woodneſborough Lane, being the property of R. S. Leggatt, Eſqre., M.R.C.S.; the other, called *Laureſton Houſe*, being the property of Mr. Matſon, but the reſidence of Miſs Toker, who has much improved the houſe, and laid out the grounds with taſte and effect. Attached to this houſe, and in front of it, is a pleaſant meadow containing 4a. 1r. 32p. Both Laureſton and Walton Houſes have garden entrances into the foot-path which runs from the Schools to Statenborough. Part of this path is ſometimes called the *Lover's Walk* from its being ſo quiet and ſecluded ; and the upper portion of it, nearer the Schools, is occaſionally uſed as a rope walk.

After paſſing Laureſton Houſe we come to *Eaſtry Street*, or as it is now entitled the *High Street*. This is the principal part of the village, and from hence branch off Church Street, Brook Street, what was formerly called Reaper's Row (which is properly a continuation of High Street, and leads paſt the Fairfield to Buttſole), Mill Lane, Gore Lane, and the Roads to Sandwich and Woodneſborough.

In High Street one or two places are worthy of mention.

On the left fide of the ftreet there is a place called *the Square*, fome cottages being built in that form; and a little further on is a foot-path leading directly to the Schools and Church, called *Church Lane* or *Collarmaker's Alley*. On the fouth of this lane is a meffuage, now the property of Mr. Wanftall, of Nonington, from which arifes the yearly rent charge of 12s. payable to the vicar and churchwardens for the benefit of the poor of Eaftry, under the laft will and teftament of Richard Thompfon, of Minfter, in Thanet, who died 1673. For further particulars refpecting this houfe fee under "*The Parochial Charities*." This houfe is now in the occupation of Edward Godden, grocer, and is ufed as a baker-and-grocer's fhop. South-ward of this is a houfe formerly called "the Nunneries," but for what reafon I know not; there are no ruins of any kind near the place, nor was there ever any fuch religious eftablifhment in Eaftry. It formerly confifted of two cottages in three dwellings, defcribed in a deed of 1567, as being at a place called "le Nunnerye." In 1609 they were purchafed by Paramor, of Statenborough, then called "the Nunnerys," and by this name they were bequeathed by John Paramor, of Statenboro', gent., his defcendant, in 1735, to his fon John Paramor, Efq., who fold it to John Matthews, of Eaftry, collarmaker (*Botel. MSS.*, vol. A., p. 65). It was rebuilt in great part by the above-named John Matthews, and is a neat houfe in two dwellings, occupied refpectively by Jofeph Bowman, parifh clerk, and Thomas Cullen. The property now belongs to John Court, of Eaftry, milk-man. Southward of this houfe is a meadow called *The Playing Clofe*, which has certainly been ufed as a place of recreation for upwards of the laft two hundred years, fince, in a rental of the year 1633, it is called "*the play clofe*." Still there is not the flighteft foundation for the idea, once prevalent, that this "playing clofe" formerly belonged to Goddard's Cha-rity. So early as A.D. 1567 it was private property, and belonged then to

Roger Churche: in 1606 it was the property of John Robins, Junr., yeoman; in 1640 it belonged to Edward Parboe, gent., and then formed part, as it did until recently, of the Street Farm over the way, once the property of the Petmans, but now divided up and fold. In 1868 this clofe was purchafed by John Iggulden, of Deal, Efqre., and now forms part of his Eaftry Houfe eftate.

Adjoining the "playing clofe" fouthward is the old *Schoolhoufe*, left by Mrs. Chriftian Goddard, 1574, for the ufe of the parifh clerk of Eaftry for ever, on condition of his inftructing one boy (see "*The Schools*"). This is now in the occupation of Thomas Young.

Next to the old Schoolhoufe is the *Bull Inn*. This has probably been the name and fite of the village inn for fome centuries. As early as A.D. 1573 it is mentioned; and, in 1633, it is fpoken of as "adjoining Goddard's Houfe for the Clerk, in Eaftry Street:" whilft the church-wardens' accounts often make mention of money "fpent at the Bull."

In A.D. 1573 Richard Huffam paid quit rent to the manor of Eaftry for the Bull. John Whitfeild, and after him Edmonde Baker, had been the previous owners. And again, in A.D. 1633, Thomas Huffam paid for the Bull. It is now the property of Meffrs. Liney and Evenden brewers.

It may not be uninterefting if we give the names of the fucceffive

HOSTS OF THE BULL.

1693, William Hall.
1702, Thomas Adams.
1725, Ingram Durhan.
1763, William Culler—then his widow.
1771, John Solley.

1791, Richard Ruffell.

1806, John Eaftes.

1816, John Ferrier.

1855, Charles Lepine.

1860, Edward Manfer.

This lift is complete as far as it goes back.

On the right hand fide of the ftreet oppofite to Collarmakers' Alley is a houfe and forge the property of the Drayfon family, and now in the occupation of Wm. Twyman, blackfmith. The houfe is comparatively new, having been built in 1861; but, on or about this fpot, there has been a forge for many centuries, where fucceffive generations of Drayfons have worked as fmiths. Will Drayfon figns the "Sefs made the 14th day of October, Anno Domene 1685," and there are frequent entries in the churchwardens' accounts of that period of payments made to the Drayfons "for iron work" or "fmith's work." By the fide of the forge there is a field path, which leads either to the Mills or to Gore.

A little higher up the ftreet, and oppofite the playing clofe, is *Eaftry Houfe*, the property of J. Iggulden, of Deal, Efqre., in right of his wife, the daughter of J. Hatfeild, Efqre., who, in or about the year 1832, bought it of the Petman family, in whofe poffeffion it had been for fome generations, being part of that old farm originally called *Swayne's*, which is now entirely divided up. This houfe is now in the occupation of Mr. John Netherfole.

Proceeding onwards paft the poft-office (foon to be made alfo a telegraph-office), a few more fteps bring us to *The Crofs*. This is the name given to that flightly open fpace where Brook Street and Mill Lane, High Street, Reaper's Row, and Church Street, meet together, and where, doubtlefs, in days gone by, there ftood the Village Crofs. In the old churchwardens' accounts frequent mention is made of thatching and other repairs done to "the Crofs Houfe" at the expenfe of the parifh. Hitherto I have been unable to identify this, and am rather inclined to think that it has difappeared, unlefs the Vicarage Cottage formerly bore that name. "The Crofs houfe" is not to be confounded with the houfe of "the Crofs Farm," formerly the property of the Kite, and now of the Boteler, family: nor yet with "the Clerke's houfe" above-mentioned in the High Street, nor with "the Sexton's houfe," which formerly was the end houfe of the Goddard's Charity, neareft and oppofite to the vicarage. At the end of the High Street neareft to "the Crofs" there is a pond which fupplies the neighbouring farmers and others with water for their cattle, and which rarely runs quite dry. Whilft on or about the fpot now occupied by Mifs Bayly's draper's fhop, formerly ftood the parifh ftocks—the terror of evil doers. Thefe were afterwards removed to a pofition nearly oppofite the church gates, beneath two elms growing in the clofe adjoining the boys' fchool. Latterly they were little ufed, and about A.D. 1828 they difappeared.

Proceeding from "the Crofs" towards the church, we pafs on the right a cottage formerly ufed as the barber's fhop, and once belonging to the Dean and Chapter of Canterbury, but which was made over to the Vicarage in or about the year 1853.

Two fteps more bring us to the VICARAGE, a large and comfortable houfe, which dates from the year 1821, when the old Vicarage was pulled down and rebuilt by the Rev. G. Randolph, then vicar. But the *foundations* of the houfe are *ancient*, and they may perhaps have formed part of the original building affigned for the ufe of the vicar in A.D.

1367, and confirmed to him in A.D. 1368, when an agreement was come to between the Prior and Convent of Chrift Church, Canterbury, on the one fide, and " Sir" Thomas, Vicar of Eaftry, on the other, " that the faid Sir Thomas, the Vicar, fhall have to his own proper ufe the hall, chambers, and kitchen, of his Vicarage aforefaid, which belonged and pertained to the Almoner and his office of old, and alfo the other buildings erected upon his fite, together with a garden and . . . . . thence arifing (the dovecote and certain wafte places, fituate below the clofe of the faid vicarage, being referved to the Almoner and his Rector in perpetuity)." It was then agreed that " the fame Almoner fhould, moreover, make and keep in fufficient repair a certain wall between himfelf and the Vicar aforefaid, beginning from the king's highway on the fouth fide of the faid Vicarage, and extending to a certain ftable of the faid Almonry of the Rector over againft the north part . . . ."
The wall here referred has been pulled down, in order that a piece of ground, which formed part of the farm yard of the Almonry, or Parfonage as it is now called, might be added to the Vicarage. The piece of ground here fpoken of is now ufed as a kitchen garden. But with regard to the wall which has difappeared; it commenced clofe to the gate which leads to the kitchen door, paffed the back door of the Vicarage, and extended to the ftables of the Parfonage. Thefe ftables ftill exift, having probably been renewed from time to time on the old fite. The Vicarage is furrounded on all fides by a narrow ftrip of garden, that portion which lies eaft of the houfe being the largeft, and having a confiderable fall. The view from the dining-room window towards the Lynch bank is very pretty. The garden contains two magnificent, and fome fmaller, yew-trees, a handfome ilex, and a very ancient claranut-tree, long paft its prime

—which has probably ftood here for fome centuries—befides numerous walnuts.

The Vicarage is bounded on the weft by Church Street, on the fouth by Brook Street, on the eaft by the garden of the Parfonage, and on the north by the yard and ftables of the fame.

Immediately oppofite the Vicarage gates are the five dwellings of *Goddard's Charity* (see "*The Parochial Charities*"). Originally left to the churchwardens for the ufe of the poor, in A.D. 1574, they would feem to have undergone comparatively little alteration, although they were formerly thatched and plaiftered, &c., from time to time, at the expenfe of the parifh. Unfortunately there is now no fund available for keeping them in repair. The end houfe neareft the road was for many years appropriated to the ufe of the fexton.

Adjoining the Vicarage is the houfe now called *the Parsonage*, but formerly the *Almonry* or *Aumbry*. This houfe ftands on, and forms part of the Rectorial property which once belonged to the Priory of Chrift Church, being appropriated to the ufe of the Almonry. After the Reformation it formed part of the endowments of the Dean and Chapter of Canterbury, but it is now in the hands of the Ecclefiaftical Commiffioners.

The great tythes of the parifhes of Eaftry and Worth, which belong to the Rectory of Eaftry, were formerly let, as well as the lands, to certain leffees. Now, however, the Ecclefiaftical Commiffioners keep thefe in their own hands, but let the lands. The lands belonging to the Rectory, or as it is commonly called "Parfonage," confift of 52a. 2r. 33p. of glebe in Eaftry; 15a. 3r. op. in Tilmanftone; oa. 2r. 24p. in Worth; in all 69a. or. 17p. To this Parfonage belongs a fmall manor called the Manor

of the Priory or Almonry, which receives quitrents from the houses and
land in the ftreet, contained within Eaftry Street and Church Street, reaching
down almoft to Little Walton. It receives alfo from the houses built on the
wafte in Reaper's Row or (as that part of the ftreet is now more commonly
called on each fide of the way), the Fair Field, and from a trifling quantity of land at or near Brook Street. The receipts of the whole are very
inconfiderable, as will be feen from the following rentals of 1573 and
1633, which I here extract from the *Botel. MSS.*, on account of the
information they give refpecting the inhabitants of Eaftry in thofe days.

" A Rentall conteyning as well the Rents of dyvers Tenñts, Lands, belonging to the Awmery or Parfonage of Eftrie, knowledged by the Tenñts
there in fundry Corts tempore nuper Regis H. viii[vi] and laftlie in cur :
tent : ultimo die Septembris anno xxx[mo] ejufdem nuper Regis As alfo a
Terror [Terrier] of all the Glebe lands belonging or aperteyning to the
faid pfonage with the Rents as well in money as in Corne toguether with
the Renouacions of their names ever as the fame is now anfwered and
paid to me Willūs Partheriche ffermor there hoc anno regni Elizabeth
xv[mo] et anno 1573, viz. :

" Rents of the tenñts belonging to the faid Awmerie." The abbre-
viated fubftance of which is as follows :—

		£	s.	d.
The poor houfe	Chryftian Goddarde widow holds a Tenement & Garden, late her father Thomas Parkers, lying in the Street over ag[ſt] the Vicarage at the payment yearly of		1	2
	Same Chryftian holds likewife a piece of land in Walton containing one rood two perches late y[e] faid Thos. Parkers at		1	1½
	Same Chryftian holds likewife a garden containing 16 perches at			1¼

H

nowe Rich. Austen Rich. Lawrance farmer	Heires of James Parker hold a Messuage, Garden & Dove house late J^{no}. Parkers lying over against the Parsonage Gate Henry Vincent farmer at	2	11

nowe Rich. Austen
Rich. Lawrance
    farmer

Heires of James Parker hold a Messuage, Garden & Dove house late J^{no}. Parkers lying over against the Parsonage Gate Henry Vincent farmer at   2   11

nowe Rich Huffam

Edmonde Baker—a tenement wth a garden contain^g 21 perches late J^{no}. Whitfields in the high Street   1   2

Willm Friende—a Kitchen wth half a stable cont^g 8 perches being parcell of the Lords tenement at the corner house leading from the Cross to the Churchwardes   6

nowe John Robins

Roger Church's widow—a crofte cont^g 5 roods ; to a close belonging to the Awmery East, to the Highway west   3   4

Said widow likewife for two acres in Walton   2

nowe John Whitfeild . . . . . . Pyfing—holds two tenements
wth their gardens cont^g 35 Perches in right of
his wife Thos. Whitfeilds widow   6^d

Said . . . . . Pyfing likewife for ½ an
acre in Walton   6^d

Said . . . . Pyfing likewife for 3
Roods in Walton   9^d 2   9

Said . . . . Pyfing likewife for a garden containing 1 Rood & 14 Perches
called Howtings   1^s

William Parromor—a tenem^t. & garden plotte late Silvester Goulds in the Street leading to the Church   1   6¼

Now Wm Parromor

John Harrys in right of his wife the widow of Jno. Paramor, pays for a tenem^t wth a garden cont^g ½ an acre 14 perches wherein the said John dwelt also one acre in Walton, also an ½ acre late Silvester Gold's, also a garden there containing 10 perches   4   9½

Saufferaic Parromor pays for a tenement and garden contain^g 20 perches late W^m. Stones &

John Arrowes lying in the high Sreet adjoining to a tenem¹ in the occupation of Thoˢ. Friend being Robᵗ. Paramors — 2½

Now Thoˢ. Frynd   Roger Frende holds a Tenem¹ and a garden containᵍ 23 perches which is now a Stable & lies over againſt his houſe in the High Street, & wᶜʰ he lately bought of Robᵗ. Frende formerly one Fydyans — 1   7

Total of the Rents   1   3   2½

Almery Manerm̄ in Eaſtry   " A Rentell made yᵉ 20ᵗʰ day of Auguſt 1633 of all the Quittrents of money due to the ſaid Mannor yeerly."

                                                        s.   *d.*

Imprimis Michˡ. Auſten Houſe & garden in Eaſtry Street — 2   2

Thos. Horſfield   Heirs of Wᵐ. Friend late Gilbert Wright for a houſe & garden on the Eaſtſide of Eaſtry Street — 1   2

Richᵈ. Stacy   Heirs of Mʳ. Hammon for the butchers ſhop in Eaſtry — 6

Thos. Huffam for the Bull in Eaſtry — 1   2

Heirs of Arnold modo Mr. Nicolls for a Houſe & certain Lands in Brook Street in Eaſtry — 3   4

Heirs of Roger Church modo Mr. Parbo for an acre of land in Eaſtry called the Play cloſe — 3   4

Joſua Parromer Tenem¹ & garden oppoſite the Smiths forge — 4

Joſua Parromer nuper Thomæ Berry jure uxoris ejus for another Tenem¹ & garden at the same place — 4

Jnᵒ. Kite
Abraham Stuppel   Stephen Thomſon Tenem¹ & garden in Eaſtry — 3
Morris

Heirs of Andrew Whitfeild, Tenem¹ & garden at the lower end of Eaſtry Street — 3

Thomas Freind Tenem¹ & garden at yᵉ ſame place — 1   7½

Sum   14   5½

After much inquiry I can learn little or nothing about the payment of these quit rents in modern times, and they would feem to have lapfed, owing probably to their very fmall amount.

The prefent Parfonage, which is a clean and comfortable looking, red brick houfe was built in A.D. 1825, on much the fame fite as the old houfe, defcribed by Mr. Boteler in the following terms : " The Parfonage Houfe is large and ancient. In it, as well as in Eaftry Court, is a fpacious Hall. In the old Parlour window, now a lumber-room, is a fhield of arms in painted glafs, containing Parthericke impaling Quarterly 1ft and 4th Gu. within a border fa. fpotted with Bezants a demy Lion argent, for the family of Line according to Harris—2nd and 3rd Ar. 3 Mullets fable, for Hamerton." In A.D. 1573 Wm. Parthericke farmed the Aumbry lands and lived in the houfe. He defcribes himfelf, as we have feen, as *Willūs Parthericke ffermor there.* From the parifh regifters it appeart that he buried his wife Alice in A.D. 1570 ; but he must have married in no long time after, as a fon Edward was born to him in A.D. 1573. The feveral tenants of the parfonage, after Parthericke, would feem to have belonged to the families here named in fucceffion. Argent—Denne —Fuller—Rammell —George—Singleton. The prefent tenant is Mr. George Terry.

Proceeding onwards a few fteps we reach the CHURCH, which will be more particularly defcribed hereafter. And now, leaving the Church on o. r right hand, an I the Schools at fome little diftance on our left, we enter the gates of EASTRY COURT, once the ancient feat of the Kings of Kent, the feene of the murder of the young princes Ethelbert and Etheldred, the favourite refort of Archbifhop Becket, and his hiding place for fome days after his flight from Northampton, and now a large farm belonging to the Dean and Chapter of Canterbury, who, on the refettlement of

their eſtates by the Eccleſiastical Commiſſioners in A.D. 1868, choſe to
keep this in their own hands. The lands formerly attached to the Court
conſiſted of 587a. or. 29p., which were all in Eaſtry, excepting ſome
27½ acres in Worth. At preſent, however, there are only 416a. 1r. 19p.
attached to the Court, the reſt having been ſold. About 21 acres of this
are paſture and brook, the reſt arable.

The houſe, which is large, and probably at one time covered the three
ſides of a ſquare, ſtill gives evidence of great antiquity, although from time
to time it has undoubtedly undergone much repair and great alterations.
Mr. Boteler ſays that in his time could be ſeen " in the ſouth wall the
letters T.A.N. in flint in large capitals—the initials of Thomas and Ann
Nevinſon." Mr. Iſaac Bargrave new fronted the houſe, and his ſon, alſo
named Isaac (who was born in 1721, bred to the profeſſion of the law and
practiſed for ſome years in London with conſiderable ſucceſs), put the
whole in complete repair about the year A.D. 1786. In doing this he
pulled down a conſiderable part of the ancient building, conſiſting of ſtone
walls of conſiderable ſtrength and thickneſs, and brought to light ſome
ancient Gothic doorways of ſtone.

The chapel, mentioned by Philipott, and which had been reſtored by
Henry de Eaſtria when Prior, is at the eaſt end of the houſe, and for
many years paſt has been uſed as a kitchen. The eaſt window conſiſting
of three compartments, may ſtill be traced, although the ſpaces between
the mullions are bricked up, and the whole is overgrown with creepers.
At the north-weſt angle of the houſe, juſt under the roof, there is a ſmall
chamber wholly dark, there being no window in it, although there is an
ample fireplace. The approach to it is ſomewhat intricate, and were the
entrance once cloſed, as might eaſily be done, the exiſtence of the chamber

would not even be fufpected. It is not unlikely that this fecret chamber may have been ufed as a hiding place in former times, perhaps during the *Civil Wars*; fince it does not appear to be fufficiently old to have formed *Becket's* place of concealment. In the cellar there is a fubterranean paffage, fuppofed (and with every probability) to lead to the Church. This, however, has been bricked up for fome years, as it was confidered danger-ous. George Gardner, Efqre., the prefent tenant, has thoroughly repaired and confiderably improved the houfe, buildings, and garden, which laft he has laid out with much tafte and fkill. From the garden a doorway leads into the churchyard, whence the inhabitants of the *Court* formerly gained access to the Church by the north door, now clofed up. The fucceffive leffees of Eaftry Court, from the 34th year of Henry viii., when *Chriftopher Nevinfon*, LL.D.,[*] was leffee, have belonged to the families of :—

Nevinfon till A.D. 1617—*Palmer* in A.D. 1641—*Bargrave* from A.D. 1647 to A.D. 1805—*Bridger* till A.D. 1859.—

The Nevinfons, originally of *Bridgend*,[+] in *Wetherell*, co. *Cumberland*, refided for many years at *Eaftry Court*, and many of them lie buried in the Church. They bore for their arms, *Argent, a chevron between 3 eagles difplayed azure.*

The *Bargraves* who, for more than 150 years, lived at *Eaftry Court*, were originally of *Bridge*, and afterwards of *Patrixbourne*. Their ancef-tor, Dr. *Ifaac Bargrave*, Dean of *Canterbury* (A.D. 1625—A.D. 1643), was the younger brother of *John Bargrave* who built *Bifrons*. Their arms were—*Or, on a pale gules a fword, the blade argent pomelled or, on a*

[*] See *Hafted*, vol. iv., p. 217, note *k*.

[+] *Hafted*, vol. iv., p. 217, note *k*, where he gives much information refpecting the families of *Nevinfon* and *Bargrave*. For Arms and Pedigree of the Bargraves fee also *Arch. Cant.*, vol. iv., p. 252.

chief vert 3 *bezants.* A Court Leet and Court Baron are fuppofed to be held every year for the Manor of *Eaftry Court,* which claims over the greater portion of the Parifh of Eaftry, part of the Parifhes of Word, Ripple, and Ewell, a great quantity of land in the Borough of Ged-dinge in the Parifh of Wotton; the Borough of Barnfole in the Parifh of Staple; the Borough of Craythorne in the Parifh of Til-manftone; the Denne of Toppenden in the Parifh of Witterfham; the Denne of Bromeland in the Parifh of Stone; the Dennes of Sarrenden and of Great Walkherft, in the Parifh of Benenden; and the Dennes of Little Hen-fell, of Pipifden, of Foxhole, and of Congeherft, all in the Parifh of Hawk-herft. The value of the quit rents, or rents of affize, paid to the lords of the Manor in A.D. 1693, amounted to £56 18s. 9¾d. At the end of a rental made in that year by John Coppin, gent., fteward of the manor, and fworn by the homage then and there prefent, viz., William Drayfon, Benj. Kite, William ffalkner, John Blowne, Michael Auften, Richard Woodwarr, Thomas Elgar, Thomas Pettit, and Thomas Stace,[*] occurs the following; " Memorand that uppon the death of every Tenant there is due by the cuftome of this Mannor to the Lords for a Releife the moytie of their quittrents. And uppon every alienacon of lands holden of this Mannor whereby an eftate of freehold paffeth there is due to the Lords the moytie of the quittrent of the lands foe aliened in the name of a releife. John Coppin, Steward."[†]

The Manor Pound is fituated at the end of the *Eaftry Court* barns and ftables, juft oppofite the Schools, and on the right hand of Church Lane, as you go down towards the ftreet.

But let us now retrace our fteps as far as the *Crofs,* and turn down *Brook Street,* which is the fteepeft hill in Eaftry, and prefents a very

---

[*] *Botel. MSS.,* vol. A., p. 200.   [†] *Botel. MSS.,* vol., A., p. 214.

passed to *Morgan Lodge*, Gent., who, in A.D. 1695, demised it to *Richard Knight*. In A.D. 1716 *Knight* sold the property to *Thomas Fuller*, gent., who built the present house and resided there himself. On his death it came into the possession of his daughter *Mary*, a single lady, who, dying in A.D. 1783, bequeathed it by will to her nephews *Thomas* and *Edward Rammell*. But *Edward Rammell*, dying in A.D. 1785, his brother *Thomas* became the sole possessor. He enlarged the house, and resided there for some years. Upon his death the property came to his sister *Elizabeth Rammell*, the founder of the Charity of that name still existing in the parish. She was an intelligent, but somewhat eccentric person. On one occasion, during her occupancy of the *Lynch*, the house was broken into by burglars, who would seem to have carefully laid their plans before hand. Towards the morning of a dark and windy night, they rode into *Eastry*, and dismounting near the top of the *Lynch Bank*, fastened their horses to the trees. Thence they proceeded on foot to the house, where they found Mrs. *Rammell*, who always sat up late, in the act of closing the shutters of the lower room before retiring to rest. The servants, it must be mentioned, were sleeping in a detached portion of the house, beyond the reach of any alarm. Anticipating Mrs. Rammell's intention of putting down the bar, they ran a pike through the window and so prevented it, at the same time slightly wounding her on the arm. She raised no alarm, and the thieves at once effected an entrance. Setting a guard over her, they ransacked the house, and discovered a considerable sum of money, which they carried off, together with a quantity of valuable plate. Some of the plate the robbers brought back before they started with their plunder, and other articles were found on the *Lynch Bank*. A large black chest containing crowbars, masks, &c., was seen next morning floating in *Butsole* pond, and this the robbers must have been obliged to leave behind them, probably on account of its being too great a weight for their horses. They were

tracked acrofs the country to Maidftone, the purfuers being aided in dif-
tinguifhing the tracks by finding that one of the robbers' horfes had on a fhoe
of peculiar fhape. The robbers were eventually fecured, and one of them
named *Webb* was even hung for the part he had taken in robbing the *Lynch*.
The Lynch is now the property of the Boteler family, and is in the
occupation of Mrs. Chas. Turner.

Paffing the feveral cottages at *Puddle-dock* and *Farthing-gate*, and afcending the hill, we come to *Little Hay*, a fmall farm of about 20 acres,
formerly the property of a family named Auften. John and Robert
Auften fold the eftate to Lewis, Lord Rockingham, from whom it
defcended to the Earl of Guilford, who, by his will dated 1779, directed it
to be fold. In 1802 *R. Tournay Bargrave*, Efqre., purchafed the property,
but fold it again in 1809 to Mr. *Richard Halford*, Junr.—thence it paffed
to Mr. *Solomon Wood* in 1817—then to Mrs. *Anna Hills*, who, in 1851,
fold the property to W. Boteler, Efqre.

Proceeding onwards from *Little Hay*, we foon reach the ftone which
marks the boundary of our parifh in this direction, whence a green way
runs to *Updown*, where the boundary of the parifh paffes through the porch
of Updown Houfe, the refidence of W. H. James, Efqre., J. P.

And now turning to the left, along the road leading to *Ham* and *Word*,
a few fteps bring us to *Great Hay*, a farm containing about 80 acres,
once the property of *Robert Marfh*, and then, in A.D. 1693, of *Richard
May*, Gent. In A.D. 1722 the heirs of *Richard May* alienated it to Mrs.
Ann Payne, who brought it in marriage to . . . . . *Dowdefwell*, of
London, and furviving him, left it by will to her nephew *Edward Stratton*,
of *London*, Efqre., whofe widow afterwards married *John Brickenden*, M.D.,
Efqre., one of the phyficians to the *Weftminfter* Infirmary. Mrs. Sarah
Brickenden, after the death of her hufband, fold the eftate, which fhortly
afterwards came into the poffeffion of the Boteler family.

Once more let us retrace our fteps to the *Crofs.* Here, on the left hand of the road leading to *Butfole,* has ftood for many generations an inn called " *The Five Bells.*" The following is a lift of " mine hofts " from the year 1693 :—

> 1693, Michael Sampfon.
>
> 1707, John Cock.
>
> 1733, William Vidgeon.
>
> 1769, Daniel Vidgeon.
>
> 1771, William Pittock, Junr.
>
> 1806, Widow Pittock.
>
> 1822, John Wilfon.
>
>   Widow Wilfon.
>
> 1848, Edward Fagg.
>
> 1853, Jofeph Silver.
>
> 1856, Elias Culver.
>
> 1866, George Foord.

Further down the ftreet, on the oppofite fide of the way, there was formerly a fmall farm, once the property of the *Idley* family. At the beginning of this century it formed part of the poffeffions of Mrs. Elizabeth Rammell, of the *Lynch,* and is now the property of Mrs. Benjamin Moat, widow. The houfe, which is old and fubftantial-looking, is now in three cottages—of the land fome has been fold, and fome is cultivated as gardens.

Adjoining this property on the fame fide of the way is the *Fairfield,* where, fince A.D. 1450, there has been held annually on *S. Matthew's* Day (fince the change of ftyle it has been held on *Old S. Matthew's Day*) a ftatute fair. The chief bufinefs done at this fair is now in cattle and articles of pedlery. Oppofite the *Fairfield* is the meeting-houfe called

"Zion Chapel," erected in 1824; and a little lower down we come to *Southbank*, a neat cottage refidence, ftanding in a pretty little garden and fhrubbery, and commanding a very pleafing view towards Bettefhanger and Updown. It forms part of the *Boteler* property, and is now in the occupation of Mrs. Voules. At the bottom of the hill, paft the turn-pike, we come to *Butfole Pond*, a large pond formerly on the left hand of the road, but altered to its prefent pofition during the con-ftruction of the *Dover, Walderfhare*, and *Sandwich* turnpike road. It derives its name of *Butfole*, firft from the circumftance that in the days of archery, when every Englifh man and boy was expected to be expert in the ufe of the bow, the archery *butts* were erected near this fpot, on a portion of land now belonging to the Boteler property and ftill called *the Butts*; and, fecondly, from an old Eaftry family named *Sole* (mentioned by *Hafted*, vol. iv., p. 224, note *s*.). Or may it have been *Butts hole*, the hole or pit near the butts? I leave this for the folution of my readers.

Turning to the right along the valley we come to *Wendeftone, Wenftone*, or *Wenfon*, a hamlet of two houfes, one of which is a fmall farm of about 50 acres, formerly belonging to one *Nicholas Freefby*, afterwards to the *Rammell* family, then to the *Petmans*—now *Henniker*.

Afcending the hill, and croffing the down, we come to *Shrinkling*, commonly called *Shingleton*, a farm confifting of about 237 acres in *Eaftry*, and 200 in *Nonnington*; great part of it being very light and chalky land. It is in the Borough of *Harnden*, and from the moft remote times it has always accompanied the *Knowlton* eftate. In *Shingleton* wood, near the fouth eaft corner, were formerly to be traced the foundations of the chapel referred to in the Endowment of the Vicarage of Eaftry (fee "*Appendix*"). Mr. Boteler thus writes of it in April,

A.D. 1784 :—" Upon a diligent fearch I have difcovered the foundation of the Chapel of Shryngelyngg juft within the wood. . . . . It ftands eaft and weft, is in length withinfide 38 feet—in breadth 19 feet, walls uniformly 2 feet in thicknefs." " Upon clearing away the earth the plaftering withinfide is ftill to be feen. The building was of the fame fize throughout without any diftinction of Nave or Chancel." Thefe foundations of the chapel are now grown over with grafs, and no trace of them is to be feen; but numerous wells—indicating the exiftence of a confiderable hamlet here in days gone by—have, from time to time, been difcovered in the wood. The Chapel of Shrinkling had fallen into decay previous to the diffolution of the Priory of *Chrift Church* (*temp*. Hen. viii.) Probably on the lands becoming attached to the *Knowlton* eftate, the Chapel was difufed by the Lords of the Manor of *Knowlton*, as having their own parifh church clofe at hand. *Shingleton* farm, on which is the *Wood* called *Pilholt*, is now the property of Admiral *D'Aeth*, of *Knowlton Court*, and is in the occupation of Mr. *William Wilfon*, farmer.

About a mile northward from *Shingleton* is the diftrict now commonly called *Harnden*, or *Hernden*, but anciently written *Hardenden*, or *Heronden*. Concerning the *name*, Mr. Boteler fays,—" I cannot find any authority for Philipotts naming this place Heronden. That this hamlet, as in other places, gave a furname to the principal family refiding there, and that the Boteler family became poffeffed of it by marriage with the female heir of that name, is exceedingly probable: but I have never, in writings of any antiquity, met with it written Heronden, but conftantly Hardenden, Hardindenne, &c." (*MS. C.* pp. 157, 158.) Neverthelefs, would not the arms of this family, *Argent a heron with one talon erect, gaping for his with fable*, feem to have *fome* reference to the name *Heronden*? *Hafted* fays that one of this family lies buried in the Church, *near the Chancel*, and that in the time of *Robert Glover, Somerset Herald*, his portrait and coat of arms in brafs remained fixed to his tombftone. This monument, it is believed, ftill remains *near the chancel*, viz., towards the fouth end of the crofs aifle, and *nearly in* the Chapel of *S. John Baptift*. The brafs, however, has long fince difappeared. The diftrict of *Heronden*, containing fome 330 acres, is in the upper half hundred of *Eaftry*, and pays quitrent to the Manor of *Adifham*. It now confifts of three farms, the Upper, Middle, and Lower.

This property anciently belonged to the family of the fame name; and fo far back as A.D. 1228, we find one *Robertus* de Hardindene owning land here. From the *Hardindens* the eftate paffed, probably by marriage, to the *Botelers;* who, however, did not acquire it all at one time, but would appear to have added to the original eftate by feveral fmall purchafes, until at length the whole diftrict of *Heronden* belonged to their family. For an account of the Botelers fee *Brook Houfe*, where I have fpoken of them more at length. It continued with the *Botelers* for many generations, until *Jonathan Boteler*, the eldeft fon of Richard Boteler, dying unmarried in A.D. 1626, the whole property came to his only furviving brother *Thomas Boteler*, of *Rowling*, who upon this removed to *Heronden*, and in no long time after fold that part of the eftate now called the *Middle Farm* to *Henry Parnell*, from whom it came into the poffeffion of the family of *Reynolds*, who, about the middle of the laft century, fold it to *John Dekewer*, of *Hackney*, Efqre., whence to *Frampton*—now Mr. *Stephen Clark*, yeoman. It confifts of about 116 acres, and is now in the occupation of the prefent proprietor.

Another part of the ancient *Heronden* eftate, now called the *Lower Farm*, after being heavily mortgaged, was fold by *Thomas Boteler* to . . . *Capell*, from whom it paffed into the family of *Johnfon*. In

A.D. 1693, it was in the poſſeſſion of *Thomas Johnſon*, Gent. *Daniel Kelley* (eldeſt ſon of *John Kelley*, who bought the Upper Farm, of whom hereafter) purchaſed this farm of *Edward Johnſon*, and by will, dated 11 Sept., 1724, bequeathed it to his ſecond ſon *Richard*, who, dying in 1768, the property came to his two ſons *Richard* and *William*. William died at Harnden, and was buried in Eaſtry Church ; Richard died at Canterbury, and was buried at S. Stephen's, near Canterbury. He left this property, together with his other eſtates, to his widow, on whoſe death it came to their only child, Elizabeth Clariſſa Kelley (now Croaſdill).

The *Kelleys* appear to have been a reſpectable old family originally deſcended from the *Iriſh* family of *O'Kelley*. They have monuments in the Churches of *Eaſtry*, *S. Mary's Sandwich*, and *S. Lawrence* ; and in Southwell and York Minſters there were formerly memorials of this family in the windows. They bore for their arms : *Argent two lions rampant combatant gules, holding in their paws a caſtle in chief vert.*

The remaining portion of the *Heronden* eſtate,—now in the occupation of Mrs. Grimaldi, and commonly called *Harnden*, or *Hernden Houſe*,—conſiſting of about 106 acres, remained in the poſſeſſion of *Thomas Boteler* above-mentioned until the time of his death in 1650. But being, by his will, directed to be ſold for the purpoſe of making a proviſion for his wife *Johan (Joan)*, and five ſurviving children, it was accordingly conveyed, in 1657, to *John Kelley*, of *Aſh*. In 1669 *John Kelley* bequeathed the eſtate to his ſon *Daniel*, after charging it with £40 per annum to his eldeſt ſon John, and £20 per annum to his ſecond ſon Jeremy. *Daniel Kelley* died poſſeſſed of it in 1733, and by his laſt will bequeathed it to his eldeſt ſon *Daniel*, who, dying in 1751, left the property to his ſon *William*, who, in 1766, pulled down the ancient manſion and erected the preſent handſome houſe, after the deſign of Weſtgate Houſe, Canterbury, on much the fame fite, and a few years after, viz., in 1784, alienated it to *John Harvey, Efq.*, Captain in the Navy, who occafionally refided at it, and who, dying June 30th, of the wounds he received in an engagement with the *French* fleet, on 1ft June, was buried in this church, July 5th, A.D. 1794.

Captain *Harvey* was of that ancient family which, as early as Edward IV.'s reign, were poffeffed of the Manor of *Barfield*, now *Great* and *Little Barville* in the parifh of *Tilmanftone*, and which has given fo many of its fons to the fervice of our country. The family were afterwards of *Eythorne*, then of *Dane Court*, in *Tilmanftone*, and afterwards of *Barfrefton*. "Capt. *John Harvey*," fays Hafted, "was born at *Elmington*, in the neighbouring Parifh of *Eythorne* in 1741; his fingular courage and attention to his duty marked his conduct throughout life, and never fhone more confpicuous than in the memorable engagement of June 1, abovementioned, in which, being commander of the *Brunfwick*, of 74 guns, he fuftained the fire of three *French* line-of-battle fhips, and deftruction feemed to menace him on every fide; but in this terrible conflict, by his intrepid bravery his fhip fingly funk one fuperior in force, and left two others abfolute wrecks upon the water; which individual conduct may truly be admitted to have contributed very materially to that victory, upon which the fate of his country in a great meafure depended, and will ever render his memory dear to it." By Capt. *Harvey's* will the *Harnden* eftate was devifed to his wife *Judith* for her life, with remainder to his eldeft fon *Henry Wife Harvey*, from whom a portion of it has defcended regularly to his great grandfon *John James Harvey*, Efqre., J.P.

The Harveys bear for their arms, *Argent, on a chevron gules, three crefcents or, between three lion's gambs erafed fable, armed of the fecond.*

Referring again to the eftate of *Harnden*, Mr. Boteler fays :—" In

K

1289 I find a part of *Harnden* lands were called *Woghope.*   *Richard de Woghope* was then the principal poffeffor—perhaps this family by extending its poffeffions, might affume the general name of Hardenden. *Woghope,* I think, I have fince feen written *Woodhope.*   Lands in the fouth part of Harnden Bottom are called Woodhope now."   In the laft century there was found in thefe grounds, ftuck on the tooth of a harrow, a gold fignet ring, which weighs 19 pennyweights, and has the *Boteler* arms, and the motto *do not for to repent* engraven upon it.   This is ftill in the poffeffion of the family, who have been kind enough to fhow it me.

And now proceeding about a mile northwards acrofs the fields we come to *Selveftone, Selftone,* or as it is now called *Selfon.*   This diftrict contains *Upper Selfon, Lower Selfon, Wells,* and *Gore,* all in the Manor of *Adifham.   Upper Selfon,* confifting of about 110 acres, all in Eaftry parifh, formerly belonged to the family of *Harflete,* from whom it was purchafed by Mr. *Richard Harvey,* of *Weft Studdall,* who refided here and died poffeffed of it A.D. 1675.   His fon *Thomas* refided here likewife, and dying poffeffed of it, A.D. 1696, bequeathed it to his fon *Robert Harvey,* who, in A.D. 1733, fold it to Sir *Robert Furnefe,* Bart., from whom it has defcended with the other eftates, and is now the property of the Earl of *Guilford,* and in the occupation of Mr. *Belfey,* farmer.

Lower Selfon confifts of two farms, one of which, containing about 70 acres, was formerly in the poffeffion of the *Whitfields,* a family of yeomen of property in this neighbourhood, from whom it came into the *Manwood* family, then to that of *Hardres.*   Thence it paffed to   .   .   . *Laflett,* who in turn fold it to *W. F. Woollafton,* Efqre, the prefent proprietor.

The other farm, containing about 60 acres, was for many generations in the poffeffion of the family of *Philpot.* It is now the property of Mr. *Beal,* yeoman, who refides there.

Wells, a farm of about 70 acres, was formerly the property of the *Friends* and *Whitfields,* from whom it paffed to the *Terrys*—then *Gibbs.* This alfo is now the property of *W. F. Woollafton,* Efqre.

Gore, a fmall farm confifting of a meffuage and 21 acres, belonged, in 1576, to the family of *Ower.* In A.D. 1594 *Richard Ower* fettled it on his fon *Boys Ower,* who by will, in 1623, bequeathed it to his three fons, *Edward, Matthew,* and *Thomas. Edward* and *Matthew,* the two furvivors, in 1641, conveyed the premifes to *Richard Harvey,* of *Selfon,* gent., whofe grandfon *Robert,* with others of the family, conveyed it in 1735, to *John Paramor,* Junr., of *Sandwich,* and afterwards of *Statenborough,* gent., from whom it paffed to *Wm. Boys,* Efqre. It now forms part of the Statenborough eftate.

The large farm at *Gore,* now called *Gore Farm,* formerly belonged to *Thos. Friend.* The houfe was built in the laft century. This is now the property of Mr. *George Terry,* of the Parfonage.

And now, retracing our fteps to the *High Street,* we come into *Woodnefborough Lane,* where, in the garden of *John Foord,* bricklayer, there is the entrance to a moft ingenioufly conftructed CAVERN or grotto, dug out of the chalk by the father of the prefent *Foord,* and containing numerous paffages, cells, and other ramifications, which extend for a confiderable diftance under the adjoining lands. It is fometimes lighted up with candles on the *Fairday,* or fome other like occafion, when it prefents a very fairy-like appearance. It is really well worth a vifit.

The *Union Workhoufe,* of which I have as yet made no mention, ftands in *Mill Lane.* It was originally erected in A.D. 1794, for the united Parifhes of *Eaftry, Northbourne, Shepherdfwell, Tilmanftone, Coldred,*

Lydden, Waldershare, Knowlton, Betteshanger, Swingfield, Denton, Wootton, and *Chillenden* (*Hasted.*, vol. iv. p. 224). The present *Union* was built in 1835-6, on the system known as Sir *Francis Head's*, and was first occupied in 1836. The following 31 parishes are those now included in the Union, viz.:—*Ash, Barfreston, Betteshanger, Chillenden, Deal, Eastry, Elmstone, Eythorne, Goodnestone, Ham, Knowlton, Great Mongeham, Little Monge-ham, Nonington, Northbourne, Preston, Ripple, S. Bartholomew S. Cle-ment S. Mary and S. Peter, Sandwich, Sholden, Staple, Stourmouth, Sutton, Tilmanstone, Waldershare, Walmer, Wingham, Woodnesborough,* and *Worth.* The following are the names of those who have filled the office of Master of the Workhouse up to the present date, viz.:—Messrs. *Watts, Lafflet, King, Walker, Fisher, Rigden,* and *Hetherington.* The usual number of inmates is from about 250 to 300; but there are now more than 400.

On the opposite side of the road stands the Wesleyan Methodist Chapel, erected in 1821, and close adjoining are the fix cottages of the *Greville's Charity,* of which a more particular account, as well of the past and present occupants, as of the original foundation, will be found under " *The Parochial Charities.*"

At the corner of *Mill Lane,* just where you come once more to *the Cross,* stands the house and buildings of the *Cross Farm.* This belonged for many generations to the *Botelers* of *Hardenden.* In A.D. 1630 *Thomas Boteler,* Gent., sold the premises, consisting of a messuage and about 50 acres, to *James Franklyn,* of *Maidstone,* Gent., and *Arthur Franklyn,* of *Badlesmere,* Gent., who, in 1638, conveyed it to *Richard Marsh,* of *Maidstone,* Gent., who, in 1654, conveyed it to *Thomas Kite,* of *Dover,* mariner, in whose family it remained for many generations, until it was at length repurchased by the *Boteler* family.

There is also added to this another small farm, the house of which is now pulled down, which was acquired by the faid *Thomas Kite*, of Eaftry aforefaid, in the year 1680, paffed with the reft of the property to his defcendants, and at length came into the poffeffion of the *Botelers* in the year 1837. The Crofs Farm now contains about 74 acres, and is in the occupation of *Baker*, farmer.

And now let us retrace our fteps as far as the turnpike on the Sandwich Road, and turn down the lane which leads to *Felderland* (commonly called *Fenderland*) and *Worth*.

A little diftance along this road, on the left fide of the way, we come to a comfortable-looking old-fafhioned houfe, with high-walled garden, and a few acres of land attached to it. This was formerly the property of the *Philpot* family—then it came to the *Dares*. On the death of Mrs. *Dare*, *Felderland* was purchafed by Mr. *Henry Matfon*, of *Sandwich*, banker, who added about 8 acres of land to it; and, on his death in 1815, it was fold to Mr. *John Hoile*, of *Sandwich*, brewer, who eventually conveyed the property to Mr. *John Harnett*, the prefent owner and occupier, in the year 1850. There are now about 11 acres of land belonging to *Felderland*.

> *So in and out, and round about,*
> *Through mead and copfe, by park and pale,*
> *Paft grange and hall, and ftede and mote,*
> *By bank and dyke, o'er hill and dale,*
> *On foot, on horfe, they take their courfe,*
> *Until the day begins to fail.*—Yᵉ PILGRIMAGE.

The Church, Dominical Circle, Frescoes, Ornaments, &c.

CHAP. III.

" This is none other but the House of God, and this is the Gate of Heaven."
GEN. xxviii. 17.

THE CHURCH, which is situated in a somewhat commanding position on rising ground, is dedicated to *S. Mary* the B. Virgin. It consists of a fine Chancel, a Nave with north and south aisles, a south Porch, and west Tower, with the aisles prolonged on either side of it.

The Tower and west doorway would appear to be the most ancient portions of the *present* church : for that there have been a succession of churches on the same site admits of little doubt. The earliest of these was probably built by one of the Saxon kings of Kent, whilst as yet their palace was at Eastry Court. Thus we may fairly claim for our Church a royal foundation.

From the narrow zigzag moulding round the semicircular arch of the west door, and certain diaper patterns cut in the stones of the tympanum of the same doorway, as well as from the solid piers which support the tower arch, we may judge the lower part of the tower to date from the end of the XIth or beginning of the XIIth century.

The ground outſide the weſt door has been ſlightly raiſed in recent times, and you now deſcend into the tower by five ſtone ſteps. The extenſion of the ſouth aiſle, which is now curtained off and uſed as a veſtry, is only acceſſible from the tower : the former entrance into it from the ſouth aiſle being blocked up by a huge buttreſs, which the ſettlement of the ſouth piers of the tower rendered neceſſary for the ſafety of this portion of the church. Mr. White ſuggeſts that "this ſettlement may have been cauſed, and the buttreſs required, by the breaking through of the arch for this extenſion ;" but Mr. W. S. Walford thinks that the extenſion was added to hide the buttreſs. The correſponding extenſion of the north aiſle is of later date, and formerly had a floor dividing it into two ſtories, the upper one being uſed as a *Parviſe* or Prieſt's Cham-ber. Mr. White thinks the ſouth extenſion may have been added as a Bap-tiſtery, and the north as a Galilee with a Parviſe over it. The organ now ſtands in this north extenſion ; as alſo a ſhort flight of wooden ſteps giving acceſs to the tower ſtaircaſe at the northeaſt *exterior* angle of that ſtructure. This door of the tower ſtaircaſe was evidently at one time outſide the church. At the northeaſt interior angle of the tower this ſtaircaſe projects into the church, and above the arches it is carried acroſs the angle upon a deeply receſſed arch and corbel table, with very intereſt-ing detail.

South of the organ ſtands the font, new in 1869. It conſiſts of a bowl of Caen ſtone carved, ſupported by four pillars of red granite placed at the corners, with a central ſhaft of light grey Purbeck.

The Nave, with its clereſtory, is of the early Engliſh period, and is divided from the aiſles by "an arcade of ſix." The four pillars on either ſide are circular with moulded capitals, one only excepted, viz., the ſecond pillar from the weſt on the ſouth ſide, which is octagonal, probably dating from the early part of the XIVth century. On the fouthweſt face of this pillar, immediately below the moulding of the capital, is the dominical circle defcribed hereafter.

Above the arcades are five clereſtory windows, with rounded trefoil heads, placed over the ſpandrils of the arches: thoſe on the ſouth ſide being filled with modern "quarry" glaſs. The lower and ſide windows of the nave, which are in three lights, with pointed trefoil heads, each window being under a ſemicircular arch, are all of the late Decorated period, with the exception of the two moſt weſterly ones in the north aiſle, which are Perpendicular. Many of theſe windows are filled with modern ſtained glaſs, and the different dates at which they have been put in will be found in the *Appendix.* The eaſt end of the ſouth aiſle was formerly a chapel with its own ſeparate altar dedicated to S. John the Baptiſt; and its *piſcina* ſtill remains, although the ſtone ſhelf within it, which ſerved for a *credence,* has diſappeared. At preſent the pulpit and prayer-deſk form a "two-decker" on the ſouth ſide of the chancel arch, but it is hoped that in time theſe may be renewed and reſtored to their proper poſition, viz., the pulpit on the ſouth ſide of the arch, and the prayer-deſk as one of the ſtalls, of which there were formerly eighteen in the Chancel of this Church. Theſe were probably arranged in the ſame way as thoſe in S. Clement's, Sandwich, that is to ſay, ſeven on either ſide of the Chancel, and two "return" ſtalls at the ends towards the weſt.

The Rood-loft and ſcreen, which at the Archbiſhop's viſitation in A.D. 1512, "lacked great reparation," have long ſince diſappeared, but indications of them ſtill remain, and their poſition may be traced. In this loft hung the rood or large crucifix with a light conſtantly burning before it, and from hence the Goſpel and Epiſtle were ſometimes read, and the ſermon occaſionally preached. The ſcreen was probably in a line with the centre of the chancel arch, which is pointed with a chamfered foffit. The arcades extend flightly beyond the line of the eaft wall of the nave, which is finifhed with a fquare quoin intercepting the curve of this arch. The eaft end of the north aifle was formerly the chapel of the B. Trinity, and contains a *credence* and *pifcina*, a ftone corbel apparently for fupporting an image, and an *Eafter fepulchre*.

In the wall, on either fide above the chancel arch, are two fomewhat unufual openings cut right through from the nave to the chancel, and apparently intended to take away from the bare appearance of the large blank wall above the arch. On the fide towards the nave thefe openings are quartrefoil in shape, on the chancel fide they are fquare with rounded trefoil heads.

Immediately above the arch are two rows of feven medallion FRESCOES, which will be defcribed hereafter.

The Chancel—which inclines confiderably towards the north, and is, therefore, not in a line with the nave—is raifed one ftep above it, and is moftly paved with graveftones. It is a good fpecimen of fimple Early Englifh; all the windows, with one exception, belonging to that ftyle. On the north fide there are five lancet windows, and on the fouth four lancets, and one two-light Decorated window, which was probably altered from a lancet in order to allow of the window-fill being ufed for the *fedilia*. The lancets on the fouth fide are filled with fingle figures in ftained glafs reprefenting refpectively S. Peter, S. John the Apoftle and Evangelift, OUR LORD AND SAVIOUR JESUS CHRIST, and the B. V. Mary (reading from weft to eaft). The Sanctuary is raifed two fteps above the reft of the chancel, and is feparated from it by a maffive oaken bar refting on iron ftandards. In this High Chancel there are, fingularly enough, no traces of a *pifcina*, though both the chapels in the nave have them. The

L

niche in the fouth wall which, meafuring 3ft. 1in. by 2ft 1in., was at one time fuppofed to have been a *credence* and *pifcina*, has recently been examined, and is now believed to have contained a *paxbread*,[*] or a lift of benefactors to the church, or perhaps a crucifix. Similar niches may ftill be feen in the Churches of *S. Clement's*, Sandwich, *S. Mary Magdalene*, Holloway, Bath, and elfewhere. It is, I think, too fhallow to have contained an image. On the fouth fide of the chancel there is a low and narrow prieft's door. The prefent altar has been twice enlarged, and now meafures feven feet in length, two feet and-a-half in width, and three feet and-a-quarter in height.

Under the High Altar—*the Altar of* JESUS, as it was called—there formerly exifted a crypt, which was ufed as the Chapel of S. Mary the Virgin, or " the Ladye Chapel." This is referred to in ancient wills and other documents, fometimes as being *in the church*, and fometimes *in the churchyard :* but the double defcription may eafily be accounted for, by the fact of its being in the church, and yet, perhaps, approached from the churchyard, and not from the interior of the church like the other chapels. The window (?) of this Chapel of S. Mary in the crypt, may ftill be traced on the fouth fide of the exterior portion of the chancel wall. It is almoft unneceffary to ftate that the crypt has long fince been filled in.

The eaft wall of the chancel is pierced with a triplet of lancet windows (with fhafts and trifoliated excoinfon arches) which have been filled with ftained glafs by the parifhioners and others within the laft few years (fee *Appendix*). The fubjects of thefe three windows are as follows :—

---

[*] Ufed for conveying the " kifs of peace," and frequently made of filver or fome other precious material. See *Arch. Cant.* vol. iv., pp. 226, 230, for mention of a filver paxbread bequeathed, A.D. 1417, by John Wotton, Mafter of the Collegiate Church of All Saints, Maidftone, to the Altar of S. Thomas the Martyr.

NORTH.	MIDDLE.	SOUTH.
(i) **The** Baptifm of our B· Lord.	(i) The Refurrection.	(i) The raifing of the son of the widow of Nain.
(ii) Our Saviour talking with **the** woman of Samaria at the well.	(ii) The Crucifixion. (iii) The Adoration of the Magi.	(ii) Our B. Lord's agony in the garden. The difciples fleeping. An Angel from heaven appearing to ftrengthen Him.

On the north fide of the altar, clofe to the eaft wall, there is an *aumbry*, or locker, for the fafe keeping of the holy veffels, &c.

A little further to the weft, outfide the Sanctuary, there hangs, on an iron crook driven into the north wall, an old helmet, which is furmounted by the Nevinfon creft, viz., *a wolf paffant ar., pellettée, collared, lined, and ringed or.* Tradition ftates that the helmet was formerly accompanied by a lance and pennon belonging to the fame ancient family many of whom lie buried here (fee "*The Monuments*"). Mr. Boteler gives the following traditional verfes concerning one of this family, as being current in Eaftry in his day :—

> *O brave Sir Roger Nevinfon*
> *That with his fword did cut in fun-*
> *Der the fhoulder of Sir Harry*
> *Becaufe he wouldn't his fifter marry.*

And afks, Are thefe lines mere waggery, or can they have relation to any tranfaction previous to the marriage of his fifter Anne to Sir Henry Crifpe ?

The following defcription of the DOMINICAL CIRCLE, which is on the fouth-weft face of *the* octagonal pillar, is taken from the Archæological Journal, and is by Wefton Styleman Walford, Efqre., a gentleman who has often examined and carefully ftudied the various features of our church.

" Mr. W. S. Walford exhibited a rubbing from a carving on a pillar in Eaftry Church. It is a little more than five feet from the floor, and at a convenient height confequently for infpection, on the fouth-weft face of an octagonal pillar (being the fecond pillar from the weft) between the nave and the fouth aifle. It confifts (fee fketch) of three concentric circles an inch apart, the outer one being eleven inches in diameter. The inner and middle circles are divided by radii into 28 equal parts, and in each of the compartments fo formed between thefe two circles is one of the firft feven letters of the alphabet, and above every fourth is another of thefe letters in a compartment formed between the middle and outer circles by the radii being there carried through to the outer circle. In this manner the letters A, B, C, D, E, F, G, are arranged fo that each of them occurs five times: but the order of them is the reverfe of alphabetical, the letters between the outer and middle circles being to be read immediately before thofe over which they refpectively ftand. Such is the order in which the Dominical letters fucceed each other, the two letters one above the other correfponding with thofe of the biffextile or leap years.

" As after every 28 years, which is the period of the folar cycle, the Dominical letters occur again in the fame manner, that cycle has been aptly reprefented by a circle divided into 28 parts. The refult was a table whereby, if the two Dominical letters for any leap year were given, the Dominical letter for any other year before or after it might be readily found, according to the then ftate and underftanding of the Calendar.

" The pillars of the church having been fcraped a few years ago, this carving, which had been covered over, was brought to light again. The lines and letters appear now but flightly incifed, the confequence probably

DOMINICAL CIRCLE IN EASTRY CHURCH.

of the fcraping : but they may all be made out. Mr. Walford could not learn that it had been explained before fince its difcovery, and, as far as he has been able to afcertain, it is an unique example of fuch a table. The church is a very good fpecimen of plain early Englifh architecture, but the pillar on which this carving exifts has the appearance of being fomewhat more recent in ftyle than the others, as if, from fome caufe it had been renewed, though it is hardly later than the early part of the fourteenth century ; and, fince the letters are what are generally termed Lombardic capitals, there is great reafon to think the carving, if not contemporaneous was executed but a few years after the pillar itfelf."— *Archæological Journal*, vol. ix., p. 389.

The feven MEDALLION FRESCOES, immediately over the chancel arch, are defcribed by Mr. Walford in the following terms :—

"About 5 years ago I had occafion to call attention very briefly to the Church at Eaftry, Kent, when I brought to the notice of the Inftitute a table for finding the Sunday letter, which is incifed on one of the piers, and of which a woodcut was given in the ix vol. of the Journal. On a recent vifit I found fome remains of early mural painting had been dif-covered there in July laft. Only a fmall part was made out and that alone continues any longer vifible ; yet, as it is of an unufual kind, I think fome account of it may not be unacceptable.

"I would firft mention that, unlefs the tower be an exception, the church is fubftantially Early Englifh throughout, though feveral windows have been fince inferted, fome of them very recently, being reftorations effected with more than ordinary care. Befides the tower it confifts of a nave with aifles and a chancel. At the eaft end of the latter is a triplet of lancet windows with fhafts and trifolated excoinfon (or hood) arches, and at the fides are fingle lancets, with the exception of the moft eafterly on the fouth fide, which is now a modern window of 2 lights, and the original was probably of the fame kind. The chancel arch is pointed with a chamfered foffit. The lower and fide windows of the nave were of 3 lights with pointed trefoil heads, each window being under a *femicircular* excoinfon arch. Thofe of the clereftory are fingle lights with rounded trefoil heads. The piers between the nave and aifles are round, with moulded capitals and bafes, except one, which is octagonal. If the tower be as fome have fuppofed 'tranfitional,' it is the oldeft portion of the building. It is remarkable for having a 'lean to' on each of the 2 fides— i.e., on the fouth and north, forming a peculiar weft 'facade,' which fhould feem to have been no part of the original defign; but to have been occafioned by an early 'fettlement' of the Tower, for the fouth 'lean to' conceals a large unfightly buttrefs, and the other was in all probability built to match it. More might be faid of the details of this interefting church, if the prefent were a proper occafion; but to proceed to the recently-difcovered remains of painting.

"The chancel arch is, as has been ftated, pointed, and on the weft fide of the wall above there was for many years fome rough wood-work, that had once fupported canvafs, on which the 10 Commandments were painted. In July laft workmen were employed in taking this down and preparing the whole weft fide of the wall for the reception of a coat of plaifter and whitewafh; when, after clearing away the wood-work, they came to fome plaifter on which were ftars on a blue ground; and, on removing this they difcovered confiderable traces of earlier painting, for the moft part too much obliterated to be made out; but immediately above the arch were 14 circular 'medallions,' nearly 18 in. in diameter, arranged in two horizontal lines of 7 each, with fubjects in them: the 4th medallion in each row being exactly over the point of the arch; the lower one indeed, was not a complete medallion in confequence of the point of the each interrupting it. The medallions are contiguous both horizontally and perpendicularly, and in the intervening fpaces are fmaller fexfoils or flowers of 6 petals. The whole had been enclofed in a rectangular parallelogram now obliterated, which like a frame feparated them from the reft of the paintings. The face of the wall above the arch now appears flufh, but the lower part was for fome little diftance thicker than the upper; it then fell back into a gentle flope, above which it prefented another perpendicular face. [In the recent reftoration of the nave roof this feature has been once more brought out. W. F. S., 1869.] This break in the furface of the wall muft have made it unfuitable for any large fubject. There were, however, traces of painting on both portions; but the rows of medallions are on the lower portion of the wall only.

"The fubjects in the upper row taken in order are as follows :—

" 1. A Lion, paffant, to the finifter.

" 2. A Griffin (a figure with the forequarters derived from an Eagle, and the hinder from a Lion), alfo paffant, but to the dexter; fo that No. 1 and 2 face each other.

" 3. Two birds, back to back, their wings clofed, their heads turned backwards, fo that their beaks almoft meet. Between them are fome traces of an object which was too much obliterated to be confidently made out, but probably a bunch of grapes on an erect ftem.*

" 4. A conventional Flower or Floral device not refembling any real flower; but fuch as is fometimes found on tiles and glafs of the 13th century, confifting of an upright ftem with a trefoil head, from which ftem iffue two pairs of oppofite fhoots, terminating in irregular petals; the upper (being

---

* See *Arch. Cant.*, vol. iv., p. 63, for a notice of tiles with a fomewhat fimilar pattern, found in the undercroft of S. Auguftine's, Canterbury.

alfo the larger) flant upwards and then turn from the ftem downwards, while the lower pair flant upwards and then turn towards the ftem.

" 5. Two Birds, as No. 3, the intervening object alfo obliterated.

" 6. A Lion as No. 1.

" 7. A Griffin as No. 2.

" The fubjects of the lower row are lefs clear, yet they appear to be the fame as thofe in the upper row, but rather differently arranged thus :—[Thefe were afterwards covered again with whitewafh.]

" 1. Obfcure, but probably a Griffin paffant, to the finifter.

" 2. A Lion paffant, to the dexter.

" 3. Two Birds as in the upper row, the intervening object wanting.

" 4. This fubject is almoft gone, but what remains is not inconfiftent with the fuppofition of its having been a conventional flower, and in all probability it refembled No. 4 in the upper row.

" 5. Two Birds, as in the upper row, the intervening object alfo wanting.

" 6. Very obfcure, but probably a Griffin paffant to the finifter.

" 7. Alfo obfcure, but probably a Lion paffant to the dexter.

" The colours are chiefly black or very dark brown, red, yellow, and a yellowifh red; the ground is buff. The medallions are formed of a thin dark circular outline, and two concentric circles of border lines, refpectively dark and either red or yellow, leaving a fpace in each of about 13 inches in diameter clear for the feveral fubjects, the outlines of which appear to have been drawn very boldly, with a full brufh and a free hand, like what are often feen in painted glafs of the 13th century. The colours feem funk into the ground, as if like frefcoes, they were laid on wet plaifter: but it is poffible that the rubbing they have fuffered, from time to time, may have given them this appearance. The yellows are very much faded,

MEDALLION FRESCOES OVER THE CHANCEL ARCH IN EASTRY CHURCH.

and the reds have loft much of their original colour, and are a good deal blackened. It is remarkable that the object between the two birds fhould in every inftance have almoft difappeared: in one it fhould feem to have been erafed, but this may be the effect of an accident or careleffnefs in removing the plaifter that overlaid it.

"Two Birds with a vafe, cup, grapes, or a vine between them, are found in the 12th and 13th centuries affociated with Chriftian fymbols in fuch a manner as to leave no reafonable doubt of their having had a fymbolic meaning of a facred character. On the old Font in Winchefter Cathedral they are to be feen at the top in two of the corners, with a vafe between them, out of which they appear to be drinking, and a Crofs is iffuing from it. They occur alfo on one fide no lefs than three times, in as many circular medallions: in the middle one they have grapes between them which they are pecking. In each of the other two medallions they are back to back with their heads reverfed, and what may have been intended for grapes, between or rather above them, which they difregard. All thefe are Doves.

"A fepulchral flab at Bifhopfton, Suffex, has on it within three circular medallions, formed of a cable moulding, a Crofs, an Agnus Dei, and two Birds (very fimilar in form and attitude to thofe at Eaftry) with a vafe between them, into which their beaks are inferted. Such Birds are not unfrequently to be feen on tiles of the 13th century, and alfo occafionally on feals with a vafe or plant between them; in moft cafes probably a mere ornament, though derived from examples that were fignificant. The device is Italian and may be traced back to the early Mofaics, as in the Church of St. Appolonus Novus, at Ravenna, which is confidered to be of the 6th century, and even to the Chriftian memorials in the catacombs at Rome, where two birds occur, as fhewn by Aringhi and others, not

M

only with a vafe or vine, but alfo fometimes with a Crofs, and fometimes with a Chriftian monogram between them, leaving no doubt of their having had a religious meaning. On a tomb, faid to be that of the Emperor Honorius, is a vafe between 2 Birds, apparently about to drink out of it; and at one preferved at Ravenna, faid to have been erected by Theodoric King of the Vifigoths, is a crofs between 2 Birds with other Chriftian fculpture; and alfo on a Sarcophagus at St. Stephen's, Bologna. Like fome other Chriftian fymbols in the Catacombs, this was, in all probability, derived from a Pagan device; but with fome modification, to give it a Chriftian fignification. On one tomb there, no doubt a Pagan memorial, are 2 Birds looking at an altar between them, on which was a fmall fire. To enter fully into this curious fubject would far exceed the limits of a paper appropriate to the prefent occafion. Affuming, as I think we fafely may, that the Birds in Eaftry Church formed part of a Chriftian fymbol, it is highly probable from what remains that the object between them was a bunch of grapes on an upright ftem, a form, however unnatural, yet fometimes met with. I am aware that a wheat ear is fpoken of as fymbolifing the Body of the Saviour, and that a bafket with apparently fruit or little cakes between 2 Birds, is to be found amongft the devices in the Catacombs; ftill grapes appear to me beft to agree with the firft traces of the object in this inftance. In the earlieft examples the Birds were moft likely intended for Doves: though in later times no particular kind of bird was uniformly reprefented. The more prevalent opinion I believe is that they fymbolized the Faithful, and the vine, cup, or grapes, the Blood of the Saviour. Some have fuppofed them to fignify the Jewifh and Chriftian churches looking to, or fharing in, the benefits purchafed by the Saviour's Paffion and Death. This feems a little too imaginative. I have, however, heard of or feen an example that I cannot now find, in which one of the Birds fronts the cup or bunch of grapes, and the other is back to it, but with the head reverfed fo as to reach it with the beak. The fymbol, if at all, would more eafily admit of fuch an explanation. Dr. Milner fuppofed the Doves on the Winchefter Font, with the vafe between them, were emblematic of the Holy Spirit breathing into phials containing the two kinds of facred chrifm ufed in Baptifm. But the early examples fhew the improbability of this : add to which that the Holy Spirit was not likely to be reprefented by *two* Doves. Now, if the Birds in queftion at Eaftry were a Chriftian fymbol, it is highly probable that the fubjects of the other medallions were fo too.

" The *Floral device*, which will be obferved, is in the middle of each row, and thus had fome degree of importance given to it, may be an emblem of the B. Virgin, who was often fymbolifed by a lily, and not unfrequently by fome conventional form of flower, having little or no refemblance to a lily, as is exemplified on many feals of the 12th and 13th centuries.

" *The Lion* may have referred to the Saviour who, as the Lion of the tribe of Judah, is fometimes fo reprefented. It is thus that the Lion has been underftood on the old Font at Winchefter before mentioned ; on one fide of which are 3 circular medallions, and in the middle one is a Lion, and in each of the others a Dove.

" To the *Griffin* it is more difficult to affign a fignification. It is rarely found amongft Chriftian fymbols. It has been not unfrequently, and even by fome mediæval writers, confounded with the Dragon, which had, not the hind quarters of a Lion, but the tail of a Serpent, and generally meant the Evil one, or at an earlier period Paganifm. I have mentioned that both the Lion and the Griffin are paffant—a peaceful attitude—and the former has no preference of place. (The Lion is sometimes found fighting with a Dragon.) A Griffin and a Lion both also passant confronting each other, and without any indication of hostility, occur on the old Font in Lincoln Cathedral, which is about contemporary with that at Winchester, judging from an engraving of the former in *Simpson's Ancient Fonts*. The other sculptures on it are not given so as to enable me to judge of their import. A writer in the *Vetusta Monumenta* speaks of there being three Griffins upon it. A Lion and a Griffin both passant and each in a circle, were two of the three animal subjects often repeated in the pavement of Tiles in the Chapter House at Salisbury. The other was the two Birds, but with a flower or plant between them. That pavement may be referred to the latter part of the 13th century. The Griffin is found too on early seals as a personal device, where it is hardly to be supposed to have had any discreditable signification, and it afterwards, we all know, became heraldic. Being composed of part of an Eagle and part of a Lion, it is likely to have been emblematic of the most honourable and admirable qualities attributed to each, and associated as it is on this occasion, we may reasonably presume it had some religious or sacred meaning, though what that was has not been discovered. What has been said of the Church, and the style of the painting, has indicated the date that I am disposed to assign to these pictorial remains. They must belong to the latter half of the 13th century, and can hardly be later than the beginning of the reign of Edward 1st. Those on the upper portion of the wall would seem to have been of a subsequent period if, as I understood was the fact, there were some fragments of black letter inscriptions on them. They may have been of the same date as the stars on a dark ground upon the plaister that overlaid the medallions that I have described. Should it appear to any one that these medallions may have reprefented part of a pavement, I would obferve that they appear too large for any fubject fuitable for the fpace, and befide that there were only two rows, and they were inclofed in a rectangular parallelogram, and there was not the flighteft attempt at anything like perfpective in the drawing.

" I may add that thefe remains have been left free from whitewafh and I have reafon to hope they will be preferved.   W. S. W." *(Archæological Journal*, vol. xv., p. 79).

Much intereft attaches to the ORNAMENTS of the Church, fince they often ferve to give us an infight into the manners, cuftoms, rites, forms, ceremonies, and religious obfervances of our forefathers.   It can never, therefore, ceafe to be a matter for deep regret that the Inventories of Church Goods and Ornaments—ordered to be made by Edward VI. in the firft and fixth years of his reign, and many of which are now pre-ferved in the Public Record Office, Fetter Lane—feem to been loft, and are now wanting, as far as our own Parifh is concerned, and, indeed, for many other Parifhes in Eaft Kent.   Had thefe Inventories been in exift-ence—as I fondly believed they were, until affifted by the officials, I had twice fearched through the bundle of Inventories relating to Parifhes in Kent, and fo convinced myfelf of their abfence—we fhould have been able to folve not a few minor queftions relating to the Church, as for inftance, how many Bells there were here in Ante-Reformation times, what became of the plate, &c., at the Reformation, what images there were in the Roodloft, &c., &c.

By the word *Ornament* we are to underftand Veftments, Books, Croffes, Cloths, Chalices, Patens, Relics, and even Organs and Bells.   The following is lift of fome of the principal Ornaments, &c., *now belonging*

to our church, with the names of the pious donors and date of prefentation.

Paten, Chalice, and Flagon, of filver prefented to the Church by
Vicar Creffener in A.D. 1718. There is no device, engraving
nor infcription either on the Paten, or the Chalice; but the Flagon,
which is very handfome and maffive, bears the words DEO SERVATORI
deeply graved on the fide within a floriated border, and at the bottom
" Eaftry, 1718."

Two Alms Bafins, the bowls of wood, covered with crimfon velvet
on the infide, the feet or pedeftals of filver. These were prefented to the
Church by Vicar Randolph, and bear the following infcription :--DEO ET
ECCLESIÆ CHRISTI A.D. MDCCCXXXV.

Two Altar Chairs of wrought oak, plain and fubftantial, given to the
Church for the ufe of the Clergy by the late Mrs. Charles Wood (formerly Jofephine W. M. Moore) in 1849.

An Organ prefented to the Church by R. Springett Harvey, Efq.,
in 1851.

An Eight-day Clock given to the Parifh by the fame generous benefactor in 1853.

An Alms' difh of beaten brafs, 18 in. in diameter, burnifhed and lac-
quered, with jewelled centre, prefented to the Church by the Miffes
Boteler, of Brook Houfe, in 1868.

A double Lectern of oak, handfomely carved, prefented to the Church
by the Rev. V. S. Vickers, in Advent, 1868.

Two Alms' bags of crimfon velvet embroidered, prefented by Mifs
Hatfield, Eafter, 1869.

Two Altar Candlefticks of wrought brafs, enamelled and engraved, 25
in. in height, given to the Church by the Miffes Boteler, of Brook

Houfe, in 1869, and firft ufed at Evenfong on Eafter day of that year.

A fet of 3 Altar Service Books—viz., a folio containing all the offices *entire*, faid at the Altar, and two quartos containing refpectively the Gofpels and Epiftles only. Thefe are bound in dark blue morocco with fimple gilt clafps; and have been illuminated by Mrs. Knapp and Mifs Voules, of Southbank, in this parifh.

DIMENSIONS OF THE CHURCH.

	Feet.	Inches.
Height of the Tower from the ground at weft door to the top of the coping	66	0
Length of each fide of Tower, at top within the walls	24	0
Length of interior Tower area below	18	6
Width „ „ „ „	18	9
Depth of Tower area below ftep of weft door	2	5
Thicknefs of piers feparating Tower from Nave	4	0
Length of Nave	77	10
Width „ „	40	0
Height of Nave from floor line to top of wall plate	30	0
Height of Nave from top of wall plate to point of rafters	16	0
Total height of Nave from floor line to point of rafters	46	0
Height of Chancel arch from floor to point of arch	18	6
Thicknefs of arch between Nave and Chancel	2	2
Length of Chancel	46	0
Width of Chancel	19	1½
Height of Chancel from floor line to top of wall plate	18	0
„ „ from top of wall plate to under part of ceiling at centre	9	6
Total „ from floor line to ceiling	27	6
Size of Prieft's door :—Height	5	6
Width	1	11½
„ West door :—Height	7	4
Width	3	11¼
„ North door :—Height	5	4½

	Feet.	Inches.
Size of North door :—Width	2	11½
,, South door :—Height	6	0
Width	3	6
Total length of Church internally	148	6
Extreme length on the outfide, including both the Tower, and		
Chancel, Buttreffes	162	0
Extreme width externally	44	0

References to the Ground Plan of the Church.

A The Weft Door.

BB Buttreffes forming the fides of the weft porch, traces of which may be feen, but which is not yet reftored.

C Extenfion of the north aifle containing a flight of wooden ftairs, giving accefs to the Tower ftaircafe at *c.*

D Extenfion of the fouth aifle, now the Veftry.

E North door, now clofed up.

F South Porch, from which there is a defcent into the Church by fteps.

G Chapel of the Holy Trinity.

H Chapel of S. John the Baptift.

I Prieft's door.

a The Organ.

b The Font.

c Entrance to newel ftaircafe.

d Holy water ftoup infide fouth door.

e Pifcina in Chapel of S. John Baptift.

f Pulpit.

g Pifcina and credence in Chapel of the Holy Trinity.

h Eafter Sepulchre in Chapel of the Holy Trinity.

i Niche in wall, fuppofed to have contained a lift of benefactors or crucifix.

k Sill of window formerly ufed for fedilia.

l Aumbry.

m Traces of a door or window, formerly communicating with the Ladye Chapel, and now blocked up.

n Lectern.

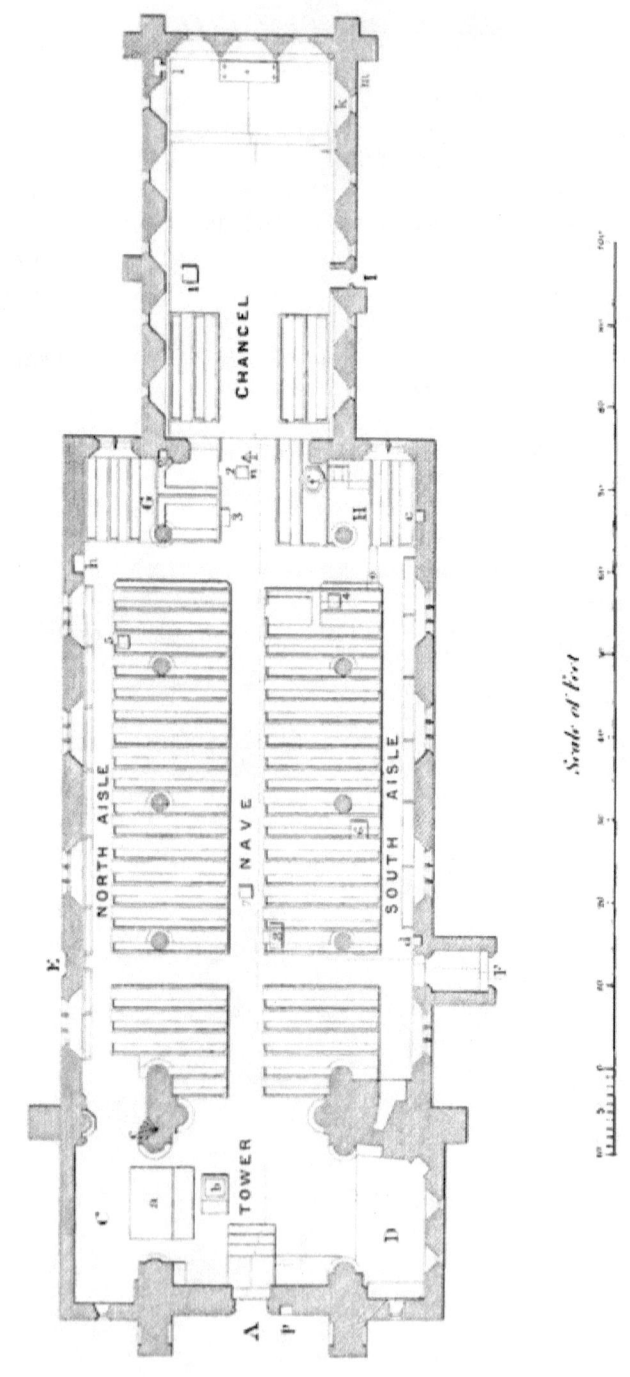

Scale of Feet

o Graveſtone belonging to Heronden family.

p Holy-water ſtoup outſide the weſt door.

1 The Bargrave and Bridger vault.

2 The Bargrave vault.

3 The Hatfeild vault.

4 The Greville or Statenborough vault.

5 The Boteler vault.

6 The Dare vault.

7 Capt. John Harvey's vault.

8 The Springett and Harvey vault.

> *In maſſive ſtrength it proudly ſtood,*
> *Some three miles off the Eaſtern flood :*
> *Reared unto God in days of old,*
> *By ſires new gathered to the Fold*
> *Of Chriſt His Church : a goodly pile,*
> *With Porch and Nave, and Tower and Aiſle ;*
> *A noble Chancel too, and ſtalls*
> *For eighteen monks againſt the walls.*
> *Its Altar High, of JESUS yclept,*
> *Stood over Mary's in the crypt,*
> *Enriched with gems and hangings rare,*
> *Rood, ſconces, tapers, chalice fair,*
> *And all things that required be*
> *To celebrate God's Mystery.*—Yᴇ Pɪʟɢʀɪᴍᴀɢᴇ.

N

The Monuments in the Church and Churchyard.

CHAP IV.

INSCRIPTIONS ON THE TABLETS AND GRAVESTONES IN THE CHURCH:

Supplied from the Boteler MSS., where they are now illegible.

IN THE CHANCEL.

Sacred to the Memory of
John Broadley, Gent.
Many years Surgeon at Dover,
Who died July the 4ᵗʰ 1784, Aged 79.
A Man of the higheſt Honour and liberality of Sentiment ;
of the Stricteſt Integrity,
And moſt approved ability in his Profeſſion,
of General Knowledge,
And particularly diſtinguiſhed for his Taſte in the polite Arts.
Frances his Wife,
Daughter of Iſaac and Chriſtian Bargrave,
in Teſtimony of her Affection
And in grateful Remembrance of his Merit,
has cauſed this Monument
to be erected.

In the Family Vault near this Tablet
Are depofited the Mortal remains of
William Bridger
of Eaftry Court in this Parifh Efquire
Who expired the 19th January 1855
Aged 81 years ;
Leaving an afflicted Widow
And Four Daughters
To lament their Irreparable loss.
His Piety was fincere and unobtrufive :
His Amiable and upright Character
Endeared him to a large circle of Friends.
Alfo of Chriftian Tournay his Widow
Daughter of
Robert Tournay Bargrave,
of Eaftry Court, Efquire,
Who departed this life 9th September 1858
Aged 5 years.
" Them which fleep in Jefus will God bring with him."
1ſt Theff. 4 : 14

Near this place
Lie the remains of Charles Bargrave, Efqʳ,
Who died Novʳ 1713 Aged 62 ;
Elizabeth his Wife who died Decʳ 1732.
Dame Frances Leigh, Relict
of Sir Francis Leigh of Hawley in this County,
Who died Feb. 1726 Aged 60 ;
Ifaac Bargrave Efqʳ, Eldeſt Son
of the faid Charles and Elizabeth,
Who died March 1727 Aged   .
Chriftian Relict of the faid Ifaac Bargrave,
And Daughter of the aforefaid
Sir Francis Leigh and Frances his Wife,

Who died Oct[r] 1772, Aged 74 ;
Isaac Bargrave Esq[r], Only Son of the aforesaid
Isaac and Christian,
Who died 24th of May 1800, Aged 77.
Sarah his Wife, Daughter of George Lynch, M.D.
Who died the 16th of April 1787 Aged 63.
Christian Wife of
Robert Tournay Bargrave Esq[r],
And Daughter of the Rev[d]. Claudius Clare
And Christian his Wife
Who died the 23rd of September 1806 Aged 55.
Robert Tournay Bargrave, Esq[r]
Who died the 19th May 1825 Aged 68 Years.
Bargrave the only Son of
William and Christian Bridger,
Who died the 13th Aug[t]. 1822, Aged 9 Years.

(*A Coat of Arms.*)
Near the remains of her Husband
is interred
Frances Broadley.
A sound understanding
And
a retentive Memory
were Faculties
for which she was distinguished.
And
from Christian principles and motives,
she was
Religious and Charitable.
This Testimony
of Esteem and Affection
is recorded by
Her Brother Isaac Bargrave.

(*A Coat of Arms.*)

Here is interred all that was Mortal of
Mrs. Chriſtian Kirk.
A Woman from a religious principle and hope,
Patient and reſigned during a long Illneſs
Which removed her out of this World
28ᵗʰ Feby 1796, in the 78 Year of her Age.
She was the elder and laſt ſurviving daughter
of Iſaac and Chriſtian Bargrave.
The Revᵈ. Claudius Clare
was her firſt Huſband.
Her ſecond Robert Kirk, Eſqʳ,
A Captain in the Royal Navy.
*Who from his affectionate regard and
Concern for an excellent Wife*
Inſcribes this Memorial.
Where alſo are depoſited the remains of the
Above Captain Robert Kirk who died
the 20ᵗʰ of May 1802, Aged 70.

(*On a Braſs Plate.*)

To the Glory of God. in Memory
of John Fuller Spong, B.A. of Caius
Collᵉ Camᵉ and Curate of this Pariſh
Who died Octʳ 13ᵗʰ 1844, Aged 25
Theſe four Windows are erected by his only Surviving Siſter.

Edward Boys M.D.
And Elizabeth, his Wife
Placed this Memorial
of their beloved Infant
Edward George Boys
Born 15ᵗʰ January
Died 15ᵗʰ July 1801.

UNDER THE CHANCEL ARCH.

(A Coat of Arms.)

Sacred to the memory of

The Rev^d. Ralph Drake Backhouse, M. A.

late fellow of Clare Hall, Cambridge,

12 Years Vicar of Eaftry with Worth,

And Rural Dean.

He departed this life December 24th 1853,

Aged 52 Years,

Leaving a Widow and Seven Children

To lament his Irreparable lofs.

This Tablet

Is erected by them, as a record of

Their deep Sorrow for their bereavement

And their warm Attachment

To A beloved Hufband and Father.

My hope hath been in thee, O Lord: I have

faid thou art my God.   Pfalm xxxi. V. 16.

ON THE FLOOR OF THE CHANCEL.

On a flab of grey ftone, now almoft obliterated.

(A Coat of Arms.)

Here lyeth interred the Bodie of Jofva Paramovr Gent, he was buried Aprill 2 1630 aged 60 Yeares.

An honeft, holie, harmleffe Life he led,

and then Death brought him to this Grave his Bed

Heere fleepes his Bodie and his Soules at reft

Where Joyes & Pleafures crowne him ever bleft.

(A Coat of Arms.)

On a Plum Pudding Stone abutting to the above Eaftward were cut a coat of arms, very much defaced in Mr. Boteler's time but now wholly obliterated.

Southward of the above is a fmall oval piece of marble bearing this infcription :—

E. G. B.

1801.

---

*On a ſtone adjoining to the above northward is the following inſcription on
a braſs Plate :—*

Here lyeth intoombed the body of Sʳ Roger Neviſon, Knight, who deceaſed
the 25ᵗʰ Day of Ivly in ye Yeere of ovr Saviovrs Incarnation 1625.

---

*On a ſtone adjoining the above northward are the effigies of a man in armour
and a woman, alſo the following inſcription on Braſs Plates :—*

(Coat of Arms.)

Here lyeth the Bodie of Thomas Nevynſon of Eſtrye Eſquier who died ye
xxvii Day of July 1590 beynge att the tyme of his Death Provoſt Marſhall and
Scoutmaſter of ye Eſt Partes of Kent & Captayne of ye lyghte Horſes of the
lathe of Sᵗ. Auguſtines, who had to Wife Anne the Daughter of Richarde
Tebolde, Eſquier deceaſed by whom he had Iſſue ſix Sonnes and four Daughters.

Under the inſcription have been braſs plates for the Sons and Daughters, now torn away.

---

*On a grey Stone by the ſide northward of the foregoing, almoſt oblite-
rated :—*

Here lieth buried Anne Theobald, the Wife of Thomas Nevinſon and Edward
Fagge, Eſquires, the Mother of thirteene Children by them both, Happy both in
her Choice and Iſſue but in her Death, the End of mortal Happineſs, moſt happy.
She died the 21ˢᵗ of November 1594.

Heading the Graveſtone of Sir Roger Nevinſon is one of black marble,
on which were formerly the Portraitures of a man and woman in Braſs,
together with other plates.   All now torn away and loſt.

This was probably to the memory of Lady Mary Nevinſon, wife of
Sir Roger, by whom ſhe had iſſue 7 Sons and 6 Daughters.

Againſt the north wall, near the eaſt end of the chancel, is affixed an

Helmet of iron with the Nevinfon Creft, from which formerly depended a Banner.   The helmet remains; the lance and pennon have been loft.

(A Coat of Arms.)

Near this place are interred the remains of
Margaret Wife of the Rev. D^r. Pennington
Rector of Tunftal in this County
And Daughter of the Rev. D^r. Carter, late of Deal.
She was Born October 17th 1725,
and died February 18th 1798.

In grateful remembrance of the beft of Wives
and the beft of Mothers, and impreffed with a deep fenfe
of her many Virtues her Husband and only furviving Children
Thomas and Montague have caufed this Tablet to be erected.

(This Tablet was removed from the South fide of the Chancel to its prefent pofition in A.D. 1865.)

(A Coat of Arms.)
In memory of
William Dare Efq^r
late of Fenderland
in this Parifh
Who died the 7th September 1770
Aged 35 Years
Alfo of Eleanor his Wife,
Who died January the 6th 1806
Aged 73 Years.
And of Mary Read Sifter of
the above Eleanor who died
April the 27th 1812, Aged 75 Years.

(This Tablet was removed from the South aifle of the Church in A.D. 1865.)

(A Coat of Arms.)

In a Vault
In the middle Aifle of this Church
Are depofited the remains
of
Captain John Harvey
late Commander
Of His Majefty's Ship the Brunfwick,
who,
After glorioufly fupporting the honor
of the Britifh Navy,
On the Memorable firft of June
MDCCXCIV,
Under Earl Howe,
Died at Portfmouth on the 30th of the fame Month,
in confequence of the wounds he received
in the engagement,
Aged 53 Years.
The Houfe of Commons
To perpetuate his moft gallant conduct,
On that Day of Victory
Unanimoufly voted A Monument to his Memory
In Weftminfter Abbey.
His untimely Death only
Prevented his being honored in the Flag Promotions
Which took place on that occafion.
In him his afflicted Family and numerous Friends
Have fuftained an Irreparable lofs
His public Character being only equalled
By his private Virtues.
Alfo of Judith his Wife
Daughter of Henry Wife Efq of Sandwich ;
She departed this life On the 4th of September 1817,
in the 75 Year of her Age.
This Monumental tribute to departed worth

O

Equally displayed in both their Parents,
Is affectionately raifed and infcribed by their furviving children,
Henry Wife, John, Edward, Mary, Fanny, & Sarah.

(This Monument was removed from the Southfide of the Chancel in A.D.
1865.)

(A Coat of Arms.)

In memory of Mr. Richard Kelley, late of this Parifh who died the 5th of
May 1768, aged 89 Years & is interred near this Place.   Alfo of Mary his
Wife who died the 6th of Dec[r] 1775 aged 72 years.

I left this World in good old age
with all its giddy Train
By honeft Deeds when on its Stage
A better World to gain.

Near this Place
lie interred the remains of
William Kelley,
Son of Richard Kelley,
late of this Parifh ;
He died 18th July 1799
Aged 59 Years.

At the bottom of a Stained Glafs Window is the following :—

In Memory of Thomas Caftle
Born 3rd May 1790 Died 29th April 1860.

(A Coat of Arms.)

Juxta Sepultus Eſt

Gulielmus Boteler Armiger, S. A. S.

Hujuſce Parochiae, quae eadem illi Natalis erat,

Ab Adoleſcentia Ad Proveƈtiorem uſque Ætatem incola

Vir literis humanioribus deditus

Hiſtoriae et Topographiae Cantii Peritiſſimus :

In Magiſtratu, Caeteriſque Muneribus Publicis Fungendis,

Firmus et Sedulus :

In Privata Vita,

Summi in ſuos Amoris ;

Integerrimae Erga Omnes Fidei :

Cantuariae Mortuus eſt iv Die Septembris,

A.D. MDCCCXVIII. Aet lxxiii.

Uxores Duxit, Priorem, Saram, Thomae Fuller, Armigeri Filiam : Alteram, Mariam, Johannis Harvey, Armigeri, et Regi e Navarchis, Filiam ; ex illa Filius Unicus, Gulielmus Fuller, ex hac ſex Filii, Ricardus, Henricus, Johannis Harvey, Thomas, Edwardus, Robertus, Quinque Filiæ, Maria, Eliza, Julia, Agnes, Bertha ; Suſcepti, aliis Immatura Morte Abreptis, Patri Superfuerunt.

Maria, uxor Altera,

Mortua eſt xxiv. Die Oƈtobris

A.D. MDCCCLII. Aet. lxxxix.

Et Juxta Sepulta.

On a Braſs Plate.

In Memory of William Fuller Boteler, Q.C.
who died 23ʳᵈ Oƈtʳ 1845 Aged 68 Years.

On a Braſs Plate.

In Memory of William Boteler Son of the Above
William Fuller Boteler Born 23ʳᵈ Oƈtober 1810
Died 6ᵗʰ July 1867. "Remember me O my God for good."

(A Coat of Arms.)

Near this place are interred the remains of Sarah the Wife of William Boteler, of this Parifh, and Daughter of Thomas Fuller Efq, late of Statenborough.

She Died January 9th 1777 Aged 29.
Leaving Iffue (alas) one Son,
William Fuller Boteler.
How dire the purchafe, how fevere the coft,
The Fruit was faved the Parent tree was loft.
This Monumental fhrine, thefe plaintive lays
This laft fad debt, A weeping Husband pays :
Not that thy praifes, Virtuous fair, require
The breathing Marble, or the vocal lyre ;
But as a fmall, a juft return for love
Tender, unfeigned, and ratify'd above.

(A Coat of Arms.)

To the Memory of Thomas Boteler, Efq Commander, R.N.
Fifth Son of the late W. Boteler of Eaftry Efqr
Who having loft the greater part of his Officers and Men In H.M.S. Hecla while on a furvey of the weftern Coaft of Africa,
Fell himfelf a Victim to that Peftilential climate
Amidft difficulties, which even to the laft
His high fenfe of duty impelled him to refift
With unfhaken conftancy, fortitude and Perfeverance.
He Died off the Old Calabar River 28th Novr 1829, Aged 32.

This Tablet is erected to the Memory of
Lieut Colonel Richard Boteler,
of H.M. Corps of Royal engineers,
who after many Years of fervice at home,
And in Africa, South America, Spain, Portugal and Canada,
And laft as commanding engineer at Halifax in Nova Scotia,
Perifhed at Sea in H.M. Packet Calypfo

On his paſſage to England on leave of Abſence,
In the beginning of the Year 1833, at the age of 46 Years.
And Alſo to the Memory of
The Revᵈ. Edward Boteler M.A.
Sometime fellow of Sidney Suſſex College, Cambridge
And afterwards Vicar of the Pariſh of St. Clement, Sandwich,
Who departed this life Auguſt 9ᵗʰ 1831 Aged 32 Years,
And is Buried
In the Vault beneath.

In the Vault beneath
Are depoſited the remains of
Charlotte Boteler,
The Wife of William Fuller Boteler Eſqʳ. Q.C.
She died Novʳ the 18ᵗʰ 1839. Aged 57 years.
Her Husband hath cauſed this Tablet to be erected,
To record her deep Piety towards God,
And her great goodneſs as a Wife,
A Mother, and in all other relations of life,
And to teſtify his Grief for the loſs
Of his affectionate, and faithful, Conſort and Friend
Through a period of upwards of thirty Years.
This Tablet is alſo Sacred to the Memory of
Anne Boteler
Their Youngeſt Daughter
A Child carefully trained by her Mother
In her own ſteps of Piety and Virtue,
And of A rare union of Strength and
Simplicity of Character :
She died in Gower Street in the County of Middleſex,
May the 1ˢᵗ 1839. At the Age of 19 Years.

THE FOLLOWING ARE IN THE SOUTH AISLE OF THE CHURCH:

Sacred to the Memory of
Captⁿ. James Remington,
of the H.E.I. Companys 12th Reg^t. of Bengal N. Infantry,
Eldeft Son of David R. Remington, Efq^r.,
of the City of London,
And Martha his Wife.
He died at Cawnpore in the Eaft Indies
September 16th 1842 Aged 34 Years.
The Officers of the 12th Reg^t. Deeply Regretting
The lofs of an affectionate Companion and Friend,
Have caufed this Tablet to be erected, as a record
At once of their Sorrow and of the high Eftimation
In which he was held by them for his many
Manly and Generous Qualities.

Thomas Pettman
Born 1733,
Died 1809;
Defervedly Efteemed
For his many Chriftian Virtues.
This Tablet is erected
As A Memorial of Affection
By his Son.
Alfo William Son of the Above Born 1768, Died 1830.
Elizabeth his Wife Born 1766, Died 1819.

Alfo 3 Sons & 1 Daughter of the above Willm & Elizth Pettman
By Thomas Born 1790 Died 1853; Edward Born 1796 Died 1851
William Born 1798 Died 1818; Sufan Born 1791 Died 1818.

In A Vault in the Church Yard
At the Weſtern entrance to this Church
are depoſited the remains of Sarah
The Wife of Mr. Thomas Pettman of this Pariſh,
Who died the 30ᵗʰ of July 1797, Aged 64.
Alſo Thomas, Son of the Above named
Thomas and Sarah Pettman,
Who died the 12ᵗʰ of March 1783 Aged 21 Years.
Alſo of Sarah Suſannah,
Daughter of the Above named
Thomas and Sarah Pettman,
And Wife of Mr. Edward Cowley,
Who died the 25ᵗʰ of July 1792, Aged 27 Years,
With her infant Child.
Alſo of Elizabeth,
Daughter of the Above named
Thomas and Sarah Pettman,
Who died the 2ⁿᵈ of July 1799, Aged 31 Years.
Alſo of Philip, Son of the Above named
Thomas and Sarah Pettman,
Who died in his Infancy.

(A Coat of Arms.)

In Memory
of Thomas Boteler,
late of this Pariſh, Gentⁿ, who died
the 24 Sepʳ 1768, aged 54 Years.
Alſo of Richard Son of the above ſaid
Thomas Boteler by Elizabeth his Wife
who died the 29ᵗʰ of Janʸ. 1773,
aged 33 Years.
Alſo of 7 other Children,
5 of Whom lie buried at Eythorn, who all
Died in their Infancy.

Also of Elizabeth Wife of the abovesaid
Mr. Thomas Boteler,
and Daughter of Salmon Morrice, Esq'.
of great Betshanger.
She died the 6th of August 1775,
aged 65 Years.
This Monument was erected in the Year
1774 by their surviving children (viz)
Sarah, Elizabeth, Mary, & Catherine.

(A Crest.)

Sacred to the Memory of
The Rev'. Philip Brandon Backhouse, M.A.
Chaplain on the Hon. E.I.C. Bengal Establishment,
Formerly Vicar of St Mary's Sandwich,
Tenth Son of the late
Rev'. J. B. Backhouse, M.A. Rector of Deal.
He died at Agra in the East Indies, after A few
Hours' severe suffering on the 30th March 1841,
Aged 33 Years.
His afflicted Widow has caused this Tablet to be
erected as A tribute of her affectionate regard
For his Memory, and to testify her deep sorrow
for her bereavement,
" Go ye into all the World and Preach
the Gospel to every Creature."
Mark 16 Verse 15.

(A Coat of Arms.)

M. S.
Rev'. Druc-Astly Cressener A.M.
Hujus Ecclesiæ, per annos xlviii, Vicarii
Viri sanè
Plurimis nominibus Memorandi ;
Nulla Literarum Studia
Non libavit ;

Theologiæ fuæ, facrifque Paginis
Penitùs Incubuit,
Ecclefiæ Anglicanæ, Fideique Catholicæ
Propugnator Impavidus
Cœlebs, Parcius Forfan, fed Honeftè Parcius
Vitam inftituit :
Non ut Inutiles Coacervaret Opes,
Sed ut benificentiæ, ut pietatis officiis
Largiori manu administraret.
Deo Servatori, infuper, Arifque ejus
Tam in hac, Quam in alterâ Illâ
Ecclefiâ de Worth,
Vafa Argentea Dicavit.
Et
Quod Omnium longè Palmarium eft,
Doctrinam Chrifti
Vitæ Integerrimæ Sanctimoniâ
Morumque Simplicitate Primitivâ
Exornavit.
Ob'. Sept. xxvii. A.D. MDCCXLVI Aetat LXXXII.

(A Coat of Arms.)

Here lieth interred the Body of Jane Daughter of John Paramor of this Parifh Gent. and Jane his Wife, and Wife of John Hayward of Sandwich Gent. who departed this life the 18th of April A.D. 1720 Aged 24 years. Alfo the Body of the faid Jane, Wife of the faid John Paramor, who departed this life the 3rd Day of May 1732 Aged 57 Years. Here lieth the Body of John Paramor of this Parifh Gent, who departed this life the 25 day of April Anno Domi 1737 Aged 65 Years.

This Monument was removed from the South fide of the Church A.D. 1865.

The following is on a Brafs Plate beneath a memorial window) :—

Sacred to the Affectionate Remembrance
of A good Sifter, Wife and Mother,
Thomafina Fanny Kenrick,
Wife of John Bridges Kenrick Efq^r.
Died Feby 22nd 1859.
The gift of her Sifter C. M. Jofephine Toker.

(A Coat of Arms.)

In the Vault near this Place,
lie the remains of
Anne Maude Harvey
Youngeft Daughter of
The Rev^d. Richard Harvey,
and Catherine his Wife.
She died 10th March 1850,
Aged 81 Years.
Alfo thofe of her Sifter,
Frances Ann Elizabeth Harvey
who died 4th June 1852.
Aged 88 Years.

To the Memory of
Mrs. Ann Harvey
Daughter of Solomon Harvey Gent.
formerly of this Parifh
who departed this life the 12th of April, 1751,
Aged 64 Years.
Mary, the Widow of Mr. Henry Ellis,
and youngeft Daughter of the faid Solomon Harvey,
Died in London the 8th of Auguft 1776
Aged 73 Years.
And was Buried in the Church of
Allhallows Staining, She left Iffue
One Son William Ellis A.M. Rector of that Parifh.

(A Coat of Arms.)

In the Family Vault near this place lieth the Body of
John Springett Harvey
A Bencher of the Honourable Society of the Middle Temple and for feveral years one of the Mafters in Ordinary, and Accountant General of the high Court of Chancery.

Who departed this life the 1ˢᵗ Day of Auguft 1833,
In the 80 Year of his Age ;
Leaving iffue by Matilda his Wife (Daughter of Mr. William Burton Rayner, and Widow of the Revᵈ. John Lightfoot) one Son Richard Springett Harvey.
In the fame Vault lieth the Body of the Above named
Matilda Harvey
Who departed this life the 28ᵗʰ Day of December 1835
In the 76 Year of her Age.

———————

The porch and part of this South aifle were rebuilt and the Church was repewed, At the expence of the Above named Richard Springett Harvey
During the Years 1854-7.
In Acknowledgement of which two Stained glafs Windows were put up in this aifle by fubfcription of the Inhabitants in June, 1857.

———————

(A Coat of Arms.)

In Memory
of Thomas Fuller, Gent, of Eaftry,
who died 24ᵗʰ June 1748, Aged 79 Years ;
and Mary his Wife (Daughter of
Richard & Elizabeth Terry) who
died 16 November 1748, aged 78 Years ;
They left four Children, John, Thomas,
Mary, and Elizabeth.
Alfo of their two Sons, John Fuller,
Gent, of Eaftry, who died 12ᵗʰ Oĉtober
1760, aged 64 Years ; & Thomas Fuller Efqʳ,

of Statenborough, who died 17 May,
1773 aged 67 Years : and of Mary Fuller
a Daughter of the laſt mentioned
Thomas, who died 28 March 1754
Aged 18 Years.
Alſo of Mary Fuller of Eaſtry
Daughter of the firſt mentioned
Thomas Fuller, who died 11 July
1783 aged 86 years.

(This Monument was removed from the South ſide of the Chancel in A.D.
1865.)

On the Pillar adjoining to the foregoing in Marble :—

(A Coat of Arms.)

Near this Place in a Vault
lieth the Body of Catherine,
Wife of John Springett,
Citizen & Apothecary,
of London.
She died the 16th December 1762
Aged 74 Years.
Alſo of her Grandſon,
Richard Maud Harvey, Son of
The Revd. Richard Harvey
Vicar of this Pariſh,
He died 26th Decr. 1758, aged 4 Months.
Alſo of the ſaid
John Springett.
He died Jany 13th 1770
Aged 73 Years.
(This was erected in A.D. *1763.)*

On the adjoining Pillar eastward, and opposite to the last-mentioned, a similar neat marble monument.

(A Coat of Arms.)

To the Memory of
The Rev^d. Richard Harvey,
Who was
14 Years Vicar of this Parish.
He died 6th March 1772,
Ætat: 42
Also of Catherine his Wife,
only Daughter of John Springett.
She died 25th May 1809,
in the 85 Year of her Age.
They left Issue 2 Sons & 4 Daughters
John Springett, Richard, Mary,
Sarah, Frances Ann Elizabeth & Ann Maude.

THE FOLLOWING ARE ON THE NORTH WALL OF THE NAVE.

(A Coat of Arms.)

Sacred to the Memory
of Edward George, of Statenborough House
in this Parish, Esqr.
Who departed this life April 19th 1810
Aged 69 Years.
His duty to the Almighty was exemplified
by the fortitude, and pious Resignation,
With which he sustained a long
and severe Illness.
To his Neighbour he ever conducted himself
with the strictest honour,
and was on all occasions
The Poor Man's friend.
To record his Virtues and her affection,

His Grateful Widow erects
This Monument.
Alfo of Mary George, relict of the
Above mentioned Edward George,
Who departed this life April 28ᵗʰ 1820
Aged 50 Years.

(A Coat of Arms.)

Sacred to the Memory of
James Hatfeild Efqʳ, late of this Parifh, who died 10ᵗʰ Janʸ 1842, Aged 62
Years. He was the eldeft Son of John Hatfeild, Efquire, late of Norwich,
Banker, and has left Surviving A Widow and Daughter, who as a fmall tribute of
Affection for one of the beft of Hufbands and kindeft of Fathers, have caufed
this Tablet to be erected.

Alfo Sarah, Widow of the above-
named James Hatfeild, Efqʳ,
who Departed this life the 13ᵗʰ
of February 1846 Aged 75 Years.

THE FOLLOWING ARE ON THE SOUTH WALL OF THE NAVE.

(A Coat of Arms.)

Robert Bargrave Efqʳ. of this Parifh died 17ᵗʰ Decʳ. 1779, Aged 84. Elizabeth
his Wife Daughter of Sʳ Francis Leigh of Hawley in this County, died 2ⁿᵈ July
1737 Aged 32. Robert Bargrave their only Son, Proctor in Doctors Commons
died 14ᵗʰ Feby 1774, Aged 39.

Whofe fole Surviving Daughter Rebecca, Wife of
James Wyborn of Sholden, hath caufed this Tablet to be Erected.

(*A Coat of Arms.*)

In the Vault,
With the remains of his Father
Captain John Harvey, R.N.,
and of his Mother Judith,
are depofited thofe of their eldeft Son
Henry Wife Harvey,
of Harnden, Efquire, in this Parifh,
Who died 13th May 1852, aged 83 Years ;
Alfo the remains of Margaret his Wife,
Who died 14th June 1847, Aged 76 Years ;
And thofe of their five Daughters ;
Catherine died 23rd June 1808, an Infant.
Elizabeth,
The Wife of Captain George Hilton R.N.
Died 25th February 1819, Aged 26.
Margaret died 28th December 1819, Aged 16.
Mary died 8th September 1820, Aged 24.
Fanny died 8th April 1824 Aged 23.

In the Vault beneath,
Are depofited the remains of
Sarah,
Relict of the late
James Leigh Joynes, Efq',
of Gravefend in this County,
And third Daughter of the late
Revd. Richard Harvey
(Vicar of this Parifh),
And Catherine his Wife.
Obiit 27th October 1843
Aged 84 Years.

On a Grave Stone near the west door on entering the Nave :—

Near this place lies the body of Richard Keble, of this Parifh, Yeoman, died
21ſt of Auguſt 1740 Aged 61 Years. Alſo Mary relict of the above died 28th
Auguſt 1765 aged 82 Years. Alſo Mary their Daughter wife of Thomas Pettman of this Parifh died 25th December 1735 aged 27 Years leaving Iſſue Thomas
and Sufanna. Alſo Thomas Keble of this Parifh Yeoman Son of the above
died 23rd April 1763 aged 48 Years : alſo Martha Relict of the above died
2nd March 1787 aged 73 Years : Alſo 2 Children, Richard died 12th Auguſt 1756
aged 5 Years, Edward died the 9th March 1773 aged 19 Years : Thomas and Mary
Survive them.

Near this place lies the Body of the Above
Thomas Keble of this Parifh Yeoman
Died 15th October 1798, Aged 49 years.

Alſo Ann, Relict of the above died 11th March 1802 Aged 54 Years ; Alſo 2
Sons Bunce, died 11th December 1792, Aged 4 Years ; Thoˢ. Herman died
12th Decr. 1792 Aged 11 Years. Left Surviving John, Ann, Mary and Richard.

Here lieth the Body of
Richard Keble, late of this Parifh,
Died 20th Feby 1816,
Aged 30 Years.
Alſo on the Right, lieth the Body of
Ann Mary Keble, late of this Parifh ;
Died 20th October 1821
Aged 40 Years :
Alſo on the Right lieth
The Body of John Keble,
late of this Parifh, Yeoman ;
Died 22nd December 1832
Aged 53 Years.

The entrance of
The Family Vault
of Captain John Harvey.

On a Grave-ftone in the middle Aifle :—

Here lyeth the Body of Ralph Rennalls of this Parifh Yeoman Who departed this Life the 28ᵗʰ day of Febʸ 1661 Aged 73 Years.

In the fame aifle Eaftward adjoining to the above :—

Here lyeth the Body of John Kelley Gent. who departed this life the 18ᵗʰ Day of January in the Year of our Lord 1669 Aged 80 Years ; and alfo of Daniel Kelley, Gent. his Son who departed this Life the firft of June in the Year of our Lord 1733, in the 87 Year of his age.

In the Paffage from the Body of the Church to the Chancel on a Grave-
ftone of black marble :—

The Body of Anne, the Wife of John Auften & Daughter of William Nayler and Anne Finnit, being aged 68 Yeare, Dyed Febʸ 19ᵗʰ 1656, lyeth here waiting for the Refurrection of the juft.

In the Crofs Aifle, at the Eaft End of the Body of the Church, are three
adjoining Graveftones with Coats of Arms and Infcriptions on Brafs Plates :—

Here lyeth buried the body of William Boteler Efqʳ.
Who dyed the 22ⁿᵈ of May Aᵒ. 1614 Ætat. fuæ 50
Chriftus mihi Vita : mors mihi lucrum.

On a Graveftone of Black Marble :—

Here lieth the Body of Thomas Boteler late of this Parifh Gent, only Son of Richard and Sufan Boteler, Gent. who departed this life May 12ᵗʰ 1737 aged 61 leaving Iffue by Elizabeth his Wife, who alfo furvived him,
three Sons and three Daughters.

Likewife the Body of Elizabeth Wife of the above Thomas Boteler and Daughter of Ralph & Elizabeth Philpott who died 14ᵗʰ June
1749 Aged 61 Years.

On an adjoining Graveftone :—

Here lyeth the Body of Richard Boteler Gent. who departed this life the 22ⁿᵈ of May 1682 Aged 52 Years. Here lieth the Body of Sufan Boteler Wife of the above Richard Boteler, Gent, and Daughter of Saphire & Margaret Paramor, of this Parifh, Gent, who departed this Life Sepᵗ the 11ᵗʰ 1724 Aged 82 Years.

In the Crofs aifle above-mentioned there are three other graveftones belonging to the Boteler family befides thofe already mentioned. On thefe there were formerly brafs plates with Arms and Inscriptions, now torn away and loft. One of thefe has fince been recovered from another Church, where it had been turned over and ufed for fome other family. It has the following infcription :—

ARMIGERI QVI MORTEM OBIJT TRICESSIMO
RTIJ ANNO DOM : 1580. ET RICHARDI BOTELER
RI FILIJ EIVS QVI MORTEM OBIJT TRICESSIMO
VARIJ ANNO DOM : 1600. ET RELIQVIT QVIN=
LIOS ET DVAS FILIAS SVPERSTITES.

from which it will be feen that a portion of the plate and of the infcription are loft. Concerning thefe memorials of his family Mr. Boteler fays :—

"Some of them with arms retained their places within memory, and becoming loose, were afterwards thrown carelesly with some others in a hole under the staircase of the Tower, where they remained till a knavish sexton thought proper to sell them to a brazier at Sandwich for old brass. I have no difficulty in assigning them to the memory of Henry Boteler who died anno 1580. Richard, his son (the brother of William mentioned above), who died anno 1600, & Thomas, his grandson, who died 1651. All of whom were in possession of and lived at Heronden. Henry was the first of this family who was buried at Eastry, their more ancient burying-place for many preceeding generations being in S. Peter's Church, Sandwich."

At the south end of this aisle there is another gravestone (marked o in the plan), which, from its coffin-like shape, is doubtless of considerable antiquity. Mr. Boteler says concerning it: "I have no doubt but that it is the stone mentioned by Philpot that had formerly the Arms and Portraiture of one of the Family of Heronden affixed to it, though from time to time its surface is so scaled off as not to leave a trace of it. There is no other in the Church will admit of the conjecture; its situation near the chancel answers his description; besides the Botelers, in whom this family ended, appropriating this aisle to their burying-place, strongly favours the opinion; from the extinction of this family the stone cannot be of later date than the time of Richard II. [A.D. 1377-1399], probably not much earlier."

There are in the Church the following vaults—viz.:

In the Chancel:—The vault numbered 1 in the plan, being for the Bargrave family, in which also many of the Bridgers have been interred. There is also a vault on the opposite side belonging to the Paramours, which is not shewn on the plan, as the entrance is unknown, because the timber that fupported the ftones of the entrance of this vault giving way, it was bricked up in A.D. 1788.

In the Church:—Mr. Robert Bargrave's vault numbered 2 in the plan.

No. 3 being the Hatfeild vault.

No. 4. The Greville or Statenborough vault—very large.

No. 5. The Boteler vault.

No. 6. A very fmall one made in A.D. 1770 for the interment of W. Dare, Efq.

No. 7. Capt. John Harvey's vault.

No. 8. A vault for the families of Springett and Harvey.

INSCRIPTIONS ON GRAVESTONES IN THE CHURCHYARD.

We now come to the Churchyard.

In the year 1847 a piece of ground was taken from the Hammel Clofe, by the permiffion of the Dean and Chapter, added to the Churchyard, and confecrated by the Archbifhop. This new ground is already nearly filled.

Oppofite the South Porch there is an ancient yew tree which, amongft the old inhabitants of Eaftry, goes by the name of " the Palm tree "—it was fo called in Mr. Boteler's time—and has in all probability borne this name fince the day in which it was planted. *The origin* of the name would appear to be, that in ante-Reformation times branches of yew were ufed inftead of palm branches in the services of the Church on the Sunday next before Eafter, commonly called *Palm Sunday*. In the fame way, in other parts of the country, branches of willow, with the catkins on them, are called "palm," and were probably ufed as a fubftitute for the real Eaftern palm tree in former days.

There are in the Churchyard the following vaults :—

1. A vault belonging to the family of *Petman* near the weftern entrance of the Church, under the gravel-path, on the fouth of the main path to the weft door. This is of confiderable fize, and was enlarged fome 50 years ago.

2. A vault holding fome 8 or 10 coffins, belonging to the *Baker* family, commonly called *Sharpe's vault*, at the extreme north-weft corner of the Churchyard, adjoining Eaftry Court.

3. A vault belong to the family of *Rae*, of Walton Houfe, made to contain 9 bodies. This was made in A.D. 1843, and is on the north fide of the Church.

4. The *Sayer* vault, on the fouth fide of the Church, and eaft of the fouth porch, conftructed in 1851 to hold fome 9 bodies.

5. A large vault belonging to the family of *Rammell*, lying on the fouth fide of the Church, to the weft of the Chancel door.

6. The *Fuller* vault, which has not been opened within memory, lying on the fouth fide of the Church, eaft of the Chancel door.

Mary Wife of John Matfon, and only Child of Stephen Goldfinch d. 22nd May 1701 Aged 29.

Stephen Goldfinch d. Nov. 18th 1722 Aged 83.

James Harvey d. 18th January 1820 Aged 90.
Efther Wife of the above d. 24th Jany. 1819 Aged 84.

Mary Wife of John Elgar d. Nov' 12th 1796 Aged 67.

William Smeeth, 28 Years the faithful Baliff of Henry Wife Harvey Efq. of Harnden, in this Parifh, By every branch of whofe Family he was much refpected He died on the 15th of February 1831. Aged 62 Y's.

He proved this truth in the path he trod,
An honeft Man' the nobleft work of God.

Mary Ann Wife of Morris Upton d. 8 April 1796 Aged 27. Alfo 2 Children d. in their Infancy, Viz John and Mary.

All you that come my grave to fee
As I am now fo muft you be
Prepare to die make no delay
I in my prime was fnatch'd away
In love I liv'd in peace I died
When God thought fit for to divide.
Alfo the above named Morris Upton
Died 20th October 1832 Aged 67.

Sufan Wife of Robert Mann, d. 27 Auguft 1861 Aged 24.

Elizabeth Wife of John Moat d. 10th July 1793 Aged 36.
Alfo the above said John Moat d. 5 June 1794 Aged 39.

Sarah Wife of Robert Gardener D. 27th Nov' 1830 Aged 28.

Thomas Mann Eldeft fon of Thomas & Elizabeth Mann, d. 28th June 1839 Aged 20 Y's.

In love he lived in Peace he died
In hope with God he fhall abide.

Alfo Thomas George Eldeft Son of James and Lucy Mann of Sandwich Grandfon of the above Thomas & Elizabeth Mann
Died 6th January 1861 Aged 8 Y's.

Betty Wife of Thomas Mann d. Novr 3rd 1864 Aged 68.
She is not dead but sleepeth
In hopes of a Joyful Resurrection.
Also the above-named Thomas Mann
Died 16th May 1869 Aged 77.

William Son of John & Mary Moat
Died 22nd December 1821 Aged 10 Y^{rs}.
Also Mary Ann, their Daughter D. 3rd May 1829, A. 1 Y^r. 8 M^{hs}.

Robert Mann Son of Thomas & Betty Mann
Died 3rd December 1826 Aged 1 Y^r & 9 Months.
Robert Thomas Richard Eldest Son of Robert and Sarah Mann D. 18th April
1867 Aged 19 Months.
Ere sin could blight or sorrow fade
Death came with friendly care
The opening bud to Heaven conveyed
And bade it blossom there.

Lawrence Marsh D. 23rd February 1812 Aged 69
Also Mary Wife of the above Lawrence Marsh
Died April 30th 1861 Aged 68.

Jane Daughter of Thomas & Charlotte Foord
Died July 2nd 1825 Aged 17
Henceforth be every tender tear suppress't
And let us weep for Joy that she is blest
From grief to bliss from Earth to Heaven removed
Her memory honour'd as her life beloved.

Charlotte Seath, Relict of the late Thomas Foord
Born 9th Novr 1777 Died 17 May 1850.

Thomas Foord D. 20ᵗʰ June 1809 Aged 45.

Simon Cock D. 27ᵗʰ July 1814 Aged 75
Alſo Sarah his Wife D. 21ˢᵗ May 1819 Aged 80.

Sarah Moat Wife of Henry Branfert
Died 28ᵗʰ March 1793 Aged 32.

Ann Moat D. 15ᵗʰ January 1835 Aged 63.

Jane Daughter of Richard & Jane Marbrooke
Died 18ᵗʰ Auguſt 1808 Aged 16.

Richard Marbrook D. 8ᵗʰ Febʸ 1830 Aged 75.

Thomas Fillis D. Febʸ 20ᵗʰ 1802 Aged 70
Alſo Sarah his Wife D. 4ᵗʰ Febʸ 1801 Aged 67.

John Phillis D. 13ᵗʰ March 1836 Aged 66
Alſo Charlotte Wife of the above John Phillis
Died 1ˢᵗ July 1850 Aged 84
This ſtone was erected by their Son
Mr. James Phillis, of Adelaide, Auſtralia.

Ann Wife of John Pittock D. April 8ᵗʰ 1780 Aged 38
Alſo the above John Pittock D Octʳ 5ᵗʰ 1834 Agᵈ 87
Alſo Ann, his Second Wife D. Octʳ 31ˢ 1835 A. 84.

William Pittock D. 7ᵗʰ Novʳ. 1775 Aged 76
Alſo Elizabeth his Wife D. 1ˢᵗ June 1774 Aged 80.

Ann Wife of Willm Pittock D. Feby 26th 1806 Aged 77
Alfo the above W. Pittock D. Auguft 18th 1811 Aged 88.

William Pittock D. March 12th 1841 Aged 45,
Alfo Sufanna Wife of the Above D. March 29th 1845 A. 52.

John Devefon D. March 29th 1853 Aged 77
He left Surviving Elizabeth his Wife and 13 Children
Viz. 10 Sons and 3 Daughters
Remembrance long will feel a pang fevere
And o'er this Grave Affection drop a tear.
Alfo Sufannah Downard Daughter of the Above
Died February 10th 1856. Aged 38.
Alfo Elizabeth Wife of the Above John Devefon
Died April 26th 1859. Aged 81.

William Belfey D. September 15th 1803. Aged 79
Dorcas Wife of the above William Belfey,
Died April 4th 1798 Aged 78.

Sufanna Wife of John Simmons D. 13th October 1780 Aged 62. Alfo the above faid John Simmons D. Sepr 23rd 1800 Aged 77.

Richard Fagg D. 22nd April 1727 Aged 55.

Edward Fagg D. Decr 6th 1780 Aged 61
Elizabeth his Wife D. 11th Auguft 1778 Aged 57.

Sarah Wife of Richard Fagg D. 22nd Decr 1799 Aged 50
Alfo the Above Richard Fagg D. 20th March 1810 Aged 64
Alfo three Children died in Infancy.

R

Ralph Pittock D. Novr 25th 1813. Aged 57.

Harriet Daughter of Willm & Mary Ann Pittock
Died 15th July 1809   Aged 14 Months.
Alfo William their Son Died 11th Feby 1810
in early Infancy.

Stephen Church D. Jany 16th 1798 Aged 60
Alfo Mary Wife of the Above Stephen Church
Died October 19th 1832 Aged 83
Likewife James Son of the Above Stephen & Mary
Church Died July 9th 1797 Aged 21.

Jane Arnold D. June 20th 1824 Aged 83
Alfo William Arnold Hufband of the Above
Died 8 June 1825 Aged 85.

William Ledner D. 26th Feby 1795 Aged 85
Alfo Sarah, his Wife D. 16th Novr. 1798 Aged 82.

James Hudson D. 25th Auguft 1819 Aged 65
Alfo Mary Wife of the Above D. Sep^t 11th 1846 Aged 90
Alfo William Son of the Above D. Decr 6th 1846 Aged 50.

Jane Daughter of Michael and Mary Cock
Died 10th November 1794 Aged 25.

Richard Soames D. 29th May 1805 Aged 53
Alfo Sarah Wife of the Above D. 8th Augt 1832 Aged 80.

Richard Soames D. 6th November 1850 Aged 72.

———————

Dilnot Sladden of the City of Canterbury, Solicitor,
Son of Isaac Sladden of Selson in this Parish
Died 25th June 1839 Aged 25.

———————

Elizabeth Wife of Isaac Sladden D. 2nd March 1816.
Aged 34. Also the Above named Isaac Sladden
Died 25th March 1861 Aged 79.

———————

Thomas Kelsey, Gent. D. 29th August 1829 Aged 85.
Also Mrs. Catherine Kelsey, Widow of the Above
Died 20th July 1836, Aged 86.

———————

(*On a flat stone railed round.*)
Thomas Castle D. 29th April 1860 Aged 69
Also Caroline & Charlotte D. in their Infancy May 1821.

———————

James Hudson D. Sepr 24th 1755 Aged 48
Mary Wife of the Above D. Novr 22nd 1780. Aged 77.

———————

Thomas Beer D. March 3rd 1804 Aged 79
Also Mary Wife of the Above Thomas Beer
Died 25th May 1822. Aged 88.

———————

James Hudson D. January 14th 1816 Aged 84.

———————

Thomas Morris D. 7th August 1835 Aged 59.

This Stone is erected in Memory of Ann Rewell by the Members of a family refident in this Parifh to record their Affectionate and Grateful fenfe of her long and faithful Service, and to fhew that integrity and Diligence make the Poffeffor refpected in life and lamented in Death.

She Died 18th Auguft 1829 Aged 66.

Alfo Sarah Mills D. 2nd Auguft 1862 Aged 62.

Ann Wife of Stephen Court, Clerk, and Daughter of
William Aynott D. 28th Auguft 1826 Aged 85.

Stephen Court 55 Years Clerk of this Parifh
Died 6th June 1830. Aged 86.

William Aynott D. 26th July 1775 Aged 70
William Son of the Above D. 1748 Aged 15
Alfo Elizabeth Daughter of the Above faid William Aynott
Died 29th January 1774 Aged 39.

Elizabeth Aynott D. 30th April 1811 Aged 97.

Edward Terry D. Feby 28th 1849 Aged 71
Alfo Elizabeth Wife of the Above D. Feby 15th 1834 Aged 55
Alfo Elizabeth Daughter of the Above D. June 20th 1838 Aged 17
Alfo Edward Hacklinge Son of the Above Died
January 30th 1816 Aged 3 Y^{rs}.
Alfo 2 Children who Died in their Infancy.
William Terry Son of George Terry. D. March 3rd 1849
Aged 10 Weeks.

John Barton late of Worth. D. 20th Jany 1763 Aged 44
Alſo Ann his Wife D. 29th June 1768 Aged 45.

James Fells D. 3rd March 1849 Aged 65.

Thomas Fells D. July 8th 1793 Aged 47
Alſo Ann Wife of the Above D. Jany 13th 1835 Aged 79
Likewiſe Thomas Son of the Above D. Octr 14th 1835 Aged 55.

John Tanton D. 31^{ſt} December 1794 Aged 69.

Jeſſe Betts D. 21^{ſt} February 1829 Aged 42.

Ann Thompſon Daughter of Thomas Adams of Updown
Died 9th October 1757 Aged 69.

Thomas Adams late of Updown D. 8th July 1730 A. 69.

Elizabeth Wife of Mr. John Solly D. 24th Jany 1805 Aged 71
Alſo the Above ſaid John Solly D. Feby 4th 1811 Aged 76.

Elizabeth Wife of Richard Ruſſell D. 12th May
1798 Aged 38, Alſo the Above ſaid
Richard Ruſſell D. 15th October 1816 Aged 63.

Elizabeth Wife of Richard Sladden D. 17th June
1806 Aged 26.   Alfo James Son of the Above
Died 20th July 1806 Aged 15 Months.

Ann Wife of Charles Pott D. 23rd Sepr 1806 Aged 23
Alfo John Son of the Above D. 17th March 1808 A. 18 Months
Alfo the Above Charles Pott D. 29th Augt, 1818 Agd 33.

To the Memory of 3 Beloved Infants of James and Mary Buddle of this
Parifh who died at the refpective Ages of Ten, Nine, and 20 Weeks, William D.
8th Janr 1834 William George D. 10th Decr 1842, and Sarah Ann, D. 13th April
1845.

> I take thefe tender lambs faid He
> And lay them on my breaft
> Protection they fhall find in Me
> In Me be ever bleft.

Harriet Wife of William Solley D. 29th February 1832 Aged 32 Yrs.,
Alfo the Above named William Solley D. 9th Febr 1847 Aged 48
Alfo 2 Children William & Harriet Elizabeth.

William Hammond D. 20th Feby 1840 Aged 87
Alfo Mary Wife of the Above D. 13th Octr 1836 Agd 83.

William Coller D. October 15th 1767 Aged 39
Alfo Elizabeth his Wife D. April 29th 1773 Aged 59.
Alfo Mary their Daughter D. July 25th 1769 Aged 26.

William Silver D. December 20th 1841 Aged 54
Alfo Ann Daughter of the Above Died
June 26th 1808 Aged 5 Months.

Jofeph Silver D. 28th Feby 1801 Aged 56
He left furviving Mary his Wife and
Nine Children, who in grateful
remembrance of the beft of Hufbands
And beft of Fathers, have caufed
this ftone to be placed here.
Alfo Mary Wife of the Above D. Sepr 6th 1816 Aged 68.

Thomas Pettman D. 9th May 1762 Aged 60
Alfo Sarah his Wife D. 17th Auguft 1800 Aged 90
Alfo Sarah Daughter of the Above faid Thomas
and Sarah Pettman D. 18th June 1761 Aged 16 Y^{rs}.
And Six other Children who died in their Infancy.

Mr. Richard Pettman of the Town & Port of
Sandwich, D. 18th January 1810 Aged 71.
Alfo Ann Pettman Wife of the Above
Died 26th February 1821 Aged 87.

Richard Wallraven D. December 6th 1800 Aged 67
Alfo Ann Wife of the Above D. Octr 11th 1789 Aged 66.

David Lawrence D. 6th Sepr 1798 Aged 68
Alfo Elizabeth Wife of the Above D. 14 Novr 1806 Aged 73.

Robert Atkins D. 24th Sepr 1807 Aged 2 Y^r & 8 Months.

Sarah Wife of Robert Atkins D. 27ᵈ Oᶜᵗʳ. 1811 Aged 51.

George Hancock D. Janʸ 12ᵗʰ 1808 Aged 76
Alſo Mary his Wife D. Decʳ 28ᵗʰ 1795 Aged 63.

Stephen Marſh D. May 23ⁿ¹ 1842 Aged 55
Alſo Elizabeth Wife of the Above D. June 25ᵗʰ 1823
Aged 33, Alſo Pleaſant Marſh, his 2ⁿᵈ Wife
Died July 26ᵗʰ 1829 Aged 35.

Margaret Wife of John Stapley Eſq, late
An Officer of H. M. Ordnance, Dover, who
Quitted this Mortal life 28ᵗʰ April 1848
Aged 65 Years (Aſleep in Jeſus).
Alſo Suſannah Vandeput Daughter of the Above
Died 17ᵗʰ June 1848, Aged 32 Yʳˢ. Alſo John
Stapley Husband of the Above Margaret Stapley
Died 9ᵗʰ October 1850 Aged 69.

George Marſh of Deal, D. 15ᵗʰ July 1825 Aged 43
Alſo Ann Marſh Wife of the Above D. 6ᵗʰ April
1860 Aged 78.

Jane Fells, Daughter of Thomas & Ann Fells
Died 11ᵗʰ November 1838 Aged 47. Alſo Lydia
Daughter of the Above D. Decʳ 5ᵗʰ 1843 Aged 57.

Mr. Ifaac Sladden, late of Gore in this Parifh
Died 23rd September 1807 Aged 40. Alfo Ann
Wife of the Above Ifaac Sladden D. 27th June 1811, A. 43
Alfo 3 Children who Died Young.

Thomas Staines Sladden late of Gore in this Parifh
Died 16th October 1831, Aged 40. He left Surviving
Hefter his Wife with 8 Children, 4 Sons & 4 Daug'.

Solomon Harvey, Gen'. D. 9 November 1733 Aged 77
Alfo Catherine his Wife D. 15th March 1740 Aged 79
Alfo their Son Solomon Harvey, A.B.
Died 22nd April 1713 Aged 23.
This was erected by their beloved Daughter, Anno 1742.
Thomas Harvey D. 27th July 1696 Aged 63
Alfo Mrs. Sarah Barnard Daughter of the faid
Thomas Harvey, And late Wife of Mr. William
Barnard Citizen of London, D. 25th July 1696 Aged 32.
Alfo Ann, Wife of the above named Thomas
Harvey. Died 25th September 1716 Aged 85.

(*Marble Slab railed round.*)
Roberta Wife of Commander George Sayer, R.N.
Died 2nd October 1851 Aged 48.

(*Stone Tomb railed round.*)
Richard Shockledge Leggatt, D. 13th March 1853 Ag'. 67.

(Tomb railed round.)

Thomas Rammell D. Dec'. 16th 1759. Aged 56
Elizabeth his Wife & Daughter of Tho°. & Mary Fuller
Died March 4th 1781 Aged 72
Alfo Mary, John, & Jane, who D. in their Infancy
Alfo Sufan D. January 5th 1770 Aged 18
Edward D. May 6th 1785 Aged 38
Mary, D. Nov'. 13th 1789 Aged 41
Thomas, D. October 11th 1799 Aged 59
Alfo Mrs. Elizabeth being the laft of the Iffue
of the Above Thomas & Elizabeth, Died
September 15th 1821 Aged 78.

Ann Wife of Edward Rammell of Deal
Died 11th April 1785 Aged 71
Thomas Son of the Above faid D. 11th Feb' 1791 A. 30.

Bartholomew Spain D. 11th Feb' 1822 Aged 42
Alfo Mary Wife of the Above D. 5th March 1862 Ag'd 76
When in the Solemn hour of Death
I Waited thy decree
This was the Prayer of my laft breath
O Lord remember me.

Hannah Daughter of Bartholomew & Elizabeth Spain
D. 25th November 1811 Aged 25.

Richard Son of Bartholomew & Elizabeth Spain
Died 21ft September 1811 Aged 28.

Frances Daughter of Bartholomew & Elizabeth Spain
D. 21ʰ February 1806 Aged 18.

Bartholomew Spain D. 15th June 1813 Aged 68.
Alfo Elizabeth Wife of the Above D. 12 May 1817. Ag.67.

H. 1701.	T. H 1724.
R. H. 1708.	K. H. 1728.

(*Mr. Sharp's Vault flat ftone.*)

John Pott D. 24th January 1805, Aged 60
Alo 4 Children of the Above who D. in their Infancy
Harriet Manger Pott Daughter of the Above
D. 13th Auguft 1814 Aged 22
Elizabeth Pott, Relict of the Above, D. 29th Febʸ 1832
Aged 85.

Ann Wife of John Pott D. 14th May 1771 Aged 64
Alfo the Above John Pott D. 7 May 1775 Aged 60.

Mary Wife of John Woodruff D. 10th Sepʳ 1727 Aged 57
John Woodruff D. 4th June 1737 Aged 71
Alfo 2 Children who D. in their Infancy.

Gibeon Son of Thomas and Sufan Rammell
D. 1ʰ Auguft 1724 Aged 15.

Sufan Wife of Thomas Rammell D. 12th May
1749 Aged 74.

Thomas Rammell D. 13th March 1725 Aged 52.

Lydia Wife of Edward Emanuel Keble
Born 6th Novr 1779 D. 18th May 1859.
Alfo the Above named Edward Emanuel Keble
late of Sandwich D. 3rd March 1867 Aged 83
Ann Relict of Edward Keble D. 14 May
1773 Aged 47.

Thomas Keble D. 14th February 1793 Aged 44
Martha Wife of the Above D. 15th Sepr 1785 Aged 32
Alfo 2 Sons Edward & George who D. in their Infancy
Harriet Daughter of the Above D. 11th March 1809 Aged 30.

Sarah Wife of John Hammond D. Novr 1^{ft} 1821 Aged 86.

Robert Simmons D. Jany 22nd 1809, Aged 84
Mary Wife of the Above D. October 29th 1809. Aged 84.

Joyce Wife of Samuel Fells D. Jany 23^d 1807 Aged 66
Alfo the Above named Samuel Fells D. Auguft 13th
1807 Aged 66.

William Moat D. Feby 19th 1814 Aged 92
Elizabeth Wife of the Above D. June 25th 1813 Aged 84
Alfo Richard Son of the Above D. April 8th 1826 A. 75
Sarah Wife of W^m. Drayfon and Daughter of the
Above Willm. & Elizth. Moat, D. Augt. 10th 1853 Aged 85.

Margaret Wife of Thomas Hart of the City of
Canterbury, Wine Merchant. D. 5th Decr 1813, Aged 53.

Jofeph Belfey D. 10th October 1801 Aged 72
Sarah Belfey, his Wife D. 20th May 1806 Aged 68.

William Thomas Wood D. 21^{ft} Decr 1786 Aged 23
Alfo 2 Sons Jofeph and Thomas.

Jofeph Belfey D. June 9th 1789 Aged 18.

Mary Wellard D. 13 Novr 1808 Aged 64.

Elizabeth Wife of William Drayfon D. June 13th 1816 Aged 57 Alfo their
Son Thomas D. Octr 18th 1803 Aged 1 Year.

Frances Wife of William Cooke D. 11th October 1818 Aged 40. Alfo John Hall,
Father of the Above D. 19th April 1820 Aged 60.
Alfo Sarah Wife of the Above D. 7th May 1836 Aged 77.

Chriſtopher Hall D. 4th Auguſt 1762 Aged 77
Ann Wife of the Above D. 3rd May 1765 Aged 78.

S. R. Died 7th April 1825 Aged 9 Months.

(*Mr. Rae's Vault railed round.*)

Suſanna Wife of Thomas Buſhell, & Daughter of Henry & Pleaſant Buſhell D.
2nd February 1838 Aged 22.
Juſt as the blaſt cuts off the blooming flower
She here reclines by Deaths reſiſtleſs power
Learn reader here and with it onward paſs
This leſſon (hard to learn) all fleſh is graſs.

Henry Buſhell D. 24th April 1835 Aged 69
Alſo Pleaſant Wife of the Above D. April 19th 1846 Aged 65
Alſo Mary Daughter of the Above named
D. 22nd October 1850 Aged 31.

John Ferrier D. Feby 15th 1847 Aged 66
George Second Son of the Above D. 11th April 1829 Infant
Alſo Emma Jane & Caroline, Twin Daughters
of the Above D. in their Infancy.

Maria Wife of William Famariſs, D. 10th March 1842 Aged 62. Alſo the
Above named William Famariſs D. 26th April 1867 Aged 89.

(Tomb railed round.)
Richard Singleton B. 9th Jany 1799 D. 11th April 1840.

(Tomb railed round.)
John Allen Willm. Wade Efq. Died
19th September 1851 Aged 39.

Elizabeth Wife of James Leake D. Jany 27th
1814 Aged 52.

John Wilfon D. December 30th 1840 Aged 52
Maria Daughter of the Above D. Jany 13th 1832 Ag. 7 Months
John Son of the Above D. Auguft 5th 1841 Aged 18 Yn.

Robert Netherfole D. 6th May 1770 Aged 66
Mary Netherfole Wife of the Above D. 9th Septr
1771 Aged 63, John Netherfole Son of the Above
D. 14th June 1767 Aged 24.

Edward Page D. 28th December 1861 Aged 59
Alfo 2 Children of the Above
George D. 22nd March 1837 Aged 7 Yr
Mary Ann, D. 9th Feby 1838 Aged 4 Yr.

(Tomb.)
Margaret Daughter of Saphire Paramor
Died 18th July 1721 Aged 74.

(*Tomb.*)

Saphire Paramor of Statenborough in this Parish, Gent.
Died September 27th 1693 Aged 77.

(*Tomb.*)

Joshua Paramor of Statenborough in this Parish
D. June 4th 1705 Aged 66 Also Mary Wife of the
Above D. Dec[r] 4th 1727 Aged 70. Margaret Paramor
Daughter of the Above D. March 38[h] 8764 Aged 67.

Eliza Wife of Richard Harvey, Gent, and
Daughter of Mr. Saphire Paramor D. 6th August 1688 Ag. 35.

Thomas Harvey, eldest Son of Captain Richard Harvey
Died 30th October 1696 Aged 19.
Wisdom and Innocency Both were joyn'd
And both in blooming Youth had fully form'd his Mind
When he to God his spotless Soul resign'd.
He saw A temping world with sin draw nigh
And fearing more to live than Criminals to Dye
He timely chose a blest Eternity.

Thomas Kite D. 22nd December 1795 Aged 36
Also Thomas Kite Son of the Above D. March 18th 1796 Aged 6 Y[rs]
And 2 Children who Died in their Infancy
Also Mrs. Sarah Kite Wife of the Above
Died 14th September 1826 Aged 64.

Arthur Son of Thomas & Mary Sutton D. May 28th 1835 Aged 5 Years Alſo Heſter Daughter of the Above D. Decr 11th 1841 Aged 13. Alſo Harriett Daughter of the Above D. April 6th 1842 Aged 23.

Mary Wife of Mr. Thomas Sutton of Sandwich
D. 7th May 1850 Aged 58. Alſo the Above named
Mr. Thomas Sutton D. 4th October 1866 Aged 71.

John Wood D. 20th October 1824 Aged 36.

(Tomb railed round.)
Jane Wife of Ephraim Prior D. March 29th 1849 Aged 28.
All you that come my grave to ſee
Remember Death will conquer thee
As you are now ſo once was I
Therefore I pray prepare to Die.

Edward Fagg D. December 8th 1851 Aged 38.
He left ſurviving Amy his Wife.
Farewell farewell yet not a long adieu
For I if faithful ſoon may be with you
In bliſsful regions where no ſin no pain
Nor parting pangs ſhall ſunder us again.

Mary Jane Hoile D. 4th Feby 1850 Aged 31
Alſo Sarah Strotten Mother of the Above
D. 27th Decr 1851 Aged 67.

James Standen D. 1ſt April 1860 Aged 74
Ann Daughter of the Above D. 30th March 1826 Ag. 4 Yrs & 6 Months.
Sarah Wife of Henry Standen Son of the Above
D. 19th February 1862 Aged 38.

William Nower D. 18th Jany 1858 Aged 61.
Ann Nower Wife of the Above D. 9th April
1858 Aged 58.

Hannah Wife of Francis Hopper. D. Sepr 13th 1856 Ag 27.

John Farrier D. 13th Feby 1858 Aged 77.

Henry Kittams D. 5th Sepr 1855 Aged 53.

Ann Wife of John Setterfield D. 30th Jany 1861 Aged 66
When in the Solemn hour of Death
I waited thy decree
This was the Prayer of my laſt breath
O Lord remember me.

Sufannah Wife of Thomas Young D. Decr 8th 1862 Ag^d 56
Affliction fore long time ſhe bore
With pain ſhe was oppreſt
Till God did pleaſe to give her eafe
And take her Soul to reſt.

(Tomb railed round.)
Sarah only Daughter of John & Sufannah
Bowes, Born 30th May 1830, D. 18th Feby 1853
Alſo John Bowes Father of the Above named
Sarah, Born 28th Jany 1792 D. 4th Decr 1865.

(Tomb.)
Thomaſine Fanny Wife of John Bridges
Kenrick D. 22nd Feby 1859.
Clara Florence their Daughter D. 7 May 1859 Aged 7.

Cranmer Kenrick Born 19th Jany 1849, D. 11th July 1860.

William Horton D. 19th Feby 1867 Aged 38
Alſo Ellen, Agnes, and Lizzie Daughters of the
Above who Died in their Infancy.

(Tomb.)
Agnes Daughter of William and Mary
Boteler Died October 8th 1857 Aged 57.

Eliz : Corney Romanis, D. 26 Augt 1855 Aged 41.

Elizabeth Barbara Wyver D. 23rd Jany 1862 Aged 62.

(Tomb railed round.)
Henry Upton D. 4th Auguſt 1850 Aged 64.
Henry Matſon Son of Henry & Mary Upton,
Died 26th Feby 1860 Aged 33.
Mary Upton D. 1st Novr 1863 Aged 70.

(Marble ſlab railed round.)
Elizabeth Wife of Captain George Hilton R.N. and Daughter of Henry Wiſe
Harvey, of Hearnden, Born in Sandwich 2nd October 1792 Died in Canterbury
25th Feby 1819 Buried in Eaſtry Church.   Alſo Eliza the only Child of the
Above Born in Canterbury 15th May 1817, Died in Bruſſels 26th July 1856.
Buried beneath this Tablet.

(Flat ſtone railed round.)
Margaret Ann Maria Wife of Robert Gordon Duglaſs Eſq. Lieut. R.N.
Daughter of Henry Wiſe Harvey of Middle Deal. Died 17th May 1858,
Aged 28.

(Tomb.)

Sarah Daughter of William Fuller
Boteler and Charlotte his Wife D. 19th May 1857 Ag 42.

(Tomb.)

William Boteler Born October 23rd 1810
Died July 6th 1867.

Olliff Julia Wyborn. D. 15th April 1864 Aged 9 Yrs.

(Marble Tomb.)

Stacey Grimaldi was born Octr 18th 1790, in the Parish of St. James London.
And died March 28th 1863. At Hernden House Eastry, leaving A Widow,
Their Six Sons and three Daughters.

"Bleſſed are the dead who die in the Lord"

To the beloved and Honoured Memory of Stacey Grimaldi Eſq. F.S.A. of Maize
Hill, Greenwich, Kent, Third in lineal Deſcent from Alexander Marquefs Grimaldi of Genoa, Who fettled in England A.D. 1683. Stacey Beaufort Grimaldi
Eldeſt Son of the above, Born in York St. London 30th September 1826, Died
in Otago New Zealand unmarried 23rd Octr 1866.

Mary Elizabeth, Wife of Henry Famarifs of Wells Farm in this Parish D.
1ſt Decr 1855 Agd 25.
Alſo Elizabeth Daughter of the Above died in her Infancy.

Jane Martha Daughter of Mark and Mary Kingfland D. 9th Auguſt 1853
Aged 18 Yrs.

Mark Kingfland late of Wells Farm in this Parish D. 1ſt March 1853 Aged
54. Alſo Mary Wife of the Above D. 18th April 1852 Aged 43 Yrs Left Surviving 7 Children Viz Mark William, Mary Elizabeth, William Thomas, Jane
Martha, Court, Emily, & James.

William Charles Monlas Courtney born May 8th 1865 : d. April 29th 1869.
"Perfected for ever."

Arthur-Mand, Carus-Wilson Born March 16th
1857 Died October 15th 1859.
" He fhall gather the Lambs with his Arms."

· Mary Wife of James Buddle, D. July 17th
1850. Aged 45. Leaving 3 Sons & 3 Daughters
She was a good and tender Mother
A true and faithful Wife.
Alfo Sufannah Daughter of the Above
D. Sep[r] 24th 1852 Aged 22 Y[n].
Alfo James Husband of the Above D. Oct 6th
1864 Aged 75.

(Tomb railed ronnd.)
Commander Charles Hougham Baker R.N.
late of this Parifh D. 29th March 1854 Ag[d] 42
much Beloved and refpected.
The Lord gave & the Lord hath taken away
Bleffed be the name of the Lord.

Richard Devefon D. 12th Auguft 1864 Aged 64.

Phineas Gilham 20th Feb[y] 1850 Aged 52 Y[n].
Alfo Mary Gilham Wife of the Above D. 20th September 1868 Aged 75.
" Bleffed are the Dead which die in the Lord."

(Tomb railed round.)
Here lieth the Mortal remains of the late
Rev. Ralph Drake Backhoufe, M.A.
12 Years Vicar of Eaftry with Worth
And 29 Years A Zealous Minifter of God's Word
Born 6th January 1801, Died 24th Dec[r] 1853.
" And their Works do follow them."

---

7 MONUMENTS IN THE CHURCHYARD,

(From the Boteler MSS.)

1ˢᵗ.

At the Northside of the Church in the angle formed by the Chancel.

Virtus post funera vivit

Here lieth buried Margaret the eldeſt Daughter of Joſhua and Suſan Paramore, and Wife to Bartholomew Fletcher of Kent Gent. She was born Auguſt 21ᵗʰ 1614 married September 18ᵗʰ 1632, and Died July 10ᵗʰ 1633.

Sir Transit Gloria Mundi

a Jewel rare		
In Earth its place	ſhall appeare	
(When Graves be open'd		Day of doome)
Earre to ſurpaſſe	of this tombe	
Strive then Spectator		
To views ſo riche or rare a diamond.		

2ⁿᵈ.

Here lyeth entomb'd the Body of Ann Bonner, late Wife of Wᵐ. Bonner of Lee, in Eſſex Mariner, by whom ſhe had Iſſue one Daughter. She was the Daughter of Joſhua and Suſan Paramor of Eſtry in Eſt Kent She drew her firſt Breth April 26ᵗʰ in the Year 1625 and drew her laſt Breth the 4ᵗʰ of May in the Year 1644

To Mourn or joy I ſtand in equal plight
Thy Loſſe deere friend to mourning doth invite
Thy Loſſe oh no my Loſſe of ſuch a Friend
Muſt needs coſt teares but yet thy happie end
Made friends at thy death both glad and ſorry
Sad to recount theire Loſſe glad for thy glory.

3ʳᵈ.

Here lieth interred the Body of Samˡ. Paramor Gent. who departed this life yᵉ 22ⁿᵈ of April 1679 Aged 29 Years

The Memory of the Juſt is bleſſed. Prov :
Look envious Eyes & ſee what's done
Low here is writ upon this Stone
An Epitaph which doth preſent
A line or two of diſconſent
For here doth lie of natures Store

A young Man and a Paramour
Lord this is thy moſt bleſt decree
To bring us one by one to thee.

4th.

Here lyeth the Body of Margaret the Wife of Saphyr Paramor of Statenborough Gent, who departed this life the 23rd of Auguſt 1679 Aged 60 Years.

5th.

Here lyeth interred the Body of Saphire Paramor of Statenborough Gent. He
was buried 27 Sepr A.D. 1693 Aged 77 Years
Waiting for the Reſurrection of the Juſt.

6th.

Here lieth interred the Body of Joſhua Paramor of Statenborough in this
Pariſh Gent. who departed this life June 4th A.D. 1705 Aged 66 Years.

Leaving Iſſue 3 Sons & 4 Daughters, by Mary his Wife Daughter of Mr.
Ralph Philpott of Word.

Alſo Mary the Wife of the aforeſaid Joſhua Paramor died Decr 4th 1727 Aged
70 Years. Alſo Margaret Daughter of the aboveſaid Joſhua & Mary died March
31^{ſt} 1764 Aged 67 Years.

7th.

Here lieth interred the Body of Marg^t. ye Daughter of Saphir Paramor of this
Pariſh Gent, who departed this life the 18th of July A.D. 1721 Aged 74 Years.

---

*On an altar Monument near the middle of the Churchyard on the North
Weſt ſide of the foot-path.*

Here lieth the Bodyes of Thomas Fawlchner, and William Fawlchner, Which
Thomas dyed 22nd day of Aprill 16   William dyed y^e of October 1616.
(The Inſcription is almoſt obliterated) Eaſtry Regiſter ;
Burials 28 April 1610 Thomas Fawlchner Paterfamilias 11 Oc^t 1616
W^m. Fawlchner Pat.

Richard Prett Died Decr 20th 1749.   Aged 50.
Jane his Wife Died 2nd Octr 1753.   Aged 56.
  Death is the fate of all you fee
  And will ere long your Portion be.
  Happy are they in Chrift that die
  To live with him eternally.

William Parker died 5 Feby 1782.   Aged 86
Elizabeth his Wife died 11th April 1778 Aged 86.

Ann Barton;
Wife of James Beal,
Born 22nd Auguft 1806,
Died 6th April, 1855.
Alfo
Sufannah Philpott,
Wife of Alfred T. Wright,
And Daughter of the above
D. 12th Jan^y.
1869, Aged 23.

Mary Beal.
D. March 4th 1857,
Aged 76 Years.

Jofeph Patten Baker,
Born 26th July, 1813,
Died 11th Novr. 1869.

 . . . . *From the ruined fhrine he ftept,*
And in the moon athwart the place of tombs,
Where lay the mighty bones of ancient men,
Old knights, and over them the fea wind fang
Shrill, chill, with flakes of foam . . . .

         Mort D'Arthur.

My attention has been called by the Rev. W. S. Shaw, to some inscriptions and monuments *not now difcoverable*, which were communi-
cated in 1790 to *Parfons' Monuments of Kent,* by the Rev. Montague
Pennington. They were as follows :—

" I. On a flat ftone partly within the [altar] rails, which are fo placed over it that
part of the inscription is illegible, is—

Hic jacet quod fuit mortale Richardi Foggi arm. qui ex uxore XIV
liberorum pater fuit, etc. Obiit æt. 74. 1580.

" II. On the wall fouth of the table, on a brafs plate about 20 inches fquare
in perfeét prefervation, are the effigies of a man and woman kneeling
with uplifted hands, behind him the fon, behind her three daughters in
fame attitude. The fon has a fword by his fide. Beneath the figures is
this infcription : Pofuit Richardo Fogg armigero, viro fuo amantiffimo
chariffimoque benigne de fuis, benigniffime de pauperibus, bene de omnibus
merito, uxor Anna hoc grati animi monumentum * * * * * Vixit et
afcendit quinquagenarius aftra, nunc anima cœlos contigit ante fide. Tres
natæ, natufque unus poft fata fuperftes virtutes patrias quas imitentur
habent.

Arms above the figures. Party per pale baron and femme 1ft On a fefs between
three annulets as many mullets pierced. 2nd, quarterly —— in the finifter
quarter a crefcent, over all a bend vairy.

" III. A flatftone without the [altar] rails to the memory of Jane daughter of R.
Kingsford rector of Upminfter in Effex and Jane his wife daughter of Richd.
Fogge late of this Parifh Efquire. She married Edward Jacob of Canter-
bury furgeon, and left iffue 8 children. Ob. March 16. 1719, ætat. 33.

" IV. Alfo the faid Edward Jacob and Mary, daughter of John Chelker of New
Romney gent., his 2nd wife : he died Feb. 9, 1756, aged 76, fhe Oct. 16th,
1727, aged 33.

" V. In the body of the Church : Here lieth Ralph Smith junior of Tilmanftone who died Aug. 16, 1655.

" VI. Here lieth the body of Ralph Smith of Eaftry who died June 11th, 1664.

" VII. Ralph Smith of Thornton, Sep. 16—.

" VIII. On the fide of the chancel a handfome mural monument to M. Hatton,
Efqre., of Dane Court in this parifh, Aug. 1, 1776.

Arms. Party per pale. Azure a chevron between 3 garbs or, for Hatton. 2nd
gules three lilies proper couped, for Lilly. On a wreath of the colours a
hind at gaze or.

" IX. Another on fame fide with fluted pillars. Thomas Michael Turney, late
Student of Brafenofe. 1ft Feb. 1770, aged 19.

In the Chancel Eaft Window were thefe arms in different compartments :—

" 1. (The bafe broken) in chief azure 3 lions rampant or.

" 2. Gules a crofs argent.

" 3. Azure three bendletts argent. The efcutcheon imperfect. In the other chancel windows are feveral figures much defaced."

Whilft thefe pages have been paffing through the prefs, a handfome Latin Crofs has been erected over the Rae Vault, ftanding on three fteps, the higheft of which bears the following infcriptions cut on its feveral faces, viz :—

On the Weft face—

" In memory of
James Rae
Of Douglas Ayrfhire, N.B.
and of Walton Houfe, Eaftry.
Died February 28th, 1843,
Aged 49 years."

On the South face—

" In Memory of
Katherine Mary
Second daughter of James Rae
and Elizabeth Sophia his wife.
Died November 8th, 1842
Aged Eleven years."

On the Eaft face—

" In Memory of
Rofa Margaret
Wife of the Revd. J. R. Holmes,
Rector of Blo-Norton, Norfolk,
Youngeft daughter of James Rae.
Died November 7th, 1869.
Aged 32 years."

On the North face—

" In Memory of
Mary
Widow of William Gordon,
of Glenlivet, Banfffhire, N.B.
only daughter of Thomas Jemmitt
of Borham Wood, Herts.
Died July 16th, 1854
Aged 89 years."

The Tower and Bells.

CHAP. V.

" What mufic is there that compared may be
With well-tuned bells' enchanting melody?
Breaking with their fweet founds the willing air,
They in the liftening ear the foul enfnare."
<small>LINES INSCRIBED IN THE BELFRY OF S. PETER'S CHURCH, SHAFTESBURY</small>

HAVING carefully examined the Church, let us now afcend THE TOWER.

We fhall not go far before we come on the left to a door-way, long fince blocked up, which probably led either to the triforium, or to the outfide of the roof of the nave, of an earlier church. A few fteps more bring us to the *Ringing chamber*, where the ringers ufually affemble on Tuefday (formerly Thurfday) nights to practife, and where hangs a copy of the Rules of the Eaftry ringers, given hereafter. Immediately above this is the *Clock chamber*, which contains "the works" of a very good and ferviceable eight-day clock by Meffrs. More & Son, Clerkenwell, given to the parifh by R. Springett Harvey, Efqre., in the year 1853 ; at which time Mr. Harvey alfo gave a telefcope for the ufe of the clerk, or other perfon appointed to wind up the clock, in order that he might notice the exact time at which the *time ball* falls at Deal

<small>U</small>

and regulate the clock thereby. *Local time, which is ftill kept at Eaftry,* is 5 minutes fafter than Greenwich time. But, had our parifh been to the *Weft* of Greenwich inftead of to the Eaft of it, the probability is that "*railway time*" would have been adopted long ago. In this chamber is kept the parifh flag—a large S. George's enfign, purchafed in 1869, out of part of the proceeds of Penny Readings.

A few fteps more bring us to the *Bell chamber*, which, however, we had better pafs by for the prefent, and haften to the top of the Tower. Arrived

here we find the whole village, as it were, mapped out at our feet; whilft on a clear day a very fine diftant view may be obtained, embracing portions of the towns of Sandwich, Ramfgate, and Deal—Ramfgate Harbour, the Goodwin Sands, Walmer Caftle, Walderfhare Tower, Goodneftone, Knowlton, and Walderfhare Parks, the grounds of Bettefhanger and of Updown Houfe, and the Tower or other portions of 17 or 18 parifh churches, including thofe of Afh; Staple; Woodnesborough; Minfter; S. Clements, and S. Peter's, Sandwich; S. Lawrence, Thanet; S. George's, and Holy Trinity, Ramfgate; S. Andrew's, Deal; Upper Deal; Shoulden; Word; Great Mongeham; Tilmanftone; and fome others.

The view is fo good on a clear fummer's day, when the fun is not too hot (for then there would probably be a confiderable haze), that I think any of my readers who fhould be induced to venture to the top of the Tower would readily confefs that they were amply repaid for all the toil and trouble of the afcent.

Carefully locking the door at the top of the Tower, let us now defcend a few fteps to the Bell chamber, and take a peep at the Bells. At prefent the Eaftry peal confifts of *five* Bells. And the probability is that the Church has poffeffed this fame number for at leaft the laft hundred and fifty years—the more recent dates upon fome of the Bells, being merely the dates of re-cafting. Mr. Boteler, in his MSS., fpeaks of the Eaftry Bells as being "wretchedly unmufical" even in his day, and as time went on they probably did not much improve. At length, however, in the year 1864, through the exertions of Lieut.-Col. Rae, who is himfelf an amateur ringer, and takes a warm intereft in the bells and bellringing, they were tuned and put into a ftate of thorough repair by Meffrs. Mears & Son.

The following are the mottoes emboffed upon the feveral Bells, toge-ther with their refpective weights :—

1ˢᵗ. " Robert mot made me 1584." Weighs 7 cwt.

2ⁿᵈ. " Johannes Clarke hanc fecit Campanam 1609." Weighs 8 cwt.
WILLIAM IDLEY z THOMAS WHITFYLDE CHVRCHWARDENS."

3ʳᵈ. " HENRy WILTNAR MADE ME 1629." Weighs 10½ cwt.

4ᵗʰ. " MR. RAMMELL CHVRCHWARDEN RICHARD PHELPS MADE ME 1734." Weighs 14 cwt.

5ᵗʰ. " THOMAS KITE WILLIAm FILPOT CHVRCH WARDEnS ROBERT CATLIn FECIT 1740." Weighs 18 cwt.

Mot flourished in London from 1570 to 1603, and died in White-chapel. *Clarke* was a Chertsey founder. His lettering is similar to that of the Eldridges, of Chertsey. *Henry Wilnar* was a Kentish founder. His foundry was at Borden, near Faversham, and the father and son flourished from 1600 to 1670. *Richard Phelps* belonged to the White-chapel Foundry—the present firm of Mears and Stainback—and died in 1738. *Catlin* belonged to the Reading Foundry.

From very early times Bells have been used for the purpose of calling the faithful to the services of the church, of assembling the clergy, of lamenting the dead, and of honouring festivals.

And to the man whose soul is capable of appreciating the grand music of good bells, there is something indescribably thrilling in the deep sonorous voice of the tenor or great bell, as its solemn tones of sadness, or of warning, come through "the listening air!" Whilst the joyous *abandon* with which a merry peal bursts forth is perfectly infectious.

Of all nations the Russians have, perhaps, the keenest appreciation of good bells (see C. Piazzi Smyth's *Three Cities in Russia*), yet, strange to say neither with them, nor elsewhere on the Continent where they have fine bells, are they rung in a peal, but one bell rings at one time, another at another, without method, so that the only effect to a stranger is a per-petual tinkling! Ringing in peals—and especially change ringing—seems almost entirely peculiar to this country, and some writers have even gone so far as to attribute the title "merrie England" to this national custom.

In the olden times a day never passed without the bell being rung once or twice, and persons very frequently left money or goods by will to pay for the bell being so rung. Thus there was the matins or early morning bell, to call the people together for common prayer before going forth to their work and to their labour. And this custom is still retained in many parishes, even where the original purpofe and intention of it has been loft fight of and forgotten. Again, there was the Bell for Evenfong; and later on the Curfew Bell, warning people to put out all lights and fires for the night. A precaution moft neceffary when the cottage and the hall were alike moftly built of wood and thatched with ftraw. This cuftom is faid to have been firft *inftituted* by William the Norman, but probably the true explanation is, that he made *obligatory* that which, there feems good reafon for fuppofing, was practifed even before his time in the convents of the north.

The ancient and goodly cuftom of ringing the Curfew Bell, at 8 o'clock every evening, continued in our own parifh till the year 1824, when unhappily it was fuffered to fall into difufe, and the annual payment of 18*s.* heretofore made to the fexton "for ringing the eight o'clock bell" was difcontinued.

Again, on Sundays and holy days, at the celebration of the Holy Eucharift, when the prieft came to the words, *Sanctus, Sanctus, Sanctus, Dominus* DEUS *Sabaoth* (Holy, Holy, Holy, Lord God of Hofts), a bell was rung, called the *Sanctus* or *Saunce Bell*, from the fact of its being rung at the time thofe words were uttered.

At the Reformation of the Englifh Church this cuftom was difcontinued, and inftead thereof a bell was rung after the Nicene Creed and before the fermon, to fummon the people to hear the Word of God preached and explained to them. This cuftom is now rarely met with; but the writer remembers, as a boy going into a country church in Somerfetfhire, among the Mendips, where this *Sermon Bell* was ftill retained and had in ufe. The rope hung down in the body of the church—for the bell itfelf was not hung in the Tower, but probably juft over the chancel arch—and the clerk left his defk and tolled it for a few minutes before the pfalm was fung which preceeded the fermon. This is the only inftance of the ufe of the *Sermon Bell* in a parifh church, which I remember to have met with, though poffibly other inftances may occur to fome of my readers. Again—when any man was grievoufly fick and nigh unto death, it was anciently the cuftom to ring a bell called *the Paffing Bell*, to intimate to the neighbours that his fpirit was paffing out of this world, and to ftir them up to pray for the foul of their brother that, if it pleafed God, his end might be peaceful and without pain, and that he might be numbered with Chrift's faints in glory everlafting. And by the way in which the bell was tolled the people could learn the fex, and in fome parifhes the age alfo, of the perfon thus *paffing* away. Then immediately the breath had left the body of the fick perfon, this *Paffing Bell* was changed to a *knell*. But nowadays the *real* Paffing Bell is forgotten and difufed (though the *after-knell* is often improperly called the *paffing bell* by fome), and the bell is tolled only when the man is dead, and our prayers can no longer avail him in this world. In our own parifh, when any perfon's death is intimated by the tolling of the bell, the fex of the deceafed is fignified by the bell's being made to ftrike three times 3 for a man or boy, and three times 2 for a woman or girl. In fome parifhes a bell is always rung at feven o'clock on Sunday mornings and another at eight o'clock. Thefe were probably to call the people to early celebrations of the Holy Communion. At Eaftry the bell is now rung at 9 o'clock only, but formerly, and until within the laft few years, it was rung at feven, eight, and nine; whilft in other parifhes—though this cuftom is fomewhat rarer—they ftill keep up the practice of ringing *the Angelus Bell* on Sundays at one o'clock or thereabouts. This bell is fo called becaufe the *Angel* Gabriel is faid to have faluted the B. V. Mary at that hour with the words, " Hail thou that art highly favoured the Lord is with thee !" This

Angelus Bell was, I find, rung in our own parifh until quite recently. On Sundays the bells are *chimed*, and not rung before the fervices, thus caufing lefs fatigue to the ringers, and enabling them to come to church.

Having thus touched upon the manner and times of ringing the bells, and thinking it may intereft fome of my readers, and poffibly caufe the adoption of fuch-like rules in other parifhes, I fhall now proceed to give—

"The Rules and Regulations to be obferved by the Company of Ringers belonging to the Church of S. Mary, Eastry.

The ringers, being officers of the church, fhall confift only of Churchmen, parifhioners by preference, fuch as are known for their good character, and as are defirous by their conduct to bring no disrepute upon the office which they fill, or the church to which they belong. The belfry, being part of the church, is to be confidered as a place where decorum and propriety are to be ftrictly obferved.

2. The number of the company fhall not exceed 12, and it fhall be the conftant endeavour of the Company to keep up to this number as far as poffible. Extra, or " *trial hands*," may be allowed to the number of four. Any perfon who may be thought defirable for a " trial hand " fhall firft be fuggefted to the vicar and churchwardens for their approval, and then taught his art on the practice nights. He fhall then, if able to raife a bell, and to do his work fairly in an ordinary peal, upon the occafion of a vacancy in the number of ringers be elected by a majority to fupply the vacant place. No fuch " trial hand " previous to election fhall have any voice in the arrangements, or be fubject to the fines hereafter ftated, or fhall fhare in the profits of the company, unlefs when for want of ringers

his aid is required and given on the occafion of a gratuity being received. He fhall then take his fhare.   He fhall, however, be fubject to all the other rules of the company.

The company fhall alfo admit *honorary members* upon an admiffion fee of 2*s.* 6*d.*, and an annual payment of £1. 1*s.*   Such honorary members fhall not fhare in the receipts of the company, nor be anfwerable to the fines, but fhall have all the other privileges of members and be fubject to all the other regulations.

3. A *foreman* and one vice-foreman (to act in his abfence) fhall be annually chofen by a majority.   It fhall be the duty of the foreman to fee that all thefe rules are carried out ; to be refponfible for order and pro- priety in the belfry ; to give notice to all the ringers on the various ringing occafions, and at the end of the year to place before the company its pecuniary condition.

4. A *treafurer* fhall be annually elected by a majority. His duty fhall be to keep in a book provided for that purpofe all the accounts of the company ; to receive the various fubfcriptions, donations, and fees which may be given from time to time ; to regifter all the fines which lie againft each member, and at the end of the year to prepare for the foreman a full ftatement shewing the apportionment belonging to each.

5. The ftated days for *ringing* fhall be : Chriftmas Day, Eafter Day, Whitfun Day, Old Year's Eve, New Year's Morning ; the Queen's Birth- day ; on the occafion of the vifits of the Archbifhop ; and at the funeral of any member, when the bells fhall be muffled.   The time for ringing on other days fhall be regulated by the convenience of the ringers and the approval of the vicar and churchwardens.

6. The *practifing* time fhall be on Thurfday evening in each week from 7 to 9. But if a majority choofe to fix any other time for practifing

in addition to, or in lieu of this, they can do fo; all other rules in fuch cafe equally holding good.

7. The ufe of the bells is to be exclufively for ecclefiaftical and national purpofes, and always fubject (as provided by law) to the approval of the vicar.

8. The rates for ringing at weddings, and fuch like occafions, fhall be as follows:—

For one hour, a fee of   10*s.*

,,   two hours   ,,   20*s.*

If a higher fee be given, then more time fhall be given at the difcretion of the Ringers. It fhall be the duty of the foreman to take means to afcertain whether parties concerned wifh the bells to be rung on fuch occafions, and to acquaint them with the rates of charges. And if the ringers think fit at any time to ring without any arrangement with parties no fee fhall be expected.

9. All monies received for the company in the fhape of fubfcriptions, donations, or fees, fhall be put down by the treafurer to the common fund. This fhall be equally divided amongft all the members at the end of the year, and then each fhare fhall be fubjected to deductions in refpect of fines, which fhall be carried over to the common fund for the next year, or otherwife dealt with as a majority fhall think fit.

10. With refpect to fines, &c. :—

(1.) A ringer who has abfented himfelf from practifing continuoufly for 3 months (unlefs it have been on account of ficknefs) fhall have his name ftruck off the lift of the company. He fhall be fubject to fines up to the time of his leaving, and fhall be entitled to fuch a fhare of monies as would belong to him up to the time of his laft attendance. In the cafe of a *bonâ fide* abfence from the parifh 6 months' law fhall be permitted in order to allow for a poffible return.

(2.) On occafions of *Ringing* when a fee is given:—

(a.) Every ringer who, after due notice, is abfent (unlefs from ficknefs) fhall forfeit his fhare of the gratuity.

(b.) If he be abfent through ficknefs he fhall receive half a fhare.

(c.) If he be not in the belfry within 15 minutes of the time of meeting announced by the foreman, he fhall forfeit 2*d*.

(d.) If he leave the belfry before all is over, unlefs the majority give him permiffion, he fhall forfeit 2*d*.

(e.) If the bells be rung more than once in the day, and he be not prefent on all occafions, he fhall forfeit (in refpect of the gratuity) proportionately.

(f.) If on ringing occafions a ringer refufe to ring on account of the fmallnefs of the fee offered (unlefs it be under 10*s*.), and for want of him the 5 bells cannot be rung, he fhall forfeit all that would have been given to the company.

(3.) On *Practifing Occafions* :—

(a.) Any member who is 15 minutes after time, or is abfent alto-gether (except through ficknefs), or leaves the belfry before the bells are down (except with permiffion of the foreman) fhall forfeit 1*d*.

(b.) On fuch occafions no ringing is to commence after 8 P.M., nor to continue after 9 P.M. (except on the night of the old year) on pain of a forfeit of 2*d*. to each ringer.

11. (1.) The bells are to be rung only in the ufual and proper mode of ringing.

(2.) No one is to be allowed to touch them except ringers and trial hands.

(3.) No damage is to be done to the bells or to the machinery connected with them. Any one chargeable with this is to be held refponfible by the foreman, and to be reported by him to the vicar and churchwardens.

(4.) None but ringers and trial hands are to be allowed in the belfry except with the fpecial permiffion of the foreman. And it is to be underftood that it is a place for work and not for lounging.

12. On occafions of ringing the foreman may provide refrefhment to the amount of 1 pint of beer for each man engaged at each time of meeting: the expenfe of which fhall be put down to the common fund. On *practifing* occafions the foreman may allow members to fupply themfelves to a fimilar extent. No *fmoking* is at any time to be allowed in the belfry. Any improper behaviour is to be reproved by the foreman, and if confidered neceffary, to be charged with a fine not exceeding 2s. 6d., and to be reported to the vicar and churchwardens. Any one guilty of grofs mifconduct, or open defiance of any of thefe rules fhall by vote of the majority and the fanction of the vicar and churchwardens, be turned out of the company.

13. Any difpute which cannot fatisfactorily be arranged by the members of the company fhall be referred to the vicar and churchwardens, and their decifion fhall be confidered final.

14. A member who fhall be confidered by the majority unable to perform his work properly through phyfical infirmity or other fimilar caufe, fhall retire from the company.

15. On the occafion of the election of any frefh member, thefe rules fhall be formally read through to him by the foreman, in the prefence of the other members, and fuch member fhall, in a book provided for the purpofe, declare in writing his full affent to them.

16. The company fhall meet on fome day at the clofe of each year for the annual fettlement of their affairs.

17. Thefe rules, which were drawn up by thofe whofe names are appended, and which received the approval of the vicar and church-wardens for the time being, were made the rules of the Eaftry Company of Ringers on the 29th of March 1864. If at any time it appears defirable to make additions to them, or alterations in them, fuch may be done by a vote of the majority and the approval of the vicar and church-wardens.

But ere you enter, yon bold tower furvey,

Tall and entire and venerably grey.

* * * *

But ours yet ftands, and has its bells renown'd,

For fize magnificent and folemn found.

THE BOROUGH.

The Rectors, Vicars, Chaplains, and Curates.

CHAP. VI.

" They may rest from their labours, and their works do follow them." Rev. xiv. 13.

THE following list of clergy, who have at different times had the cure of souls in this parish, is chiefly extracted from the ancient diocesan registers in the Archiepiscopal Library at Lambeth, and the references in the notes are to the several volumes which are lettered with the names of the successive archbishops. There are also in the muniment room of the library very copious and valuable indices to all these registers, compiled by Dr. Ducarel, librarian of Lambeth in the last century. The earliest register in the Lambeth collection—viz., that of Archbishop Peckham—who was advanced to the primacy in A.D. 1278—begins in June A.D. 1279. All the earlier registers are said to have been carried to Rome by Archbishop Kilwardby, the immediate predecessor of Archbishop Peckham, when he resigned the archbishopric on being made Cardinal and Bishop of Portua. I have been informed that these Registers are no longer in the Vatican Library, but are supposed to have been removed to Paris, after the capture of Rome by Napoleon I. During the occupation of Paris, application was made to the late Duke of Wellington, for their reftoration to the Vatican, but without fuccefs.

The title "Sir," which occurs occafionally in the following lift (and which is = Lat. *dominus*), was commonly employed towards parifh priefts in olden time, *not* in virtue of their prieftly office, but of the degree of B.A. taken at the univerfity. Thofe who had taken a fuperior degree were addreffed as "Mafter." The dates in the text are corrected to the new ftyle: the old ftyle remaining in the notes unaltered, as taken from the regifters :—

The Rectors.

ante A.D. 1280 John Bacon,[1] Prefbyter.

1284 Anfelm de Eaftria,[2] Prefbyter and Cleric.

1310 Mafter Robert de Mallynggs,[3] Prefbyter.

13— William de Scottowe :[4] died *before* A.D. 1355.

1355 Sir William de Cufynton or Cofyngton :[4] died *before* 1361.

1361 Sir Stephen de Grauele,[5] Prefbyter.

[1] John Bacon or Bakon (for the name is fpelt both ways), prieft and rector of the Church of Eaftry, was fo oppreffed by the cares and refponfibilities of his cure, that he refigned the rectory 8 Id. April A.D. 1280; but feems to have accepted it again, as he was inftituted to it by the archbifhop, *with his own ring* (fuo annulo), a fhort time after.—*Reg. Pecham.* f. 48 b.

[2] *Ibid.* f. 55.

[3] *Reg. Winch.* f. 49.

[4] *Reg. Iflep.* f. 270, ftates that Cufynton was collated to the rectory of Eaftry, then vacant by the death of William de Scottowe, his predeceffor.

Reg. Iflep. f. 287, tells us that Dominus Stephen de Gravele, *prefbyter of the parifh church of Eaftry*, was prefented to the rectory of the faid church vacant by the death of the laft rector William de Cufynton. We find from the deed of endowment of the vicarage, which is dated *Aug.* A.D. 1367, that the rectory of Eaftry was *then* vacant by the ceffion of the rector, which muft have been Stephen de Grauele. Sir Stephen was, therefore, the *laft rector* of Eaftry.

THE VICARS.

1367 Thomas Molot,[6] Prefbyter.

1370 Sir John Holenden.[7]

1373 Sir John Clerk :[8] exchanged with his fucceffor.

1376 John Kyngs :[9] exchanged with his fucceffor.

1377 William Buke,[10] Prefbyter.

Thomas Goldyngton :[11] exchanged with his fucceffor.

1404 Philip Hamon :[11] exchanged with his fucceffor.

1414 Galfrid Adam :[12] exchanged with his fucceffor.

1416 John Ruton or Royton :[13] exchanged with his fucceffor.

1417 John Putteney :[14] refigned.

1421 Thomas Newman, B.A.[15]

[6] Molot was of the Convent of Stone, and diocefe of Lichfield.—*Reg. Laugh.* f. 99 b.

[7] Holenden was of Tonbrigge (Tunbridge).—*Reg. Whit.* f. 80 b.

[8] Clerk was of Alwakely.—*Regift. Whit.* f. 93 b.

[9] On the 8th July, A.D. 1376, John Kyngs, vicar of Brokefbone, dio. London, exchanged with John Clerk, vicar of Eaftry.—*Reg. Sudb.* f. 114.

[10] William Buke, Prefbyter, chaplain of the perpetual Chantry of the B. Virgin Mary, in the parifh church of Herne, exchanged with John Kyng.—*Reg. Sudb.* f. 123 b.

[11] On the 1ft April, A.D. 1404, Thomas Goldynton, vicar of Eaftry, exchanged with Philip Hamon, vicar of Benynden (Benenden) : Goldyngton, muft, therefore, have been inftituted fome time previoufly, and there feems good reafon for fuppofing that he was the fucceffor of William Buke, though in what year remains unknown.

[12] July 30th, A.D. 1414, Galfrid Adam, rector of ffrenftede (Frinfted), exchanged with Philip Hamon.—*Reg. Chich.* f. 60.

[13] Twenty-fecond October, A.D. 1416, Galfrid Adam exchanged with John Ruton, rector of Bocton Malherbe (Boughton Malherbe).—*Reg. Chich.* f. 77 b.

[14] On the 15th October, A.D. 1417, John Royton exchanged with John Putteney, Vicar of Salhurft, diocefe Chichefter.—*Reg. Chich.* f. 89 b.

[15] Seventeenth December, A.D. 1421, Thomas Newman, Bachelor of Arts, was collated to the vicarage of Eaftry vacant by the refignation of John Putteney, the laft vicar.—*Reg. Chich.* f. 128 a.

1426 John Water or Watier :[16] died.

1435 William Watier.[17]

1436 Sir John Barbour.[18]

1437 Thomas Wyles or Wylys :[19] exchanged with his fucceffor.

1440 Thomas Lawke.[20]

1451 Sir Robert Deaken or Dekyn : [1] exchanged with his fucceffor.

1455 Sir John Craller.[2]

in 1479 *Sir William Craller :[3] died A.D. 1487.

1487 *Mafter Afchowe :[3] died A.D. 1507.

   .   .   .   .

1517 Richard Maifter, S.T.B.[4]

1534 Master Richard Champyon, M.A. :[5] died A.D. 1542.

---

[16] Thirty-firft Oct., A.D. 1426, John Water, *chaplain*, was collated to the vicarage of Eaftry then vacant.—*Reg. Chich.* f. 165 b.

[17] Nineteenth Oct., A.D. 1435, William Watier was collated to the vicarage of Eaftry vacant by the death of John Watier, laft vicar.—*Reg. Chich.* f. 208 b, 209 a.

[18] Sixteenth July, A.D. 1436 John Barbour, *chaplain*, was collated to the vicarage of Eaftry then vacant. *Reg. Chich.* f. 211.

[19] Thirty-firft Aug., A.D. 1437, Thomas Wylys, *chaplain*, was collated to the vicarage of Eaftry.—*Reg. Chich.* f. 217 b.

[20] Twenty-eighth April, A.D. 1440, Thomas Wylys, vicar of Eaftry, exchanged with Thomas Lawke, rector of Bedfelde, dio. Norwich. *Reg. Chich.* f. 223 b.

[1] Fourth February, A.D. 1450, Thomas Deaken, prefbyter, was collated to the vicarage of Eaftry.—*Reg. Staff.* f. 108 a.

[2] Twenty-fecond April, A.D. 1456, Robert Dekyn, vicar of Eaftry, exchanged with John Craller, rector of Hattleport, dio. Lincoln.—*Reg. Bourch.* f. 60 b.

[3] Wills in the Prerogative Court, Canterbury.—*From the Botel. MSS.*

[4] Twenty-feventh July, A.D. 1517, Richard Maifter was collated to the vicarage of Eaftry then vacant by the death of the laft incumbent, whofe name is wanting.—*Reg. Warh.* f. 363 b.

[5] Nineteenth April, A.D. 1534, Richard Champyon was collated to the vicarage of Eaftry.—*Reg. Craum.* f. 355—and as to death *Botel. MSS.*

1542 Sir John Orgravar :[6] ftill Vicar in A.D. 1551.

1553 Thomas Sawyer.[7]

15— Mafter Robert Hill, M.A. :[8] refigned.

1558 John Lawfon.[9]

1561 *Peter Lymiter :[10] died A.D. 1581.

1581 John Seller, S.T.P. :[11] exchanged with his fucceffor.

1590 *Samuel Nicols, M.A. : died A.D. 1639.

1639 Thomas Blechynden.

1653 *Nicholas Brett,*[12] *Minifter.*

1661 *John Whifton : died A.D. 1694.

1695 *Thomas Sherlock, M.A. : died A.D. 1698.

1698 *Drue Aftly Creffener, M.A. : died A.D. 1746.

[6] *Reg. Cranm.* f. 389.

[7] He had the Queen's letters of prefentation.—*Hafted.* vol. iv., p. 230.

[8] In *Reg. Pol.,* f. 76, Robert Hill is fpoken of as the predeceffor of John Lawfon.

[9] John Lawfon, prefbyter, was collated to the vicarage of Eaftry 31ft January 1557, o.s.—*Reg. Pol.* f. 76.

[10] The date of Peter's Lymiter's *collation* is from a lift of inftitutions to beneficcs now in the Public Record Office : his *death* is recorded in the parifh regifter. *Hafted,* vol. iv., p. 230, gives the names of three vicars, here between Lawfon and Seller—viz., " *Walter Herbert,* 1571 ; *Peter Leniker,* 1574 ; and *Thomas Lymiter.* . . . . obiit. 1582." I am forry to differ from fo eminent an authority, but a careful inveftigation of the regifters at Lambeth, and of other documents, convinces me that he has fallen into error here, and has inferted the names of two men (Walter Herbert and Thomas Lymiter) who never were vicars of Eaftry.

[11] *Hafted.* vol. iv., p. 230, gives 1582 as the date of Seller's inftitution, but *Reg. Grind,,* f. 546 b, ftates that, on the 13th February, 1580 (o.s.), John Seller, Cleric, M.A., was collated to the vicarage of Eaftry, with the chapel of Worth annexed to the fame, vacant by the natural death of *Peter Lymiter.*

[12] Brett's name appears in the parifh regifter of this date (1653), and alfo in 1654 and 1655. He was probably the intruding minifter in the time of the Commonwealth. There was a Thomas Brett, minifter of Shoulden, and rector of Bettef-hanger, who was buried at Shoulden A.D. 1681—he might have been fome relation to our Brett.

1747 Culpeper Savage, M.A. :[13] died A.D. 1753.

1753 Samuel Herring : exchanged with his fucceffor.

1757 *Richard Harvey, B.A. : died A.D. 1772.

1772 Richard Harvey, M.A. :[14] died A.D. 1820.

1821 George Randolph, M.A. : preferred A.D. 1841: alive in 1870.

1841 *Ralph Drake Backhoufe, M.A. : died A.D. 1853.

1854 Charles Carus-Wilfon, M.A. : preferred A.D. 1867 : alive in 1870.

1867 William Francis Shaw, M.A.

BRIEF NOTICES OF SOME OF THE RECTORS AND VICARS.

WILLIAM DE CUSYNTON : A.D. 1355—1361.   In the time of this rector a difpute arofe between the prior and convent of Chrift Church, Canterbury, and William de Cufynton, on the one part, and Sir Richard de Monyngham, perpetual vicar of the Church of the B. V. Mary, Sandwich, on the other, with regard to a certain piece of land called Pottokefdown (now Puttockfdown). The vicar of S. Mary's claimed that this land belonged to his parifh, and accordingly feized the tythes of the fame.   But the prior and convent, in conjunction with the rector of Eaftry, brought an action againft the vicar of S. Mary's in the Archbifhop's Court at Canterbury, when the vicar was caft, and a definitive fentence was pronounced againft him A.D. 1356.   The land was

---

[13] He refigned the vicarage of Sutton Valence on being collated to this vicarage, which by a difpenfation he was permitted to hold with Stone in Oxney (*Haſted*).

[14] This R. Harvey was the nephew of his predeceffor, and alfo vicar of S. Laurence, in Thanet, which he refigned in 1793 (*Haſted*).

* The names in the above lift which have afterifks are thofe of the vicars which have been buried here.

declared to be within the parifh of Eaftry (i.e., within that part of it which now forms the parifh of Word), and the vicar was ordered to make reftitution of the tythes or their value, as well as to pay all cofts. In the fentence pronounced by Mafter John Euerleye, *auditor caufarum Archiepifcopi*, occurs this paffage : "*Willelmus de Cufington inductus fuit in corporalem poffeffionem ecclefie de Eftry ante feftum affumpcionis beate Marie Virginis proximo preteritum:*"[*] which fixes the time of Cufynton's induction pretty clearly. For, as the fentence was pronounced in Feb. A.D. 1356 (o.s.), and the Feaft of the Affumption of our Lady was on the 15th Auguft, A.D. 1356, he muft have been inducted fome time in the previous fpring or fummer.

It is very fingular to notice what a ftrange hankering the good people of S. Mary's, Sandwich, feem to have had for the above-mentioned piece of land called Puttockfdown, and how generation after generation they claimed it to be within the boundary of their own parifh. As late as A.D. 1676, we find the Rev. Afahel King, vicar, and the parifhioners of S. Mary's, affembled in veftry, afferting their right to levy a rate on this land, as part of the parifh of S. Mary's, and even voting money for any fuit that might be inftituted to try the cafe.[†]

STEPHEN DE GRAUELE: A.D. 1361—A.D. 1367. From Boys' *Hiftory of Sandwich* (vol. i., p. 350), we learn that Stephen de Gravele was inftituted to the rectory of S. Peter's, Sandwich, by Archbifhop Simon Iflip on the vi. Ides of September, A.D. 1350. This, however, he muft have refigned fome few years afterwards, fince in the year A.D. 1361, when he was appointed to the rectory of Eaftry, he is defcribed as "Prefbyter of the parifh Church of Eaftry," by which we may perhaps underftand

* See *Botel. MSS.*, vol. A.

† From the veftry minute book of S. Mary's, Sandwich, kindly brought under my notice by the Rev. A. M. Chichefter, vicar.

that he was one of the chaplains or chantry priefts attached to the church.

WILLIAM CRALLER: A.D. 1487. It is often very curious to notice the various and varying ways in which furnames were frequently fpelt in former time. The general found of the name was caught, and expreffed in various ways, whilft ofttimes the final fyllable was cut off. Thus it happens that Vicar *Craller* was often called *Crall'* or *Craule :* *Afchowe* was pronounced *Afch'* or *Afhe ;* and *Orgravar* became *Orgrav'* or *Orgrave.*

Amongft the wills proved in the Confiftory Court of Canterbury, in A.D. 1487 (fee Chap. XII hereafter) is that of " *D^{us}. Willm. Craller penciouarius Ecclē pōch de Eftric,*" who directs that he fhall be buried in the chancel of Eaftry Church. Now, as he is elfewhere mentioned as being vicar of Eaftry in A.D. 1479, he had probably refigned it, on a penfion at the time of his death.

THOMAS ASCHOWE: A.D.　　—A.D. 1507. In the will of the preceeding Sir William Craller, which is dated 14 Mar. 1487, mention is made of " Thos. Afhow " as " ppetual vicar of the faid Church " of Eaftry. And the will of John Whitefelde of Eaftry—which directs that he be buried in the church, and is dated 21ft Jany. 1507—mentions " Mafter Thos. Afhe, vicar of Eaftry." Again, the will of Jane Afchowe, of S. Bartholomew's, near Sandwich, in 1524, directs that fhe be buried in the chancel of Eaftry Church, near her deceafed uncle, Sir Thomas Afchowe, and that a ftone be laid upon her faid uncle. All traces of this ftone have long fince difappeared.

RICHARD CHAMPYON : A.D. 1534—1542. He calls* himfelf in his will Prieft, and Prebendary of Chrift Church, Canterbury. He leaves to his efpecial friend *Dr. Drom, S. Auguftine's* Works ; to *Dr. Rydlye* the preacher,

* *Botel. MSS.*

S. Ambrose, or some other like work. Also to Dr. Rydlye, the prebendary—afterwards Bp. of London, and Martyr—*Complutens Editio*, otherwise called the *Spanish* Byble, "or such like kynd of old amytye and friendship." Which two last he appoints supervisors to his will. He died in A.D. 1542, but there is no record of his having been buried here.

JOHN ORGRAVAR or Orgraver immediately succeeded vicar *Champyon* in A.D. 1542; though how long his vicarate lasted is slightly uncertain, seeing that his name does not occur after A.D. 1551 : we may, however, conclude that he held the benefice till A.D. 1553. But whether he then vacated it by death or otherwise is unknown.

THOMAS SAWYER, whose name occurs in A.D. 1553, had the Queen's letters of presentation.[*] This would seem to have arisen from the See of Canterbury being vacant at the time.

PETER LYMITER : A.D. 1561—A.D. 1581. A list of institutions to benefices belonging to the Augmentation Office, and now in the Public Record Office, Fetter Lane, states that Lymiter was collated to this vicarage in the third year of Queen Elizabeth, and we learn the date at which his vicariate ended, from the parish register, which contains the following entry of his burial :—

> " 1580   Peter Lymiter Vicar of Eastrie."
> ffebr.
> 6

His will was proved in the Consistory Court of Canterbury the 11th Feb. A.D. 1581 (new style). In it he directed that his body should be buried in the Chancel of Eastry Church; but whether there were ever any monument, brass, or stone, erected to his memory I know not : at all events, there is none now in existence.

JOHN SELLER : A.D. 1581—A.D. 1590, appears to be the only doctor

* *Hasted.* vol. iv., p. 230.

on our lift for he was S.T.P., or Sanctæ Theologiæ Profeſſor = Doctor of Divinity. Three children were born to him at Eaftry—viz., *Anne* in A.D. 1583, another *Elizabeth* in A.D. 1584, and a ſon *Thomas* in A.D. 1586. He ſeems to have exchanged this benefice in A.D. 1590 with *Samuel Nicols* for *Little Mongeham*, to which *Nicols* was preſented in A.D. 1588.

SAMUEL NICOLS: A.D. 1590—A.D. 1639. On the 16 May A.D. 1588, we find *Samuel Nicols* was preſented to the rectory of *Little Monge-ham*, and in A.D. 1590 he became vicar of *Eaftry*, probably by an exchange with his predeceſſor. He ſeems to have been poſſeſſed of ſome freehold property in the pariſh, for mention is made of ſome of *his land* as adjoin-ing the glebe, in the Terrier which I have called No. I. The pariſh regiſters furniſh us with ſeveral notices of his family, which tend to throw ſome light upon his domeſtic life. Thus, in A.D. 1592, ſome two years after his collation, we find he had a daughter born to him, who was baptized on the 9th October in that year by the name of *Suſan;* and who, on 19th September, A.D. 1609, was united to *Joſhua Paramour* in holy matrimony at the early age of 17 ! But two years before this joyous event—viz., on the 12th April, A.D. 1607, was buried " *Margaret Nicolls*, wife of *Samuel Nicols*." And in A.D. 1639 the ſcene cloſed, for there was buried in that year, after an incumbency of nearly 50 years,

" ffebru Mr. Samuell Nicols

21 Vicar of Eaftry."

It was during the vicariate of Nicols that the Regiſters were newly copied out by order of Convocation in A.D. 1598*. Two of the Terriers alſo— one being the earlieſt relating to our pariſh that is extant—were made during his incumbency, and will be found with the others in the *Appendix.*

---

* For further information reſpecting this ſee " *The Registers*," *poſt.*

JOHN WHISTON: A.D. 1661—A.D. 1694. We get at the date of Vicar Whiston's appointment to this benefice by the following note in his handwriting, which occurs in our earlieſt regiſter of burials under the year A.D. 1661 : "The wife of John Adams, *ye firſt that I John Whiſton buried after I was Vicar*, May 20." On the 1^{ſt} Jan^y., 1683, was buried " Mrs. Suſan Whiſton," probably the wife of our vicar ; but whatever the relationſhip betwixt them, he did not long ſurvive her, for on the 17th Octtober, 1694, his mortal remains were committed to the earth.

THOMAS SHERLOCK, A.D. 1694—A.D. 1698, ſeems to have been of Corpus C. College, Cambridge, and to have taken his M.A. degree in 1679. Like ſo many of his predeceſſors and ſucceſſors in this pariſh, he died at his poſt, and was buried in his own church. Vicar Creſſener, in a quaint and amuſing entry in the oldeſt regiſter book, aſſerts that he was ill-uſed and badly treated by his people, and that too in ſuch a way as to ſhorten his life. But may not grief for the loſs of Mrs. Mary Sherlock, who was buried here 30 March, A.D. 1697, have contributed in ſome degree to haſten his end ? The following is the brief entry in the regiſter reſpecting his burial : " Mr. Thomas Sherlock Vick. June 2, A.D. 1698."

DRUE-ASTLY CRESSENER : A.D. 1698—A.D. 1746, was by no means an ordinary man. Endowed with much learning and indomitable energy, he was alſo bleſſed with ſo good a conſtitution that he was vicar of our pariſh for well nigh 50 years. His long vicariate, which ſaw four ſovereigns on the throne, ſtands forth in remarkable contraſt to the ſhort incumbencies and rapid ſucceſſion of our vicars in the early part of the XVth century. He was a member of Pembroke Coll. Oxford, where he graduated in A.D. 1682.

At one time in his life Creſſener was apparently on ſomewhat bad terms with his pariſhioners, or at leaſt he entertained no very high opinion of them, as the following fingular entry in the oldeft regifter teftifies :—" Aftley Creffener Vicar Inducted by yᵉ Revᵈ. Mr. Tho: Mander December 11. 1698 among the Savages of Eaftry, who uf'd my Good Predeceffour almoft as Ill as my Self, but Death in a little Time gave him a Happy Deliverance." An entry in the churchwardens' accounts under the year A.D. 1708, may perhaps throw fome light—in the abfence of all *certain* information on the point—on the caufe of the mifunderftanding between the vicar and his parifhioners. It would appear to have arifen from fome difpute about the election of churchwardens : which difpute waxing hot was carried into court, when the parifh was defeated, and had to bear the cofts of the action.

The following is the entry referred to :—

" 1708.

 22 Apⁱ. pⁱ. to Mr. Peter Gleane Proctor his Bill on Account of Court and other Charges on the Difpute between Mr. Creffener and the Parifhonˢ in electing Churchwardens on the 5ᵗʰ Inftant, which upon hearing att yᵉ Court of Canterbury on the 13ᵗʰ Inftant before Doctor Robᵗ. Wood he ordered that the faid Bill fhould be allowed and paid by the Parifhoneners [*fic*] . . 2 8 3 "

Again, in the " Difpurfmˢ. " of " Mr. Tho: ffullar " as churchwarden for the years 1708 and 1709, occurs the following :—

" Spent att the Vifitacon when the Parifhonˢ mett att Court and had
 the Difpute about Chufing Churchwardens . . 2 19 0 "

Vicar Creffener prefented to the church a paten, chalice, and handfome flagon of filver, which are ftill ufed in the celebration of the Holy Euchariſt. There is no infcription either on the paten or chalice, but the flagon has the words " Deo Servatori " deeply graven on the fides within a floriated border, and at the bottom " Eaftry 1718." He bequeathed alfo a fum of money to be laid out in ornamenting the church, which is faid by tradition to have been employed in ceiling the chancel.

What other alterations may have taken place at this time it is not eafy to fay : though there feems good reafon for fuppofing it was about this date that "the 18 ftalls for the ufe of the monks" in ante-Reformation times, which formerly exifted in the chancel difappeared. It is much to be wifhed that thefe ftalls could be reftored again to their ancient pofition in the chancel.

Creffener alfo left £5 to be be diftributed amongft the poor of Eaftry and £5 for thofe of Worth. Thefe fums were duly diftributed amongft the poor of Eaftry and Worth by Vicar Savage on 1ᵗ Janʸ., A.D. 1748.

After a life of much activity and of diligent attention to the feveral duties of his holy office, Creffener at length fell afleep, and was buried on the 27th September, A.D. 1764, in the 82nd year of his age. He was buried in the chancel, where was placed a handfome monument to his memory, which now ftands againft the wall of the fouth aifle. An oil portrait of Vicar Creffener in gown and bands—faid by tradition to have been an admirable likenefs—formerly hung in the veftry of the church. The canvass is ftill in exiftence (1869), but as the colours are faft crumbling to pieces, and fall off on being touched, its value as a portrait is deftroyed beyond all chance of reftoration!

GEORGE RANDOLPH, A.D. 1821—A.D. 1841, on coming to the parifh found only one fervice here and one at Worth every Sunday. This he fpeedily altered for the better by engaging the fervices of a curate, and having two full fervices at each church every Lord's day. He alfo may be regarded as the founder of the National School fyftem in this parifh, for he collected a fum of money and built our firft National Schools in the year 1840 : which buildings have fince been pulled down to make way for the prefent more commodious ftructure. Again, in the early days of his vicariate, he pulled down the old vicarage houfe, and rebuilt it—

A A

much to the advantage of his fucceffors. After 20 years' labour in our parifh, he was preferred to Coulfdon, in Surrey, A.D. 1841.

But I cannot finifh thefe brief notices of our rectors and vicars without a few words refpecting *the laft vicar* of *Eaftry cum Worth.*

RALPH DRAKE BACKHOUSE, A.D. 1841—1854, was educated at the Rochefter Cathedral School, whence in due time he proceeded to Clare College, Cambridge. In A.D. 1823 he graduated as fifth Junior Optime, and was fhortly after elected fellow of his college. In A.D. 1824 he was ordained deacon and licenfed to the curacy of Little Chart. He afterwards became curate of Walmer, and upon the death of the incumbent (the Rev. E. Owen), was prefented to that benefice by Archbp. Howley, at the requeft of the parifhioners. Here he laboured earneftly for fome years, until in A.D. 1841 he was collated to the vicarage of Eaftry *cum* Worth by Archbp. Howley. On the removal of the Rev. C. Lane to Wrotham, he was appointed Rural Dean of the Sandwich Deanery. For 23 years he was alfo the evening lecturer at S. George's Chapel, Deal. During his incumbency the parifh church of Eaftry was much improved, and thofe reftorations were commenced which have fince progreffed fo fuccefsfully, and which, if thoroughly carried out, will make our church one of the fineſt in the neighbourhood. In his time alſo the church was firſt opened for weekly ſervice during Lent, and an *extra* evening ſervice eſtabliſhed on the laſt Sunday in the month when the Holy Communion is celebrated. He alſo ſtarted the evening ſchools —introduced an organ in place of violins—greatly improved the ſinging and chaunting—and, in A.D. 1847, enlarged the churchyard. For ſome years Mr. Backhouſe was chaplain of the Eaſtry Union, where he was much beloved by the poor and afflicted. He was a good ſcholar, an able and eloquent preacher, a moſt zealous and devoted pariſh prieſt, and in manner and bearing a thorough Chriſtian gentleman. His performance of three full ſervices every Sunday for many years, and his other varied and heavy duties, at length brought on premature illneſs, which cauſed his death on the 24th December, A.D. 1853. He was followed to the grave by a large number of the neighbouring clergy, and his body was interred in the churchyard, in a ſpot of ground ſelected by himſelf, being that on which the archbiſhop ſtood when conſecrating the portion of land added to the churchyard in A.D. 1847. His death was univerſally regretted, and he is ſtill affectionately remembered by many in the pariſh.

The Chaplains.

In former times there was uſually more than one prieſt attached to each church. The chief being called either rector or vicar, according to the nature of his benefice, and the other prieſts, either ſerving under him, in the Mother Church, or in chapelries in diſtant parts of the pariſh, as was the caſe here when the vicar was bound to keep a chaplain for Word, or elſe occupying a ſomewhat more independent poſition as the chaplain of a chantry chapel within the walls of the church. Such chantries being founded for the purpoſe of having maſſes ſaid for the repoſe of the ſouls

of the founders and their relations. In our own church there were three
Chantry chapels—viz., thofe of the B. Virgin Mary, commonly called
"our Lady," of the Bleffed Trinity, and of S. John the Baptift ; confequently there muft have been many priefts attached to the church. Thefe
chantry priefts were fupported by the offerings of the faithful in various
ways—e.g., by oblations and obventions, by payments for maffes and obits,
by bequefts and benefactions. And it would appear that the priefts
belonging to the chantries in Eaftry Church had fome 18 acres of land
in the parifh appropriated to their ufe and fupport, which were known so
late as 1693 by the name of "*the Chantry Lands.*" The following very
imperfect lift is all that I have been able, as yet, to difcover :—

CHAPLAINS AND CHANTRY PRIESTS.

ante A.D. 1361 Stephen de Grauele, prefbyter, afterwards rector : in
1391 John FitzRobert, clericus : *ante* 1426 John Watier, chaplain, afterwards vicar : *ante* 1436 John Barbour, chaplain, afterwards vicar : *ante*
1437 Thomas Wyles, chaplain, afterwards vicar : in 1538 William
Kene, chaplain.

THE CURATES.

By the term "curate" is now generally underftood "the minifter whether
prefbyter or deacon, who is employed under the fpiritual rector or vicar,
as affiftant to him in the fame church or elfe in a chapel of eafe within
the fame parifh belonging to the Mother Church."* Formerly, however,
it meant *all* prefbyters or deacons who had the *cure* of fouls, and in this
wide and general fenfe it is ufed in the *Book of Common Prayer* when we
pray for "all bifhops and curates." In the prefent cafe, however, we ufe
the word in its common modern acceptation.

* *Hook's Church Dictionary*, p. 289.

The earlier portion of the subjoined list is necessarily somewhat incomplete.

CURATES IN CHARGE AND ASSISTANT CURATES.

Ante A.D. 1511 H. Patryke,* parish priest of Word: in 1557 Thomas Bennett, clericus ac curatus: 1687 *Parson* Denne: 1743 *Parson* Omer: 1752 Samuel Fenner Warren: 1776 . . . Adkins: 1777 N. Nisbet, and still in 1781: 1783 Thomas Pennington, D.D., and in 1798: 1800 Philip Le Geyt: 1804 Henry Thomson: 1809 Henry Plumptre, rector of Claypole and curate of Eastry: 1817 George Fielding, M.A.: 1821 James Peto, LL.B.: 1837 Edward John Randolph, B.A.: 1840 Frederick Thomas Scott, M.A.: 1840 Henry Mapleton, Junr., B.A.: 1843 John Fuller Spong, B.A.: 1844 James Layton, B.A.: 1845 Wm. Maundy Harvey Elwyn, M.A.: 1847 John Francis Baynham, B.A.: 1854 John Buttanshaw, M.A.: 1860 Thomas Hy. Papillon, B.A.: 1861 Henry Beaufort Grimaldi, B.A.: 1863 John Erskine Campbell-Colquhoun, B.A.: 1865 Gustavus Bosanquet, B.A.: 1867 Valentine Shillito Vickers.

* *Reg. Warcham,* f. 48.

> *A good man there was of religioun*
> *That was a poure Persone of a toun ;*
> *But riche he was of holy thought and werke,*
> *He was also a lerned man, a clerk,*
> *That Christes gospel trewely wolde preche*
> *His parishens devoutly wolde he teche.*
>
> PROLOGUE TO THE CANTERBURY TALES.

The Clerks and Sextons.

CHAP. VII.

" I had rather be a doorkeeper in the house of my God, than to dwell in the tents of wickedness."—Psa. lxxxiv. 10.

IN FORMER times the clerks and sextons were generally such as had taken minor Orders, that is to say Holy Orders below the rank of Subdeacon. And then afterwards the names were retained as the distinguishing titles of these officers of the Church, even when it was no longer customary for them to be ordained by the laying on of the hands of the Bishop.

The word clerk properly meant one well skilled to read and write—a scholar. It was thus commonly applied to the clergy, who were generally able to read and write, in days when these were very rare accomplishments.

The parish clerk is appointed to his office by the vicar: and he may be duly licensed thereto in the Ecclesiastical Courts. In which case the office is a freehold, from which he cannot be removed except for some grave fault, such as immorality or neglect of duty. I have gleaned from the registers—

A List of the Clerks.

In A.D. 1573 . . Carrington: 1633 John Carrington: 1653 William Kingsland: 16 . . Thomas Wrake: *ente* 1684 Samuel Terry, buried 28 Feb., 1703: 1703 James Keble, to 1724 probably, he was buried 20 Oct., 1738.

In 1725 and 1726 appears this entry in the churchwardens' accounts for those years :—

" P⁴. the Widow Walsgrave for clark's wages 15ˢ."

1728 Hezekiah Stace, buried 6 Sept., 1745: 1745 William Aynott, buried 30 July 1775, aged 70 years : 1775 Stephen Court; he married Aynott's daughter: 1830 Joseph Bowman.

In the oldest register occur the following entries respecting Kingsland :—

" 1590 March William Kingsland pish Clarke was baptized at Ickham this yeare & month."

" The 22ⁿᵈ day of September 1653 William Kingsland of Eastry .

. was by the Maior part of the pishioners . . . elected and chosen to be the pish register, &c."

He took the oaths of his office before Peter Peke, Esqre., on the 23rd of November following, and he signs his name for the last time in the register book under the year 1660.

Further on in the same register is a notice of Wrake's baptism inserted irregularly :—

" Aprill the 12 1635 was

Thomas Wrake pish Clarke of this pish baptized."

Both in the case of Wrake and in that of Kingsland there would appear to have been suspicions that they had not been baptized, which occafioned both thefe entries. That concerning Kingfland being efpecially fingular, as the facrament would feem to have been *performed at Ickham,* not that he was brought *here* from another parifh for that purpofe. A glance at the lift of clerks will fhew that the duties of their office have not been at all prejudicial to their longevity, at least during the laft 120 years. For fince the year 1745 up to the prefent time there have been only three parifh clerks!

Mrs. Chriftian Goddard, of Eaftry, widow of Oliver Goddard, bequeathed by her will in A.D. 1574, a tenement and garden in Eaftry

THE CLERK'S HOUSE.

Street, to the churchwardens " to hold to the ufe of the clerk of Eaftry for ever, fo that the fame clerk for the time being do teach and inftruct in learning one of the pooreft men's children of the parifh being a man child from time to time for ever." Further information refpecting this houfe will be found under " *The Schools*" and " *The Parochial Charities.*" It is now unfortunately in a fad ftate of dilapidation, and has been held adverfely for many years, as againft the churchwardens, by Thomas Young, who was once for a fhort time fchoolmafter, and who has long refufed to give up poffeffion of the premifes.

The Sextons.

The title *facriftan* or *fexton* was given to that officer of the church who had charge of the holy veffels, plate, veftments, relics, lamps, &c. His duties now-a-days, as well as his refponfibilities, are fomewhat lefs than formerly. But he ftill exercifes a general care of the church and churchyard, cleans the church himfelf or by his deputy, rings the bells, and digs the graves. The fexton is elected by the parifhioners; and the office is tenable for life, fubject to fufpenfion or removal, for mifconduct or immorality, by the ecclefiaftical authorities. The following is a

List of the Sextons.

Ante 1589 James Andrew, "the fexten," buried the 8 July 1589:
. . . . William Renward, buried 23 Jany., 1644-5: 1645 George Stuppell, "houfeholder, the fexton," buried 12 Oct., 1661: 1661 James Stupell, buried, "an ancient man," 9 May, 1711: 1708 John Smith, to Jany., 1719-20: 1720 Nicholas Cook, buried 29 June 1745: 1745 Michael Cock, buried 3 July, 1767: 1767 Stephen Danton, to 1785: 1785 Michael Cock, buried 12 Feb., 1805, aged 67: 1805 James Hudfon, buried 14 Jan., 1816, aged 84: 1816 John Moat, buried 24 July, 1867 aged 83: 1834 Richard Moat.

In the Churchwardens' accounts for the year 1785 there is this entry :—

"To expenfes at choofing a fexton . . 6ᵈ."

The fexton thus chofen was *Michael Cock.*

Stephen Danton feems to have left the parifh in or about the year 1785, as I can find no mention of his burial either in that or in fubfequent years.

Goodman Cock lived in the firft of the five houfes of Goddard's Charity

—viz., the one neareſt the road, now occupied by Widow Bullock. For the pariſh ſeems to have early appropriated this as "the Sexton's Houſe," and in the churchwardens' accounts we find numerous entries of various ſums paid, from time to time, for "clay," "ſand," and "ſtraw," as well as for "thatching" and "glazing," for this houſe.

What is a church?   Our honeſt Sexton tells
'Tis a tall building, with a Tower and Bells ;
Where Prieſt and Clerk with joint exertion ſtrive
To keep the ardour of their flock alive.

Theſe for the living ; but when life be fled,
I toll myſelf the requiem for the dead.—THE BOROUGH.

The Registers.

CHAP. VIII.

THERE have been various opinions as to the precife period when
parifh regifters were first kept in England [see Burn's *Parifh
Regifters*, p. 4 : a very valuable and interefting book well worth reading.]
But Dr. Prideaux feems on the whole to be correct when he fays in his
Directions to Churchwardens : " Parifh Regifters were firft ordered by the
Lord Vicegerent Cromwell in the 30th year of King Hen. VIII. (A.D.
1538), and from thence all parifh regifters have their beginning."

Our own regifters begin in September, A.D. 1559, the firft year of
Queen Elizabeth, who iffued an injunction in that year for the better
keeping of parifh regifters. The oldeft book has the baptifms, burials,
and marriages, entered in feparate columns on the fame page. That portion of it, however, which is prior to 1598 is, like many regifters in other
parifhes, only a *copy* of the older regifters : howbeit a *correct* and *reliable*
copy, fince the entries are attefted at the foot of each page by the words
Concordat cum originali, followed by the fignatures of Samuel Nicols
[vicar] ; Nicholas Squyer, W^m. ffaulkner [churchwardens]. The title-

page of the book explains this copying, and is as follows :—" A reiefter booke for the parifh of Eaftrie of Marrages, Chriftennings, and burialls begonne in the yeare of o^r. Lord 1559 : and now this yeare 1598 newlie written according to a conftitutiō made in cōvocatiō begonne att Londō the 25 of October 1597 by the Archbifhoppe, Bifhopps and the Clergie of the Province of Canterburie."

For the original conftitution referred to in the foregoing extract fee Burn's *Parifh Regifters*, pp. 23, 24. The regifter is defective in the burials and marriages from 1645 to September 1653: the few that are entered, having apparently been put in afterwards from memory.

In other refpects, however, few parifh regifters have been fo well kept as our own.

I may here mention that the old regifter book of Worth, which probably went back to the fame period as our own, viz., 1559, was deftroyed by one Richard Read, the clerk there, who judging it to be *out of date*, and being a tailor by trade, cut the parchment into flips for meafures !

In the year A.D. 1653 an act was paffed directing Regiftrars to be chofen in every parifh, to be approved of and fworn by a juftice of the peace. [See Burn's *Parifh Regifters*, p. 29.] The following is the entry in our own regifter concerning the due appointment of one of thefe officers for the parifh of Eaftry : " The 22th day of September 1653 William Kingfland of Eaftry in the County of Kent was by the Maior part of the pifhioners of the faid pifh elected and chofen to be the pifh regifter of Eaftry aforefaid for the regiftring of all marriages, births of children and burialls of all forts of people. And to Act and doe in all things therein according to an Act of Parliament in that cafe made and provided witnes our hands

" Nicholas Brett minifter James Bunce Roger Goulder Saphir Paramor William Vigin Michael Aauften Churchwardens John Auften his ✕ marke Ri: Harvy.

"I doe approue of the faid William Kingfland to bee Regifter of the Parifh of Eaftry abouefaid according to the election abouefaid. And the faid William Kingfland hath taken his oath before me, According to the Acte of Parlieament in that cafe made and prouided. Witnes my hand heereunto fubfcribed this Three & Twenty day of November 1653.— Pet. Peke."

In the year 1666, being the 18th Chas. II., an act was paffed directing that no perfon fhould be buried in any garment that was not wholly compofed of wool under a penalty of five pounds. And fubfequently another act was paffed in 1678 (30 Chas. II., cap.3) which required every minifter to take an affidavit of the relatives of the deceafed perfon, at the time of interment, fhewing that the ftatute had been duly complied with. Thefe acts were framed with a view to the encouragement of the woollen trade : and they were eventually repealed by the 54 George III., cap. 108, fec. 1.

Of courfe, when a penalty of £5 was attached to the being buried in linen, and the fhrouds of all but the very wealthy were made of woollen, it became a mark of diftinction to be buried in cloth of the forbidden material, and fo we find that the regifter gives us, from time to time, the names of certain perfons who, from family cuftom, wealth, or other motives, were thus interred.

The following entries are extracted from the Eaftry regifters, either on account of their fingularity, their ftrange omiffion of important particulars, or from throwing fome light on matters of local intereft.

Aug. 20 1562 Jone Bakar a chryfomer daughter of W^m. Bakar buryed.

May 11 1563 Jone Cornelius chryfomer the fon of John Cornelius gent. buryed.

June 3 1564 ffrifwyth Rogers chryfomer buryed.

feb. 28 1564 John Wickā fon of Tho. Wickā buryed.

ffeb. 27. 1566 John Cornelius gent. an houfeholder buryed.

Januar. 15. 1567 A certayne ftranger whofe name was not knowne buryed.

ffebr. 4. 1572 Willam Horne the fonne of Thomas Horne of ffelderland baptifed.

Sept. 12. 1575 ffryfwyth Nevinfon wife of Thomas Nevinfon gent. buryed.

Jan. 30. 1575 John Church and Sammell ffreind maryed.

Julie 4. 1577 Sammell Bagen a mayde fervant buryed.

Jan. 19. 1577 Robert a fervant of W^m. Richards buryed.

July 23. 1577 George Taylorr and Avis Smyth maryed.

deceb. 18. 1579 Holt a poore mã who dyed in John Hatchers barn buryed.

Aprill 15. 1581 Richard Mounte a Tyler buryed.

noveb. 5. 1582 an old womã not knoŵ what fhe was buryed.

ffeb. 21. 1584 ffather ffagge a fhepherd buryed.

march 16. 1584   the fonne of Markes Whittfeild buried.

Julie 4. 1585 Williã Corell & Godley Peene maryed.

deceb. 21. 1587 Thomas Hauke & Phemina ffynch maryed.

Sept. 26. 1588 a poore wayfayring mã his name & dwelling not known buryed.

At the bottom of the page under the year 1590 appears this entry in a later handwriting : March William Kingfland pifh Clarke was Baptifed at Ickham this yeare & month.

March 24. 1591 a poore Italian whofe name was not known buryed.

decbʳ. 6. 1592 John Chandler & Remembrance Wright maryed.

June 27. 1592 martha allen chryfomer buryed.

Auguft 6. 1594 Nicholas Squire & Silvefter Lowd maryed.

Septeb. 29. 1597   Nayler of Sᵗ. Nicholas in Thanet buryed.

Jan. 3. 1598 a flemifh child buryed.

Jan. 25. 1600 Ofwal Brompton fervant to Mr. Richard Boteler buryed.

Oct. 8. 1601 a poore boy found dead in the fields buryed.

ffebr. 15. 1601 Peter Clarke paterfamilias buryed.

Oct. 1. 1604 John a ftranger whofe name was not known buryed.

maye 2. 1607 Elizabeth Cleeve daughter of Sᵗ. Chriftopher Cleeve Knight buryed.

May 29. 1610 Chriftiã Pyfing a poor old mayd buryed.

Jannar 1. 1611 W^m. Boyes gent. & Sara Sea gent. maryed.

January 26. 1616   Mocket fonne of John Mocket baptifed.

ffebr. 1. 1619 Cicilie ffrofte virgin buryed.

Julie 26. 1621 Georg Gibbō ſon of George Gibbō chryſor buryed.

Aprill the 12. 1635 was Thomas Wrake *piſh Clarke* [theſe words have been partially eraſed] of this piſh baptized.

Julie 4. 1635 Margaret Gill an Innocent buryed.

deceb. 29. 1635 Sara n mayd ſervant buryed.

Jan. 6. 1639 Jeremie Maſterſon & Marie Friend at Wordneſborrow by Licence maried.

Jan. 24. 1643 Marke ffreind aged 90 yeeres buried.

In 1645 there are only three entries of *burials*, in 1646 only one, in 1647 there are ſix; but, in 1648 none! There are none in 1649, only one in 1650, five in 1651, one in 1652, and none in 1653 up to the time of Kingſland's appointment as "*Pariſh Regiſter*." This muſt have ariſen from the regiſter being kept ſomewhat careleſſly during the "troublous times"; though, as I have ſaid before, our regiſter may compare on the whole very well with thoſe of other pariſhes.

During all the above-mentioned years the *baptiſms* ſeem to have been entered pretty regularly; but there are no *marriage* entries in 1647, 1648, 1650, 1651, nor in 1653 previous to Kingſland's appointment.

The firſt page of Kingſland's entries is headed as follows: "A regiſter of births and Chriſtnings of children, alſo of Marriages and burialls, in the piſh of Eaſtry ſince the Nine and Twentith day of September in the yeere of our Lord Chriſt One Thouſand Six Hundred ffifty and Three, ſetting downe the births of as many as I could be enformed of according to the Act of Parliament in that behalfe lately made and according to my Oath wʰ I took wᵗʰ that proviſo."

From Kingſland's time the baptiſms, marriages, and burials are in diſtinct parts of the book. Before that they were entered in three separate columns in each page.

The following are extracted from the baptiſmal regiſter:

1672 Elizabeth yᵉ daughter of Thomas Giles & *Angelet* his wife 10ᵗʰ of December.

1673 Vinſton Barbor aged about 20 yeares baptiſed the 26ᵗʰ of March.

1677   of Thomas Tedeman Eſqʳ & Ann his wife November yᵉ 11ᵗʰ.

1677   the daughter of Thomas Stacy & Jane his wife November yᵉ 19ᵗʰ.

Theſe two laſt are curious as ſhowing how the baptiſmal name was forgotten to be inſerted.

1713 17. May   Ann daughtʳ of a Traveller her name not known.

From the marriage regiſter :—

The dates in the dexter column being thoſe of the publications of banns, and in the ſiniſter of the ſolemnization of the marriage itſelf.

1654 July 2. 9. 16   Edward Harnett and Katherine Paramor mar- July 18
                       ried by Mr. Maior [the Mayor] of Sandwich and
                       afterward by Mr. Bret.

        1655   Mr. Joſhua Paramor and Mary Gurney mar-
      publications   ried by Mr. Maior of Sandwich and afterward Aprill 17
     Aprill 1. 8. & 15 by Mr. Bret at Eaſtry.

The regiſter ſtates that there were no marriages in 1659, 1660, or 1661.

1662   and Ann fforſtall both of Thanet Octob: 12

Here the *name* of the *bridegroom* is ſingularly omitted! And there are many ſimilar omiſſions either of the Chriſtian name or ſurname juſt about this time.

From the regiſter of burials :—

1665 The wife of Samuel Churchman ffebru : 18.

1667 Stephen Anſell an aged man about 95 yeares Aprill 26.

From Lady-day, 1678, to Lady-day, 1679, there was buried only one perſon. Indeed, any one carefully examining the regiſter about this period, cannot fail to be ſtruck with the fact that nearly every entry is that of the burial either of " an ancient man," " an ancient woman," " a pore old man," " ſenex," " an aged man," or of " an infant," " a young child," " a child." Thereby ſhewing moſt unmiſtakably the low average of deaths, and the healthineſs of our pariſh.

In this register occurs the singular entry in Mr. Creffener's handwriting already noticed in the sketch of his life.

In 1779, Sept. 25, was buried Thomas Nisbett. Opposite the entry of his burial in the register there are some marks, apparently a sentence in cipher, which I have not been able to make out.

> *The year revolves and I again explore*
> *The simple annals of my Parish poor :*
> *What infant members in my flock appear ;*
> *What pairs I bleff'd in the departing year ;*
> *And who, of old or young, or nymphs or swains,*
> *Are loft to life its pleasure and its pains.*
>
> THE PARISH REGISTER.

The Schools.

CHAP. IX.

" Train up a child in the way he should go and when he is old he will not depart from it."—Prov. xxii. 6.

IN the year 1574 " Chriſtian Goddard, of Eaſtry, widow of Oliver Goddard," bequeathed to the churchwardens of Eaſtry and their ſucceſſors a tenement and garden in Eaſtry Street " to hold to the uſe of the clerk of Eaſtry for ever, ſo that the ſame clerk for the time being do teach and inſtruct in learning one of the pooreſt men's children of the pariſh, being a man child, from time to time for ever."

In courſe of time, however, the ſchoolmaſter was expected to teach *four* children gratis. But this may have ariſen in the following way— ſince in the abſence of all certain evidence we are left open to conjecture : —there being no funds left for the neceſſary repair of the ſchool houſe, and the clerk himſelf being unable to bear the expenſe of keeping it wind and weather tight, the pariſh would ſeem to have interpoſed, and agreed to keep the building in repair on condition of the clerk's inſtructing *four* children inſtead of *one.* This ſuppoſition is borne out by the fact that, in the churchwardens' accounts for 1689, and thenceforward *paſſim,* occur ſuch entries as the following relating to this houſe :—

" Paid to Thomas Bigg for ffoure dayes worke the Clarkes houfe and
     about the Bells   .   .   .   .   .   .o   6   8
For Lats and Nailes and Rafters about the Clerkes houfe .   .o   1   6"

And in Mr. Boteler's time [see *Botel. MSS.*, vol. A, p. 64] all remembrance of the original bequeft of Mrs. Goddard had apparently died out, whilft yet the clerk's obligation to teach *four* children had been handed down by tradition. Again, in the year 1728, firft appears the entry of 12*s*. 6*d*. under the head of "Schoolmafter's Salary," which I have traced as far as the year 1805 continuoufly. A few years further on we find that this 12*s*. 6*d*. was a half yearly payment = £1 5*s*. a-year. Perhaps the parifh may have agreed to give the fchoolmafter for the time being this falary, befides keeping the houfe in repair, in confideration of his teaching three children over and above the one mentioned by Mrs. Goddard in her will.

The fchool-room in the clerk's houfe, convenient and well adapted for its purpofe as it was once regarded, was, however, doomed to be fuperfeded and fall into difufe.

Through the exertions of the Rev. George Randolph, then vicar, new fchools were built in the year 1840, capable of holding 170 children, at a coft of £325, including a grant of £75 from the Canterbury Diocefan Education Society. Thefe fchools, which confifted of two rooms, one for girls and one for boys, with a gallery room attached, were built on much about the fame fite as the prefent fchools ; and were formally opened on Tuefday the 29th of September, 1840, in the prefence of many of the fubfcribers, who expreffed themfelves as highly pleafed and gratified with the arrangements of the building.

The rooms of this School were, however, of low pitch, were heated only by a fingle ftove, placed at the angle where the girls' and boys' fchools met, and were floored with brick.

Thus as time went on it was felt that thefe fchools were neither fufficiently airy nor warm, comfortable nor commodious. And, therefore, like as the fchools of 1840 fuperfeded the old long room in the clerk's houfe of 1574, fo thefe too in their turn gave place to the prefent handfome and commodious ftructure, which combines a picturefque appearance with a thorough adaptation of every part to its particular ufe.

By the laudable and painftaking efforts of the Revd. Charles Carus-Wilfon, then vicar, fubfcriptions, amounting to upwards of £950, were raifed for building new fchools; and, on the 5th November, 1859, thefe fchools were opened for the reception of children.

THE NEW SCHOOLS.

The prefent fchools contain what the former did not—viz., a feparate infant fchool, in addition to the boys' and girls' fchools and claff-room. They are alfo admirably adapted for all kinds of parochial meetings, lectures, &c., inafmuch as, by means of folding and fliding doors, all three fchoolrooms can be thrown into one.

The bell which daily—with the exception of Saturday—fummons the youth of both fexes to fchool, is hung outfide the boys' fchool. It is an ancient one, is fuppofed to have been an old fhip's bell, and bears the following infcription embofled round the crown; the letters are nearly an inch in height :—

✠ AVE ○ MARIA ○ GRACIA

where we fee that the R in GRACIA has been turned upfide down in cafting. Between the AVE and the MARIA, as alfo between the MARIA and GRACIA, is the medallion of a king's head, though of what king I have been unable to difcover.

The fchools, when built in 1840, were intended for the four parifhes of Eaftry, Worth, Ham, and Bettefhanger, and accordingly the vicars of Eaftry and Worth, and the rectors of Ham and Bettefhanger, are named truftees in the truft deed. Thefe, however, affociate with themfelves feveral refident fubfcribers to the fchools for the purpofe of forming a committee of management.

The fchools are in connection with the National Society, and are united to the Diocefan Board of Education. They are fupported partly by voluntary fubfcriptions and contributions, and partly by the Government grant.

The dimenfions of the feveral fchool-rooms are as under :—

Boys' School-room: length, 36 feet; breadth, 18 feet; height 24 feet; *Girls' School-room:* length 26 feet; breadth, 18 feet; height 24 feet; *Clafs-room:* length, 14 feet; breadth, 14 feet; height, 22 feet; *Infants' School-room:* length, 19 feet; breadth, 25 feet; height, 24 feet.

> *At fchool I knew him—a fharp-witted youth,*
> *Grave, thoughtful, and referved among his mates,*
> *Turning the hours of fport and food to labour ;*
> *Starving his body to inform his mind.*
>
> OLD PLAY.

The Parochial Charities.

CHAP. X.

" He that hath pity upon the poor lendeth unto the Lord; and look, what he layeth out, it shall be paid him again."—Prov. xix. 17.

OUR parish is tolerably rich in the provision which has been made from time to time by pious donors for the relief and assistance of the poor.

But here, as elsewhere, some charities have lapsed and been lost; sometimes through a want of care on the part of those whose duty it was to attend to such matters, in days gone by; at others through circumstances which no care and trouble on their part have availed to overcome.

Elware Charity *for Church repair.*

1499. This year Thomas Elware, of Eastry, left to Roger Frynne (his executor), his heirs and assigns for ever, his tenement at Selson, with all the lands belonging, on condition that he should pay yearly to the churchwardens of Eastry 3s. 4d. towards the repairs of the said church. (See *post.*) This sum may perhaps be considered equivalent to 10s. in these days.

This bequeſt has unhappily been loſt, and there is now no fund available for church repair, beyond ſuch ſmall ſum as the churchwardens may deem fit to give to this objeƈt from the voluntary church rate.

GODDARD'S CHARITY.

1574. This year the will (for which ſee *poſt*) of "Chryſtian Goddarde, late of Eaſtrye, widow," was proved in the Conſiſtory Court of Canterbury, before Thomas Dickes, regiſtrar. By this will ſhe left to the churchwardens of Eaſtry, and their ſucceſſors churchwardens of Eaſtry for the time being, one tenement and a garden, with the appurte-

GODDARD'S CHARITY.

nances in Eaſtry, over againſt the vicarage, to hold for the uſe of Joan Frauncs, her ſervant, during her natural life, and after her death to the uſe of the poor people of Eaſtry for ever.

This tenement oppoſite the vicarage is now in five dwellings, which ſtand endways to the ſtreet, and are occupied reſpeƈtively by widows Bullock, Burton, Grayham, Wm. Fagg, and Spain. The appointment to theſe cottages reſts entirely with the churchwardens, who uſually charge the occupants a fmall yearly rent—1ft, as an acknowledgment of their tenancy; and 2nd, to help fomewhat towards the neceffary repairs of the buildings. Mrs. Goddard alfo left another tenement with a garden in Eaftry Street, for the ufe of "the clarke of Eaftrye" on certain conditions, which have been already more particularly mentioned under "*The Parifh Clerks.*" This houfe adjoins the Bull Inn and is now in the occupation of Thomas Young. Like the laft, this appointment refts with the church-wardens, but they are tied down to appoint a certain perfon—viz., the Parifh clerk, the right of appointing whom refts with the vicar.

APPLETON'S CHARITY.

1593. In this year Thomas Appleton, of Eaftry, yeoman, left £5 for the perpetual benefit of the poor of Eaftry, to be either laid out in lands, or the intereft in clothes, &c., to be beftowed at the difcretion of fix of the principal inhabitants of Eaftry. The profits, whether intereft or otherwife, were to be received 14 days before Chriftmas by the church-wardens for the time being, and afterwards diftributed amongft the poor.

BOTELER'S CHARITY.

1617. Katherine Boteler, of Eaftry, widow, by her will, proved 1617, gave to the churchwardens of Eaftry the fum of 30s. to be diftributed amongft the poor people there, and alfo the like fum to remain in ftock for the ufe of the parifh.

This is now loft. It may, however, for aught we know, have been applied to fome purpofe, now forgotten, by a vote of the veftry.

THOMPSON'S CHARITY.

1673. Richard Thompfon, of Minfter in Thanet, by his will dated

1673,[*] bequeathed a meſſuage in Eaſtry to his ſon Stephen ſubjeĉt, to the following charity, viz. that 24 poor people, at three ſeveral times in the year, Chriſtmas, Eaſter, and Whitſuntide, ſhould receive a twopenny loaf each. The annual value of this rent charge is 12s.; it ariſes from a houſe in Eaſtry Street, (now the property of Mr. Wanſtall, of Nonington, and in the occupation of Edward Godden, baker and grocer), abutting on Collarmakers' Alley, and is adminiſtered by the Vicar and Churchwardens for the time being.

Freind's Bequest.

1715. Anne Freind, of Eaſtry, ſpinſter, by will proved in 1715, gave to the poor of our pariſh £5; and to the overſeers of it and their ſucceſſors for ever, three acres and one rood of arable land, at or near a place called *Deadman's Gap*, in Eaſtry, then in the occupation of Daniel Kelley, and held of the Dean and Chapter of Canterbury.

The ſaid overſeers were to renew the leaſe from time to time, and to let or otherwiſe employ the ſame to the beſt advantage : in truſt that the yearly rents and profits ſhould be equally paid and diſtributed on Chriſt-mas Day yearly, among ſuch induſtrious poor people of the pariſh, as did not receive alms thereof.

This is now loſt—indeed, it could hardly be otherwiſe from the nature of the holding, and the ſmall extent of the land in which an intereſt was thus bequeathed.

Rammell's Charity.

1821. This year " Mrs." Elizabeth Rammell, of Eaſtry, ſpinſter, be-

---

[*] Mr. Boteler thinks this date muſt be incorreĉt, as no mention is made of this charge on the eſtate in a conveyance of 1656 (? 1676), but it is mentioned in one of 1682.—*Boteler MSS.*, A., p. 65.

queathed to the churchwardens and overseers of the parish of Eastry, and
their successors, the sum of £300 of lawful money, to be invested in their
names in trust for the poor, and the interest of the said £300 to be dis-
tributed and disposed of on the 4th of January in each year, " in bread
clothes, or money, and in such proportions as they in their discretion shall
think proper, unto and amongst such of the poor parishioners of the said
parish residing therein, as shall not have received alms or relief from the
said parish for the space of one year previously." This £300 was duly
invested, and purchased £311 5s. 8d. of New 3 per Cent. Consols.

FECTOR'S CHARITY.

1821. The late John Minet Fector, of Dover, Esq., left the sum of
£50 (secured on the Sandwich, Waldershare, and Dover, Turnpike Road,)
to the Rev. George Randolph, Vicar of Eastry, and his successors, vicars
of Eastry for the time being, " to be applied in aid of any subscription
fund or otherwise for the education of the poor, or for the benefit of the
poor, in any other manner at the discretion of the vicar, or the officiating
or other minister for the time being of the aforesaid parish of Eastry."
This produces £1 10s. a-year, and may be disposed of by the vicar at his
discretion, but is generally added to the school funds.

HILL'S CHARITY.

1829. Mary Hills, of the parish of Ash, next Sandwich, widow, bequeathed to the vicar, churchwardens, and overseers of the poor of the
parish of Eastry, and their successors, the sum of £250 of lawful money,
upon trust to invest the same in some of the Government or Parliamentary
stocks or funds of this Kingdom, and upon the 14th day of January in
every year to distribute and divide the " dividends, interest, and income,

either in bread, clothes, or money, and in such proportions as they in their difcretion fhall think proper, into and amongft fuch of the poor and indi-gent widows of the faid parifh of Eaftry as fhall be confidered the moft deferving, and who endeavour to fupport themfelves without the aid and affiftance of parochial relief." This was duly invefted, and purchafed £255 Confols.

GREVILLE'S CHARITY.

1835. At a veftry meeting held on Thurfday, September the 18th, 1834, at which were prefent—Mr. Boteler, *in the chair*, Meffrs. Harvey, Rae, Bridger, Leggatt, Caftle, Manfer, Hatfeild, Church, Solley, Jullion, Smith, Hy. Sladden, Ifaac Sladden, Upton, Sutton, John Moat, Senr., and Grayham—Mr. Leggatt made a communication to the parifh from Wm. Fulke Greville, Efqr., propofing to build certain almfhoufes for aged and infirm parifhioners; men and women of good charaćter, and to endow each with a yearly penfion, all at his own expenfe; provided that the parifh would procure land upon which to erećt the faid houfes.

This handfome offer was at once accepted—100 perches of land on the north fide of Mill Lane, were purchafed by the parifh of Mr. Kite for

£100—a quick hedge, "three feet within the boundary of the Charity Land" was planted to divide the Charity Land from Mr. Kite's land—a field gate and small entrance gate to the almshouses and land were erected —the fence next Mill Lane repaired—the land divided out for gardens and allotted to the several alms-houses respectively—and the houses themselves built and ready for occupation by the 7th of April, 1835. On this day the trustees met and placed the almsmen and almswomen in their respective houses in due form. They received their first quarter's pension on the 7th July following. The almshouses thus built and endowed by Mr. Greville are six in number, and stand endways to the Mill Lane; the numbers commencing with the house nearest the road, which is numbered 1. They are each endowed with a pension of £10 a-year; which sums arise from the interest of £2000 3 per Cent. Consolidated Bank Annuities conveyed by Mr. Greville to the trustees for that purpose. There are also two outdoor pensions of £10 each. The trustees appoint a receiver, who receives the money from the Sandwich Bank, pays the pensioners, keeps the accounts, and makes the entries in the book of record; he also takes the chair at all meetings of the trustees.

The following are the

"Directions and Rules for the establishment and good Government of the Alms Houses erected and endowed by William Fulke Greville Esqr. in the Parish of Eastry, in the County of Kent.

1st. That the Vicar, Churchwardens, and Overseers of the Poor of the Parish of Eastry for the time being, be perpetual Trustees of the Alms Houses, and that five other substantial Inhabitants of the parish be from time to time nominated trustees to act in all matters relating to the same with the perpetual trustees.

2nd. That Messrs. Wm. Fuller Boteler, Henry Wise Harvey, Richd.

Shocklidge Leggatt, Wm. Bridger and James Rae, be the firſt nominated truſtees to act with the perpetual truſtees of the almſhouſes.

3rd. That when any of the truſtees now or hereafter to be nominated to act with the perpetual truſtees of the almſhouſes ſhall die or remove from the pariſh, and ceaſe to have any houſe or lands in the ſame, or ſhall decline to act, or become incapable of acting in the truſt, one or more ſubſtantial inhabitants of the pariſh ſhall be nominated by the perpetual truſtees and other ſurviving or continuing truſtees of the almſhouſes, to be a new truſtee or new truſtees in the ſtead of the truſtee or truſtees, ſo dying, removing, declining, or becoming incapable of acting, to act with them in all matters relating to the almſhouſes.

4th. That the land purchaſed for the ſite of the almſhouſes ſhall be conveyed to the truſtees nominated to act with the perpetual truſtees and their heirs, and the ſum of £2000 3 per Cent. Conſolidated Bank Annuities intended for the endowment of the almſhouſes ſhall be transferred into the names of the ſame truſtees, or any four of them, and whenever the truſtees, in whom the charity eſtate, ſtocks, funds and property, ſhall be veſted reſpectively, ſhall be reduced to leſs than three in number, ſuch eſtate, ſtocks, funds, and property, ſhall be conveyed, and transferred ſo as that the ſame may become veſted in the whole number of truſtees nominated to act with the perpetual truſtees for the time being, or (as to the Bank Annuities) any four of them.

5th. That the government of the almſhouſes, and the management of the charity eſtate, ſtocks, funds, and property, and the diſpoſitions of the revenues thereof, ſhall be under the care of the perpetual truſtees, and nominated truſtees, for the time being, ſubject to the rules and regulations herein contained, and any future rules and regulations to be made as hereinafter mentioned, and all acts done by the trustees, and orders made by them, shall be done and made at an ordinary meeting of the trustees, of which one shall be held at the almshouses at 12 o'clock at noon on the first Tuesday in January, April, July, and October, in every year, or at a special meeting of the trustees to be called from time to time, by notice in writing signed by any two trustees desiring the same, and left at the dwelling house of each of the other trustees who shall at the time be resident in the parish, not less than four days before the day of meeting. At which ordinary or special meeting four of the trustees at least shall be present, and the majority of voices of the trustees present at the meeting, shall be binding upon the other trustees present; and, in case of an equality of votes upon any question, the chairman of the meeting shall have a second or casting vote; and all acts done and orders made at every such meeting shall be entered in a book kept for the purpose and signed by the chairman of the meeting.

6th. That as soon as the almshouses shall be erected and fit for habitation six poor persons, men or women, shall be appointed, each to inhabit one of the almshouses for life, subject to forfeiture or removal from his or her place as hereinafter mentioned. And as and when vacancies shall afterwards happen in the almshouses, by death or otherwise, such vacancies shall be filled up in every case within six calendar months after the same shall happen, provided that if at any time money shall be wanted for the necessary substantial repairs of the almshouses, the trustees may in their discretion keep one vacancy, or at most two vacancies, not filled up, until they have in their hands a sufficient sum of money for doing such repairs.

7th. That Mr. Greville fhall have the appointment of the almfmen and almfwomen in the firft inftance, and in all cafes of vacancies which fhall happen during his life, and after his deceafe the truftees of the almfhoufes fhall, from time to time, appoint the almfmen and almf-women to the fame as vacancies fhall occur.

8th. That the perfons appointed almfmen and almfwomen be parifhioners, who have been inhabitants of the parifh of Eaftry for not lefs than five years immediately preceding the time of their appointment, and who are not lefs than 50 years of age at the time of their appoint-ment, and no perfon fhall be appointed to an almfhoufe unlefs it fhall appear to the truftees that he or fhe is of good moral and religious character.

9th. That no almfman or almfwoman have any relation or other perfon to inhabit with him or her, in his or her almfhoufe, except fuch almfman or almfwoman as fhall be married at the time of his or her appointment, who may have his wife or her hufhand to live with him or her, and except in any cafe the truftees fhall give permiffion in writing to any almfman or almfwoman to have one or more relation or relations or other perfon or perfons by name to live with him or her, and in cafe any almfman or almfwoman fhall marry after being appointed to any almfhoufe, or in cafe any almfman or almfwoman fhall have any relation or other perfon to inhabit in his or her almfhoufe contrary to the directions hereinbefore contained, the truftees of the almfhoufes may, if they in their difcretion think fit, remove fuch almfman or almfwoman from his or her almfhoufe and appoint another perfon to the fame in his or her ftead.

10th. That in any cafe any almman or almfwoman appointed to the faid almfhoufes, fhall be guilty of any mifconduct which the truftees deem it neceſſary to notice in ſuch manner, ſuch almſman or almſwoman ſhall be in the firſt and ſecond inſtances admoniſhed by the truſtees, and if ſuch almſman or almſwoman ſhall, after being ſo twice admoniſhed, be again guilty of ſuch miſconduct, ſuch almſman or almſwoman, ſhall be removed from his or her almſhouſe, and another perſon ſhall be appointed to the ſame in his or her ſtead.

11th. That the dividend of the ſaid ſum of £2000 3 per Cent. Conſolidated Bank Annuities be applied in payment to each of the almſmen and almſwomen of a yearly ſtipend of £10 by four equal quarterly payments of £2 10s. each to be made on the days of the ordinary meetings of the truſtees.

12th. That the ſurplus, if any, of the money propoſed to be raiſed for the purchaſe of the ſite of the almſhouſes, and the dividends of the ſaid £2000 3 per Cent. Conſolidated Bank Annuities which ſhall become due before the firſt appointment of almſmen or almſwomen, and the amount of any ſtipends which may become due during any vacancies of almſhouſes, ſhall be retained by the ſaid truſtees of the almſhouſes, and improved at intereſt as a fund to provide for the repairs of the almſhouſes, inſurance againſt fire, and any incidental expenſes which may ariſe in the management of the charity.

13th. That the almſmen and almſwomen do keep in repair the glaſs windows, plaſtering, whitewaſhing, and other ſmall internal repairs of their reſpective almſhouſes which the truſtees ſhall from time to time direct, and do no wilful damage in or to their reſpective almſhouſes, and in caſe of default of any almſman or almſwoman in the above behalf the truſtees ſhall and may apply the whole, if neceſſary, or any part of his or her ſtipend in doing ſuch laſt mentioned repairs and making good ſuch damage.

14th. That the truftees of the almfhoufes fhall and may from time to time make any additional rules or orders for the good government of the almfhoufes, fo as that fuch new rules and orders, if made in the lifetime of the faid Wm. Fulke Greville be made with his confent, or if made after his death do not alter, and are not at variance with, the foregoing original directions and rules or any other directions and rules made during the lifetime of the faid Wm. Fulke Greville for the good government of the almfhoufes."

Further rules and regulations with the dates of their enactment numbered continuoufly :—

15th. " That the truftees do examine into the ftate of the almfhoufes at the quarterly meeting in October annually." Made Jan. 5th, 1836.

16th. "That the receiver's accounts fhould be paffed annually at the quarterly meeting in October." Ap. 4th, 1843.

17th* "That on no occafion of filling up any vacancy in the almfhoufes fhould any vote by proxy on the part of the truftees be received." July 6, 1847.

18th. " That on the occafion of filling up any vacancy in the almf-houfes votes by proxy on the part of the truftees may be received." July 1ft, 1859.

Out Pensioners of Greville's Charity.

" Wm Fulke Greville, Efq., having been pleafed to transfer the fum of £666 13*s*. 4*d*. 3 per Cent. Confolidated Bank Annuities (in addition to the fum of £2000 previoufly granted) into the names of Meffrs. W.

---

* This was altered by the fucceeding rule No. 18, and, therefore, is not now in force.

Fuller Boteler, Henry Wife Harvey, Richard Shockledge Leggatt, Wm. Bridger, and James Rae, the truftees of his almfhoufes.

The dividends of this fum of £666 13s. 4d. are to form a yearly ftipend of £10 each for two aged perfons refiding out of the almfhoufes, who, as vacancies happen in the houfes, are to be admitted thereto in their turn, and new objects, to enjoy the ftipends out of the almfhoufes, are to be nominated in their ftead; but it is not to be imperative upon the truftees to place the outpenfioners in the houfes as vacancies happen, whenever for fpecial reafons it appears to them more expedient to nominate objects to the houfes who have not been outpenfioners in preference.

All the rules and orders relating to the objects of the charity placed in the almfhoufes as regards their qualification, nomination, removal, conduct, or otherwife, which admit of being applied to the outpenfioners, are to be applicable and to be applied to them."

TABLE OF ALL THE CHARITIES NOW EXISTING IN THE PARISH: fhewing the date of their foundation, perfons who appoint, value, &c. :—

Date of inftitution.	Truftees.	Property.	Purpofe for which available.
		GODDARD'S CHARITY.	
1574.	The churchwardens.	Five cottages oppofite the Vicarage : a houfe and garden in Eaftry Street.	The cottages are for the habitation of poor people. The houfe and garden in yᵉ ftreet are for the Parifh clerk.
		THOMPSON'S CHARITY.	
1673.	Vicar & churchwardens.	An annual rent charge of 12s. on houfe occupied by Godden, the baker.	For giving a twopenny loaf to 24 poor people at Chriftmas, Eafter, and Whitfuntide.

Date of inftitution.	Truftees.	Property.	Property for which available.
		RAMMELL'S CHARITY.	
1821.	Churchwardens and Overfeers.	£311 5s. 8d. New 3 per Cent. Confols : dividend of fame.	To be diftributed in bread, clothes, or money, to poor people who have not received parifh relief.
		FECTOR'S CHARITY.	
1821.	Vicar.	Sandwich, Walderfhare, and Dover Turnpike Road Bond for £50.	For the education of the poor or for the benefit of the poor in any other way.
		HILL'S CHARITY.	
1829.	Vicar, churchwardens, and overfeers.	£255 Confols : dividends only available.	To be diftributed in bread, clothes, or money, amongft fuch of the poor widows as endeavour to keep themfelves without parifh relief.
		GREVILLE'S CHARITY.	
1835.	Vicar, churchwardens and 5 other fubftantial refidents.	Six cottages with gardens and 100 perches of land : and £2666 13s. 4d. 3 per Cent. Confolidated Bank Stock.	The houfes to be occupied by poor people who fhall receive £10 a-year each : and two perfons to receive £10 a-year without houfes.

Twelve rooms contiguous ftood and fix were near ;
There men were placed, and fober matrons here ;
There were behind fmall ufeful gardens made ;
Benches before and trees to give them fhade.—THE BOROUGH.

Appendix.

I HAVE endeavoured to gather together under this general head-ing fuch documents and information, as being of no great intereft to the ordinary reader, are neverthelefs valuable for reference. In this way fome things may be preferved which otherwife, through lapfe of time, would have been overlooked, loft fight of, and then forgotten; whilft other things may be here plainly fet forth, which are not eafily acceffible.

CHURCH RESTORATION, with dates, taken from the veftry minute book.

"Repairs and alterations made in the church by Richard Springett Harvey, Efqr., except where othewife mentioned:—

Nov. 1851. An organ was put up in the gallery at the weft end of the nave. The gallery was painted by fubfcription of the inhabitants.

Sep. 1852. A fmall fide gate at the weft end of the Churchyard was put up; and the path from it to the fmall porch made good. The way from the large weftern gates to the weft door was paved and lined on the fouth fide with curb-ftones.

Jany. 1853. A new clock was put into the tower: the old clock being quite worn out.

Augſt. and Septr. 1853. The "lean-to" on the north ſide,* and alſo that on the ſouth ſide of the tower were entirely rebuilt; the latter being converted into a veſtry. Formerly the veſtry was at the weſtern end of the ſouth aiſle of the nave. The ground floor of the tower was newly paved with tiles. The arches under the tower were brought out to view and repaired. The tower ſtairs were partially repaired. The yellow waſh over the weſt door on the outſide of the tower was removed; the flint work made good; and the diaper work over the door (i.e., in the tympanum) "picked" out and repaired. The weſtern doorway was repaired and widened about three inches, and five new ſtone ſteps were put in the place of the old ones leading down into the tower.† Three new pews were put up under the gallery. Towards theſe repairs the pariſh raiſed about £54 by voluntary ſubſcription; the total coſt being about £230.

May-July, 1854. The wall of the ſouth aiſle, from the tower eaſtwards—as far as to the window on the eaſt of the porch incluſive—and the ſouth porch itſelf were entirely rebuilt. Two windows were inſerted in this wall; that on the eaſt ſide of the porch being put in by Capt. Robert Boteler. The whole of the lead roof of the ſouth aiſle was made good. The "ſhoots" were removed from the tower and replaced by pipes.

June-Aug. 1855. The main part of the nave and aiſles—that is from the moſt weſtern pillars to the moſt eaſtern pillars excluſive—was repewed and refloored. The lower parts of the pillars were made good and the

---

* This "lean-to" was formerly in two ſtories, and the "upper chamber" is traditionally ſaid to have been uſed as a ſchool. This has now entirely diſappeared, as the roof of this "lean-to" was made to come much lower againſt the tower.

† The floor of the tower is 29 inches below the level of the ground at the weſt door.

hatpags removed. The old high pews attached to the north and fouth walls were removed, and the paffages in the north and fouth aifles were placed nearer the walls, and increafed in width to allow of a line of feats along them. The centre aifle was narrowed 18 inches for the fake of accommodation. Ten oil lamps were provided for evening fervices. The footpath through the churchyard from the fouth porch to the gate at the eaft end was widened and underdrained. A ftained glafs window was put in the north aifle by Wm. Boteler, Efqre, to the memory of his father.

1856. The Chancel was entirely repaired by the rectors—viz., the Ecclefiaftical Commiffioners;* i.e., all the windows were reglazed and their ftone work renewed where neceffary. The centre light of the eaft window was reftored from its debafed form of a double light with circular heads, to its full and proper form. The north fide of the roof was thoroughly repaired, the fouth fide of it having been repaired a few years before. Four new pews were put up in the chancel. All this was done by the Ecclefiaftical Commiffioners.

May, 1857. The wooden floor—which extended to within four feet of the north and fouth wall of the chancel—and the wooden railings enclofing it on three fides, the oak‡ panelling on the eaft wall—on which were written the Ten Commandments, the Creed, and the Lord's Prayer—and

---

* This was probably the refult of a vifit from the archdeacon, which is thus recorded in the veftry book:—"May 3, 1850. Vifited and ordered the north and fouth fide of the chancel roofs to be ripped and relaid—a window in the fouth fide of the church to be generally repaired once every year. . . . .

(Signed)   James Croft, Archdeacon."

‡ In the year 1731, the churchwardens feem to have made a kind of tour, with the purpofe of infpecting the "altar pieces" at Knowlton, Nunnington, Wingham, Ickham, Afh, &c.

alfo that on the north and fouth walls, were removed. A floor of Portland ftone was laid down extending acrofs the chancel; a light railing was inferted in front of it, and the whole fpace of wall under the eaft window was faced with Caen ftone, on which were engraved the Commandments (in 1209 letters): The Holy Table alfo was enlarged; a new crimfon cloth covering, new cufhions, new haffocks and carpet, and new books of Offices, were provided. The wall of the fouth aifle from the window on the eaft of the fouth porch (exclufive) to the eaftern corner was repaired. The fouth-eaft corner, and eaft extremity of the fouth aifle, were entirely rebuilt, and in the latter, a new window was inferted.

June, 1857. Two new windows were inferted in the fouth aifle towards its eaft end, and fitted with ftained glafs (from Powell's, of Whitefriars, London,) by fubfcription of the inhabitants, as a teftimonial to R. S. Harvey, Efqre., for the kind and benenevolent intereft which he had taken in their Church.

Auguft 1857. The pulpit was removed, from its pofition on the north fide of the moft eaftern pillar of the fouth aifle, to the weft front of the fouth pier of the chancel arch. The reading defk was removed from the fide of the pulpit to the front of it, and the vicarage pew from behind the reading defk to a pofition alongfide of it and the pulpit, facing the centre aifle. The pulpit, reading defk, and vicarage pew, as newly arranged, occupy exactly the fame fpace of ground as they did formerly. A new Bible and Prayer-Book (quarto) were placed in the reading defk by Mr. Harvey, to whom the churchwardens prefented the old folio Bible. The remaining high pews in the fouth-eaft corner of the fouth aifle were taken down and new ones put in their places. The clereftory window, fecond from the chancel arch on the north fide, was entirely renewed.

May-June 1858. The other four clereftory windows on the north

fide were alfo renewed, and the three moft weftern windows in the north
aifle were reftored to their previous form, with plain glafs. The whole of
the lead roof of the north aifle was made good, and ftone coping fubftituted
for the former brick parapet. A ftained glafs window was put in at the
eaft end of the north aifle by W. Boteler, Efq., to the memory of his two
fifters Sarah and Ann Boteler.

Sep. 1858. A new gate was put up at the eaft end of the churchyard.

1857. There was removed fome modern panelling on the weft fide of
the wall above the chancel arch. Behind it and underneath many coat-
ings of whitewafh was difcovered much painting in frefco. The whole
wall appeared to have been originally blue ftudded with gold ftars. On
a later coat of plaifter were the circles containing the early Chriftian
fymbols, which at prefent are to be feen above the arch. There were many
other circles with fimilar defigns, which were covered over again on
account of their very indifferent condition, as well as being mere repeti-
tions of thofe preferved.

A ftained glafs window was put in the centre of the north aifle to the
memory of Mr. Caftle.

1861. A ftained glafs window was put in at the eaft end of the fouth
aifle to the memory of the late Rev. R. D. Backhoufe by Mifs E. C.
Boteler.

A ftained glafs window was put in the centre of the fouth aifle to the
memory of the late Mrs. Kenrick by Mifs Toker.

The remaining block of old pews at the north-eaft corner of the nave,
which had remained unaltered at the time of the general repewing
of the church, was taken down and the fpace fitted as the reft of the
church.

1862, Chriſtmas. Stoves were introduced into the church ; the expenſe of them being undertaken by the Rev. Ch. Carus-Wilſon.

1863. The gallery at the weſt end of the nave (which had been put in 1842, and which completely blocked up the eaſt arch of the tower) was taken down and the arch thrown open. The arches under the tower on the north and ſouth ſides were alſo thrown open, and the organ (removed from the gallery) was placed under the former. The ſpace at the ſouth-weſt end of the nave (hitherto unpewed) was fitted with pews for the choir, and the ſpace on the oppoſite ſide at the north-weſt end of the nave, which had hitherto been indifferently pewed was made to correſpond with the reſt of the church. The weſt door was encloſed with a wooden framework, ſcreened with a curtain ; the ſteps were projected ſomewhat into the church, and the veſtry was ſeparated from the tower by a curtain. The arch at the weſtern end of the north aiſle was opened out into the "lean-to," and new wooden ſtairs made to the belfry. The arch at the western end of the ſouth aiſle was cleared out, ſo far as was conſidered ſafe. The funds for theſe alterations were provided by the Rev. C. Carus-Wilſon.

Stained glaſs windows and new ſtonework were put into the ſouth clereſtory, partly by Mr. R. S. Harvey, partly by the Rev. C. Carus-Wilſon, and partly by other means.

The pariſhioners by ſubſcription put ſtained glaſs (furniſhed by Meſſrs. Ward and Hughes) into the eaſt window. New ſtonework being partly provided by the Dean and Chapter of Canterbury.

1866. Miſs Spong put ſtained glaſs (furnished by Meſſrs. Hughes) into the four early Engliſh windows on the ſouth ſide of the chancel.

1868. A handſome almſdiſh of beaten braſs with jewelled centre was preſented to the church by the Miſſes Boteler.

F F

Advent, 1868. A double oak lectern was prefented to the church by the Rev. V. S. Vickers, then curate.

Eafter, 1869. Two handfome maffive altar candlefticks of beaten brafs, jewelled and enamelled, 25 inches in height, were prefented to the church by the Miffes Boteler for the purpofe of lighting the chancel, and more efpecially the precincts of the Holy Table at the evening fervices.

Aug. 1869. The Holy Table was enlarged to a proportion more in keeping with the fize and grandeur of the church. Two almfbags, of crimfon velvet, embroidered, were prefented to the church by Mifs Hatfeild."

Aug. to October. The Roof of the Nave, erected in 1687, being very much out of repair was taken down, the brick parapet above the clereftory windows removed, and an open high pitch roof, of beft Memel pine and tiled, fubftituted for it, under the direction of Wm. White, Efq., F.S.A., architect. The roof is as nearly as poffible a reftoration of the ancient roof prior to 1687, and the marks of the water-table, &c., on the eaft face of the tower, indicating the pitch of the older roof, were carefully noted and followed.

The plaifter was removed from the face of the eaft gable of the Nave, and from the weft front of the Tower, which were then frefh " pointed." A new weft door, of oak with hammered ironwork, was prefented by Mr. G. Terry, parifh churchwarden. The old Font, being much battered, containing no interefting features, and being incapable of reftoration, was replaced by a new one, and a drain was duly dug for carrying off the water. A set of three Altar fervice books, each bound in dark blue morocco, with two gilt clafps, was provided out of funds placed at the vicar's difpofal.

WANTS.

And now, whilft on the fubject of additions and improvements to the Church, it may perhaps be well to mention fome things that are abfolutely neceffary, and others that would greatly add to the glory and beauty of our Church, fhould any pioufly difpofed perfons fee fit to prefent them, or aid in their being carried out. Among the former may be mentioned, a new pulpit and reading defk; a new great Bible[*] in two parts for the two faces of the lectern, and a brafs altar defk for the heavy Communion Office book. Amongft the latter, ftained glafs windows in the Chancel in place of the prefent yellow blinds; the roofs of the aifles to be made to corre-fpond with the roof of the nave internally; the ceiling of the chancel to be divided into panels, with ribs and boffes, and picked out with colour; fome more oak chairs or fedilia within the fanctuary; a reredos at the back of the Altar; the floor of the fanctuary laid with encaustic tiles; the walls of the church cemented fo as to prevent the neceffity of whitewafh, and ornamented with diaper or other patterns in frefco; a large frefco over the chancel arch above the medallions; the tower area laid with encauftic tiles, and the old and very fingular Weft Porch reftored according to the traces ftill re-maining.

Such are fome of the reftorations which I would here fuggeft as calcu-lated to render our Church more fitting for the celebration of Divine fervice, and more worthy of His Prefence, Whofe Houfe it is.

---

[*] Whilft thefe pages were paffing through the prefs, a friend kindly promifed to prefent us with this.

TERRIERS.

The 87 Canon of the Canons of 1603 runs thus:—" We ordain that the archbiſhops and all biſhops, within their ſeveral dioceſes, ſhall procure (as much as in them lieth) that a true note and *terrier* of all the glebes, lands, meadows, gardens, orchards, houſes, ſtocks, implements, tenements, and portions of tithes, lying out of their pariſhes (which belong to any parſonage, or vicarage, or rural prebend), be taken by the view of honeſt men in every pariſh, by the appointment of the biſhop (whereof the miniſter to be one), and be laid up in the biſhop's regiſtry, and there to be for a perpetual memory thereof."

The following terriers are extracted from the archives of the Confiſto- rial Court of Canterbury :—

I.

" A Terriē of all the Gleabe lands and Tenements belonginge to the Pſonage of Eſtrie made by us whoſe names are heereunder written.

" Imprimis. A cloſe called the Buts Cloſe contayneinge thirteene acres and a halfe and eight perches abuttinge one the Eaſt uppon the Kings highway Weſt and South the Land ptayneinge to Chriſt Church North to a Cloſe of Mr. Jaleys Weſt are Dane Twelve Acres Eſt Weſt North and South Chriſt Church.

" Horſe Acre. Sixe Acres abuttinge one the South to the Lands of Henry Parramour North William Faulkner Eaſt Chriſt Church Weſt to the Tenants commō way.

" One Acre and a halfe called the Horſefayer abuttinge one the Eaſt South and Weſt to the Land of Thomas Hufham North to Sʳ Roger Newinſonn.

" One halfe Acre layeinge at the Mill abuttinge Eaſt and Weſt to the High- way North Kerby South Edmnd Parker.

" Upper Croſs Fower Acres thirtie fix perches North the Heyres of Wil- liā Nutt Eſt South and Weſt Chriſt Church.

" Skinners Gore Five Acres abuttinge on the South uppon the Lands of Edmnd Parker Eaſt and Weſt Chriſt Church Weſt Tenants common way.

One Acre one rod laying to Horſe Acres Buſh abuting one Williā Friends Land one the North Weſt Tenants common highway South the Heyres of Williā Nut Eſt Chriſt Church One Acre and a halfe layinge at Colket abut- tinge one the North and South to the Lands of Jonathan Boteler Weſt to the Cōmon way Eaſt to the Heyers of Matthewe Meares One Acre at Horſe

Acre Eaſt Chriſt Church South Mr. Jonathan Boteler Weſt the coñon Tenants way North uppon the Land of William Parker.

Three rods at Felderland South and West William Hilde North Kings Highway and Eaſt abuttinge upon the Land of William Dranton.

Six Acres at Hoyſelſewood Field abuttinge on the Kings Highway uppon the South North and Weſt Chriſt Church and uppon the Lands of Mr. Samuell Nicols one the Eaſt One Acre and a halfe at the Buts buttinge one the South uppon the Lands of John Pittocke Eaſt Chriſt Church Weſt the Highway North Thomas Huffam.

Two Acres more or leſſe in the occupaꞇon of William Paramouʳ Halfe one Acre in the occupaꞇon of William Salter One Acre layenge before the Ambry Gate.

Two rodes in the occupaꞇon of Thomas Arnolde Churchway North and Eſt South Richard Auſtin Weſt upon the Land of Edward Parker. One Acre three rods amonge the Lands of Robart Gyles.

Two acres of Land in the occupaꞇon of William Paramoʳ abuttinge uppon Chriſt Church Land one the North and upon the ſayd William Paramouʳ Land Eſt Weſt and South.

Sixteene Acres layeinge in the p of Tillmeſton in the occupation of Stephen Saffery.

One Tenement layeinge in Eſtry Street in the occupaꞇon of William Hougham.

One Tenement or Howſe layeng in Eſtrie Street in the occupaꞇon of Thomas Houghm̄.

Thomas Hilde

⋈

his mke.

William Falkener Churchwarden.

Thomas Robins ⋈ his mark.

Thom Friend   Sydmen.

Joſua Paramor."

This terrier was probably made in or about the year A.D. 1598, ſince William ffaulkner was churchwarden in that year, which was the 8th year of the vicariate of Samuel Nicolls.

II.

" A Terrier of the Tenements Gardens and Gleabe Lands belonging to the Ambry or Parſonage and Vicaredge of Eaſtry lying in the piſhes of Eaſtry Word and Tilmanſtone wch ſaid Parſonage wth the Tenements and Gleabe Lands Sr George Sondes Knight of the Bath houldeth by Leaſe from the Deane and Chapiter of Chriſt Church in Canterbury the ſaid Terrier being made and ſubſcribed the fowre and twentith day of Auguſt Anno Dm̅ni 1637 by Mr. Samuel Nicols Vicar of the ſaid piſh and Mr. Joſhua Parramore and Thomas Marſh Church-Wardens of the ſame as followeth :—

" Imprimis the Parſonage Houſes and two Acres of Land lying in the Plane and Gardens abutting to the Kings Highwaies and the Vicaredge Land towards the South and Weſt and to the Churchyard and Eaſtry Court Land toward the North and to the Lands of Mr. Joſhua Parramore towards the Eaſt.

" Item the Vicaredge Houſes and halfe an Acre and 20 pches of Land abutting to the Kings Highwaies and to the Lands of a Houſe belonging to the Parſonage in the occupaċon of Henry Richardſon South and Weſt and to the Lands belonging to the Parſonage North and Eaſt.

" Itē A Dwelling Houſe and a Garden nere the Croſſe in Eaſtry Streete lying to the Kings Streete South and Weſt and to the Vicars Garden and Land North and Eaſt.

Itē One other Houſe and Garden in Eaſtry Streete lying to the Streete Weſt and to the Land of Thomas Boteler North To the Landes of the Heires of William Freind Eaſt and to the Landes of Richard Stacy South.

" Itē nine peeces of Gleabe Land ſeverally lying in Eaſtry aforeſaid containing in the whole fifty acres a halfe and one roode.

" 1. Whereof one peece is called the Faire Feild and conteineth xxij one roode and xxix pches and lyeth to the Kings way leading towards Tilmanſtone Eaſt To the Landes of the Heires of William North to Mr. Fowlers Land North and Weſt To the Lands of Mr. Samuell Nicols late John Falkeners and to the Lands of Eaſtry Court Weſt and South.

" 2. Two other peeces thereof lying at a place called Skeymers* Gore and con-taine nine Acre a halfe and xi pches lying together to the Lands of Mr. Nutt and to the way leading to deadman gap North & Weſt To Mr. Foules Land Eaſt and South To the Faier Feild Weſt and North To the Lands of Mr. Parks South & Weſt.†

---

* Skinners Gore, now Gore. † There is no 3 in the copy from which this is taken.

" 4. Itē one other peece thereof containing one Acre one roode and xiiij pches to the Landes of Mr. Josua Parramore late Mr. Huffam North East & South To the way leading towards Tilmanstone West and North To the Lands of the Heires of Sʳ Roger Newinson East and South and to the Lands of the heires of Wᵐ. Smith and Simon Mount West.

" 5. Itē one other peece thereof containing one acre one roode and xxvij pches and lyeth to the Highway West To the Lands of Mr. Josua Parramore late Mr. Huffams toward the North To the Landes of Richard Pittocke South and to Eastry [? Court] Land called Bramble Hill Banke towards the East.

" 6. Item one other peece thereof containing fixe acres and fixe pches lying to the way leading to deadman gap West and North To the Landes of Mr. Samuell Nicols late John Falkeners North and East To the Landes of the Heires of William Parramore South and West and lyeth at or neere a place there called commonly by the name of Calcott toward the Landes called the Elderne Stumpe.

" 7. Itē one other peece thereof lyeth towards deadman gap and conteineth one acre and xxviij pches and abutteth to the said way leading to deadman gap West and North To the Lands of Mr. Nutt North and East To the Lands of Thomas Freind West and South.

" 8. Itē one other peece thereof containing one acre one roode and xxij pches and lyeth nere unto deadman gap to the said way West and North To the Land of Mr. Boteler North and South.

" 9. Itē one other peece thereof lyeth in Hasell Wood Feild and conteineth fixe Acres and xxij pches and abutteth to the way leading to Northborne South and West To Eastry [*Court*] Land North and West To the Lands of Thomas Marsh late Mr. Nicols East and South.

" Itē one peece of Land conteining one acre and xxiiij pches lying in Eastry over againſt the Church planted wᵗʰ fruite trees for an Orchard and abutteth to the Kings waies North and East To the Lands late Mr. Huffams now Thomas Botelers and the Lands of Michaell Austen South and to the Lands of Mr. Parks and the Clarkes* Garden West.

" Itē one little peece of Land conteining halfe an Acre and xxiij pches lieth at thElder Land in Word pish inclosed into the Orchard of John Hille late William Hille and abutteth to the Landes of the said John Hille South and West and to

---

* This refers to the garden given to the clerks of Eastry by Mrs. Chriſtiana Goddard. For further information concerning which see CHAPTER VII.

the Highway leading to Word Streete North and to the Lands of the heires of Stephen Danton Eaſt.

" Itē fower peeces of Land lying in Tilmanſton Conteyning in all together fifteene Acres and three roodes.

" 1. Whereof one peece conteineth by eſtimaĉon nine Acres and lyeth to the Kings way and to Pryers Cloſe South and Weſt and to the Lands of Sʳ Thomas Palmer Knight South & Weſt To the Kings way North and Eaſt To the Gleabe Land of the Church of Tilmanſtone Weſt and North to the Landes of John Dove and the Lands of John Denne North and Eaſt.

" 2. Itē one other peel thereof conteining one acre and a halfe lyeth to the Kings way South To the landes Thomas Croft Eaſt To the Lands of John Denne North and Weſt.

" 3. Itē one other peece thereof containeth two Acres and one roode and lyeth to the land of Sʳ Thomas Palmer South and Eaſt To the lands of William Jenkin Weſt and South To the Lands of the ſaid Sʳ Thomas Palmer Weſt and to the Gleabes aforeſaid Eaſt and North.

" 4. Itē one other peell thereof containeth three acres and lyeth to the Lands of Sʳ Thomas Palmer Weſt South and North To the Landes of the Parſonage of Tilmanſtone North and Eaſt To the Lands of William Jenkens Eaſt and South To the laſt mentioned peell of Gleabe Land South and Weſt.

Samuel Nicols Vic. ibide.

Joſua Paramor   ⎱
Tho : **T** Marſh ⎰   Churchwardens.
   his marke."

III.

" To the Moſt Reverend Father in God William by divine Providence Lord Archbiſhop of Canterbury.

" We the Vicar and Churchwardens of the Pariſh of Eaſtry in the County of Kent do hereby certify That the whole Quantity of Glebe Land in the ſaid Pariſh belonging to the ſaid Vicarage amounts to about one rood & thirty perches lying together & ſurrounded by two Roads and the Rectorial property—There is a Glebe Houſe Coach-houſe and Stabling upon the ſaid Glebe & no other Buildings—The living is united to that of Worth—the adjoining Pariſh—in which there is about Sixty Perches of Glebe Land but no Building thereon—The Emoluments are derived from fmall Tithes & fees. There is alfo an Augmentation of £20 per annum paid to the Vicar of Eaftry with Worth £5 6s. 8d. of which is paid by the Dean & Chapter of Canterbury & the remaining fum of £14 13s. 4d. is paid by the Leffee of the Rectorial Property.

" Witnefs our hands this fifteenth day of October in the year of our Lord eight hundred & thirty three.

George Randolph Vicar of Eaftry with Worth.

Henry Sladden }
Henry Upton } Churchwardens of Eaftry."

ENDOWMENT OF THE VICARAGE OF EASTRY, A.D. 1367.

[Ex. *Regift. Langh.*, fol. 129[b], 130.]

" Univerfis Sancte Matris Ecclefie filiis ad quos prefentes littere pervenerint, Simon, etc., falutem in Domino fempiternam. Ex parte religioforum virorum prioris et capituli ecclefie noftre Cantuarienfis nobis extitit intimatum quod recolende memorie Simon ultimus Cantuarienfis archiepifcopus defunctus immediatus predeceffor nofter ecclefias parochiales de Eaftry et Monketon cum capellis eifdem annexis ac juribus et pertinentiis fuis univerfis noftre Cantuarienfis diœcefios dudum dictis religiofis viris priori et capitulo ecclefie predicte et elemofinarie ipforum canonice appropriatas, quas quidem Baldewynus predeceffor nofter qui vir erat magne potencie prout fibi placuit aliquamdiu integraliter occupavit, ac qui collaciones dictarum ecclefiarum fibi retinuit, et medietatem fructuum utriufque ecclefie dictis religiofis viris pro elemofinaria predicta reliquit reliquam vero medietatem eciam utriufque ecclefie fuis clericis per eundem in dictis ecclefiis inftitutis affignavit minus jufte ad petitionem religioforum virorum predictorum ex caufis juftis et legitimis per ipum judicialiter approbatis omnibus et fingulis quorum intereffe poterit in ea parte primitus evocatis ac ceteris que de jure requirebantur eciam concurrentibus ad ipfos religiofos viros pertinuiffe et pertinere debere, dictos religiofos viros reftituendos et reducendos fore ad jus et poffeffionem quod et quam in dictis ecclefiis habuerunt tempore dicti Baldewini et ante, ipfofque in jure et poffeffione hujufmodi tuendos fore fententialiter et deffinitive pronunciavit decrevit et declaravit, ac ipfos quantum in eo fuit ad ftatum priftinum reduxit et reftituit

G G

per decretum, refervando fibi et fuccefforibus fuis libera facultate vicarias et porciones ipfis congruentes, cum rectores ipfarum ecclefiarum eifdem cefferint, vel ipfi
decefferint, taxandi, ftatuendi et ordinandi. Ita quod cedentibus vel decedentibus
rectoribus dictarum ecclefiarum qui tunc fuerint liceret dictis priori et capitulo per
fe feu alios vel alium eorum nomine ecclefias antedictas de Eaftri et Monketon cum
capellis fuis et poffeffionem corporalem earundem libere ingredi reintrare et read-
quirere, ac eas et earum poffeffionem pro fuo perpetuo in ufus proprios et elemofinarie predicte retinere, quodque religiofi viri fubfequenter et poft premiffa dictas
ecclefias de Eaftri et Monketon cum capellis fuis et earum poffeffionem corporalem
per ceffionem rectoris de Eastri et per mortem rectoris de Monketon qui tunc
fuerant nuper vacantes et vacuas adepti nacti funt in prefenti et ingreffi, nullaque
vicaria adhuc creata feu ordinata in eifdem, fupplicarunt nobis prefati religiofi viri
quatenus attentis premiffis et juxta ea ad creacionem et ordinacionem vicariarum
hujufmodi juxta valorem fructuum et proventuum illarum medietatum quas
rectores feculares qui pro temporibus retroactis fuerunt in eifdem percipere confue-
verunt procedere curaremus.

Nos igitur peticionem dictorum religioforum virorum diligenter confiderantes et
invenientes dictum patrem defunctum circa premiffa prout prefati religiofi viri
nobis intimarunt rite et legitime proceffiffe ac ipfas ecclefias de Eaftri et Monketon
cum capellis et pertinentiis fuis univerfis ad ipfos religiofos viros et elemofinariam
fuam predictam pertinuiffe et pertinere debere fententialiter et deffinitive pronun-
ciaffe et declaraffe, necnon ipfos religiofos viros ad ftatum priftinum quem hactenus
habuerunt in eifdem quatenus in eo fuit modo et forma premiffis reduxiffe, gefta
habitus et facta per dictum reverendum patrem defunctum circa premiffa multum
exquifite pie et devote exercita plurimum commendantes ac quantum in nobis eft ea
omnia et fingula ex noftra certa fciencia approbantes et confirmantes omnibus et
fingulis quorum intereft vel intereffe poterit in ea parte primitus evocatis, caufe
cognicione et juris ordine que de jure requirebantur circa premiffa legitime obfervatis, vicariam perpetuam in ecclefia fupradicta de Eaftri prefatis religiofis viris ut
premittitur reftituta ordinamus facimus et creamus per prefentes; porcionemque
vicarii et vicarie ecclefie fupradicte de Eaftri ordinamus facimus et limitamus fub-
fcripto modo confiftere debere in perpetuum; videlicet, quod vicarius, qui pro
tempore fuerit in eadem, habebit aulem cum duabus cameris coquinam et unum
curtilagium pro ftatu fuo competenter, cum claufura fufficienti, infra manfum porcionis quam nuper elemofinarius habuit in eadem in prefenti extantes fitas et edifi-
catas, fumptibus vicarii hujufmodi continue in futurum reparandas necnon

oblationes, legata, et obvenciones quascumque ac decimas lane, agnorum, vitulo-
rum, butiri, lactis, cafei, lini, canabi, aucarum, anatum, porcellorum, ovorum, cere,
mellis, pomorum, pirorum, columbellorum, pifcariarum, aucupacionum, venacionum,
negociatoriorum, molendinorum, feni, herbagii, filve cedue, et aliorum quorumcunque
ad ipfam ecclefiam de Eaftri feu capellas quafcumque ab eadem dependentes quali-
tercumque provenientes, decimas eciam minores de maneris de Leden dictorum
prioris et capituli quociens et quando datur ad firmam ac quinque marcas bone et
legalis monete ad fefta fanctorum Michaelis et Pafche per equales porciones a
priore et capitulo predictis annuatim perpetuo in futurum fideliter vicario qui pro
tempore fuerit in eadem perfolvendas ; que quidem oblaciones, legata, preventus
et decime prout per inquisitionem fuper valore annuo eorundem legitime captam
fufficienter fumus informati una cum dictis quinque marcis annuatim ut premittitur
percipiendis ad viginti libras bone monete communibus annis fe extendunt porcionem tamen fuam hujufmodi in dictis oblacionibus, legatis, decimis et quinque
marcis predictis ut permittitur confiftentem propter cafus fortuitos qui contingere
poterunt in futuro ad decem libras argenti duntaxat limitamus et taxamus juxta
quarum decem librarum argenti taxam vicarius qui pro tempore fuerit in eadem,
decimam in futuro ipfam ecclefiam contingentem pro porcione fua duntaxat folvet
fubibit et agnofcet, invenietque dictus vicarius unum capellanum in capella de
Worthe ab eadem ecclefia de Eaftri dependente fingulis diebus fi et quatenus
comode poterit celebraturum qui eam officiabit in divinis prout hactenus eft fieri
confuetum, inveniet eciam cereos proceffionales fuperpellicia, ligabit eciam libros
invencionem rectoris concernentes librofque hujusmodi inventos fuo periculo cuf-
todiet necnon omnia alia onera infra dictas ecclefiam et capellam per rectorem loci
confueta fuis fumptibus fubibit et expenfis, hoc excepto, quod prefati religiofi viri
cancellos dictarum ecclefie et capelle in omnibus fuis membris et particulis repara-
bunt et fi diruti fuerint reedificabunt fuis fumptibus et expenfis, ipfofque religiofos et non vicarium qui pro tempore fuerit ad inventionem unius capel-
lani in capella de Shrynglynges a dicta ecclefia dependente fi ad hoc rectores
tenebantur in antea teneri volumus et obligari : folvent infuper dicti prior
et conventus annuatim terminis fupradictis vicario memorato quadraginta
folidos fterlingorum pro fupportacione oneris clerici parochialis ibidem in-
veniendi, quas quidem ecclefie de Eaftrie predicte reftitutionem et reductionem
vicarie ordinacionem, ipfiufque vicarii porcionis limitacionem in eadem et onerum
impofitiones antedictas ipfos et eorum quemlibet ut premittitur concernentes
ac omnia alia et fingula hujufmodi reftitucionem et reductionem ordinaciones
limitaciones ac impoficiones contingentia vocatis primitus in forma juris in hac

parte vocandis ceterisque folempniis in omnibus per nos obfervatis cum plena caufe cognicione firma ftabilia et cunctis temporibus futuris firmiter obfervanda fore debere dictamque porcionem fufficientem et congruam effe vicario hujus modi pro omni tempore futuro de communi affenfu et confenfu capituli noftri pronunciamus, diffinimus et declaramus per prefentes. In cujus rei teftimonium figilium noftrum fecimus hiis apponi. Datum apud la Fford nostre dioecef: Ꝯ non : Augufti Anno Domini milleffimo ccc^m sexagefimo septimo et noftre tranflacionis primo."

The tranflation of the foregoing Ordination or Endowment of the Vicarage of Eaftry runs as follows :—

" To all the fons of Holy Mother Church to whom thefe prefent letters fhall come Simon, &c., fendeth Health in the Lord everlafting. It has been intimated to us on the behalf of thofe Religious perfons, the Prior and Chapter of our Church at Canterbury, that Simon of venerable memory the laft Archbifhop of Canterbury deceafed our immediate predeceffor, the Parifh Churches of Eaftry and Monkton with the Chapels annexed to the fame of our Diocefe of Canterbury and all the rights thereto appertaining, long fince canonically appropriated to the faid Religious Perfons the Prior and Chapter of the faid Church and the Almonry ufed by them (which one Baldewyn our Predeceffor who was a man of great Power without Juftice wholly occupied for fome time as he thought fit, and who retained to himfelf the Collations of the faid Churches and left the half of the Fruits of both to the faid Religious for the Almonry aforefaid and affigned the remainder to his own Clerks inftituted by himfelf in the faid Churches) at the petition of the faid Religious, for juft and lawful reafons judicially approved by himfelf (all and every Perfons who might be interefted in that matter being firft cited, and all other lawful Obfervances concurring) did fententially and definitively pronounce, decree, and declare, that they had belonged and ought to belong to the faid Religious Perfons, and that the faid Religious fhould be reftored and brought back to the Right and Poffeffion which they had in the faid Churches, at and before the time of the faid Baldewyn, and that they fhould be maintained in the poffeffion of the fame, and did reduce and reftore them as far as it depended upon him to their former Eftate by his decree, referving to himfelf and his fucceffors the free power of ordering, eftablifhing and ordaining the Vicarages and parts appertaining to them whenfoever the Rectors of fuch Churches fhould quit them or fhould themfelves be dead : fo that upon the Refignation or Deceafe of the Rectors of the aforefaid Churches for the time being, it might be lawful for the aforefaid Prior and Chapter by themfelves or others or any other in their name freely to enter, re-enter and re-acquire the aforefaid Churches of Eaftry and Monkton, with their Chapels, and to have the corporal Poffeffion of them for their own ufe, and that of the Almonry aforefaid for ever: and that the faid Religious confequently and after the Premiffes have now obtained acquired and entered into the faid Churches of Eaftry and Monkton with their chapels as well as the corporal poffeffion of them, being vacant by the ceffion of the Rector of Eaftry and the death of the Rector of Monkton who were at that time being; and no Vicarage being as yet created or ordained in the fame, the aforefaid Religious have fupplicated us that attending to the Premiffes we fhould take care to proceed to the Creation and Ordination of fuch like Vicarages according to the value of the Fruits and Profits of thofe medieties which the fecular Rectors who have been in times paft were accuftomed to receive. We therefore, diligently confidering the Petitions of the faid Religious and finding that the faid Father deceafed, according as the faid Religious have intimated to us, did rightly and lawfully proceed, and that he fententially and definitively pronounced and declared that the faid Churches of Eaftry and Monkton, with the Chapels and Appurtenances, did belong and ought to belong to the faid Religious and their Almonry aforefaid, and alfo that as far as he might or could, after the manner and form aforefaid, he reftored the faid Religious Perfons to their former Eftate which they aforetimes held in the faid Parifhes, very much commending whatever has been tranfacted and done by the faid Reverend Father deceafed concerning the Premiffes, as done with great Piety and Devotion, and as far as lies in us, from our certain knowledge, approving and confirming all and every of thefe Acts and Things (all and every Perfons who may and might be interefted in the fame being firft cited and the caufe, cognition, and order of juftice which were required about the premiffes being duly obferved) do ordain, make and create by thefe prefents a perpetual Vicarage in the above-mentioned Church of Eaftry, reftored as is before related to the aforefaid Religious: And we ordain, make, and limit that the Portion of the Vicar and aforefaid vicarial Church of Eaftry ought to confift for ever in the manner underwritten, that is to fay, that the Vicar, who for the time fhall be in the fame, fhall have the Hall with two Chambers, the Kitchen and one Curtilage fufficient for him with a fufficient Clofe beneath the dwelling Houfe of that portion which the Almoner lately had, now being fituated and built in the fame, to be repaired continually for the future at the Cofts of the faid Vicar, and alfo fhall have the Oblations, Legacies, and Revenues whatfoever, and the Tenths of Wool, Lambs, Calves, Butter, Milk, Cheefe, Flax, Hemp, Geefe, Ducks, Pigs, Eggs, Wax, Honey, Apples, Pears, Pidgeons, Fifh for fale, Fowling, Hunting, Merchandifes, Grift, Hay or Grafs, Herbage, Felled Wood, and of other things whatfoever to the faid Church of Eaftry, or the Chapels whatfoever depending upon the fame, howfoever arifing, as alfo the fmaller Tenths of the faid Prior and Chapter's Manor of Leden, as often as and whenfoever it may be let out to farm. And moreover that five marks of good and lawful money fhall be paid faithfully by equal portions at the Feafts of Saint Michael and Eafter yearly for ever, by the Prior and Chapter aforefaid to the Vicar who for the time fhall hold the fame, which Oblations, Legacies, Profits and Tenths, as we have been fufficiently informed by Inquifition duly made into the yearly value of the fame, together with the faid five Marks to be received yearly as above-mentioned, do amount to Twenty Pounds of good money per year. Neverthelefs we limit and reftrain the Portion of the faid Vicar (confifting in the faid Oblations, Revenues, Legacies, Tenths with the five Marks aforefaid) as is premifed by Reafon of the Cafualties which may happen in future time, to Ten pounds of Money only, according to which rate of Ten pounds the Vicar for the time being fhall only pay, anfwer, and acknowledge as his part of the Tithe for the time to come appertaining to the Church. And the faid Vicar fhall find one Chaplain in the Chapel of Worth depending upon the faid Church of Eaftry, to celebrate Divine Service, every Day, at leaft as far as it may be done with convenience ; and who fhall there officiate in Divine Things according to ufual Cuftom. He fhall alfo find waxen candles for Proceffions, and Surplices, he fhall bind the Books relating to the Rector's income, and whatever Books of this kind may be found he fhall keep at his own Peril : and alfo fhall undergo and perform all other Burdens, at his own expenfe, relating to the faid Church and Chapel that were accuftomed to be borne by the Rector of the Place ; excepting only that the faid Religious Perfons fhall repair the Chancels of the faid Church and Chapel, in all their Members and Parts, and if they fhould fall to ruin fhall rebuild them at their own cofts and expenfe. And we will that the faid Religious, and not the Vicar for the Time being, fhall be held and bound to the maintenance of one Chaplain in the Chapel of Shrynglynges* depending upon the faid Church, provided the Rectors were held

---

* In a copy of this Tranflation of the Ordination of the Vicarage in the poffeffion of the Vicar, there is the following note in Mr. Boteler's handwriting :—" Eaftry April 1784. Upon a diligent fearch I have difcovered the foundation of the Chapel of Shryngelynges juft within the wood, now called Shingleton Wood at the South Eaft

in Times paſt to the ſame. Moreover the ſaid Prior and Convent ſhall pay yearly at the times aforeſaid to the Vicar above-mentioned 40s. for the finding and maintaining of a Pariſh Clerk there. All which Reſtitution and Reduction of the ſaid Church of Eaſtry, Ordination of the Vicarage and Limitation of the Vicar's Part in the ſame, and the aforeſaid impoſitions of Burdens relating to them and any of them as is premiſed, and all and ſingular appertaining to ſuch Reſtitution and Reduction, Ordinations, Limitations and Impoſitions, we, firſt having cited according to form of law, all that in this affair ought to be cited, and all other legal Forms being in all reſpects fully obſerved by us, and having a full knowledge of the cauſe, with the common aſſent and conſent of our Chapter, do pronounce, determine, and declare by theſe Preſents to be firm, ſtable, and ſuch as ought conſtantly to be obſerved in all future Times; and that the ſaid Portion is ſufficient and proper for the ſaid Vicar in all ſucceeding times. In Teſtimony whereof we have cauſed our ſeal to be affixed to theſe preſents. Given at La Ford in our Dioceſe the ſecond of the Nones of Auguſt in the year of our Lord 1367 and of our Tranſlation the 1ſt."

In or about the year 1745, the queſtion having ariſen whether the Rector or the Vicar, of Eaſtry was entitled to the Tythe of Canary, Clover, and other ſeeds, a caſe was drawn up and ſubmitted to counſel, when the following opinion* was given:—

"I have read over a copy of yᵉ Endowment of yᵉ Vicaridge of Eaſtry and yᵉ queſtion upon it being whether yᵉ Rector or yᵉ Vicar is intitled to yᵉ Tyth of Canary ſeed Clover ſeed and other ſeeds I am of opinion that by reaſon of yᵉ general words *ad aliorum quorumcunque ad ipſam Eccleſiam de Eaſtry ſeu Capellas quaſcunque ab eadem dependentes qualitercunque provenientes* and yᵉ uſage for the Vicar to take yᵉ Tith of Canary ſeed and other ſeeds that yᵉ Vicar is intitled to yᵉ Tith of Canary ſeed Clover ſeed and other ſeeds, Canary ſeed Clover ſeed and other ſeeds being unquſtionably ſmall Tithes and not great Tiths.

" J. Knowler
" 26 October 1745."

end." The fact that it was only diſcoverable "after diligent ſearch" nearly a 100 years ago, ſhews us how long it muſt have been diſuſed and ruined.

* In the poſſeſſion of the Vicar.

INVENTORIES OF THE XVII CENTURY.

The following Inventories of Goods, extracted from the MSS. notes of
William Boteler, Efqre., of Brook Street, in this Parifh, give us a very
good idea of the furniture and wardrobe of a private gentleman of Eaft
Kent in the beginning of the xvii century :—

"A true inventory of the goods & chattels of Richard Boteler,[*] gent. late
of Eaftrie deceafed made & prized the xix day of March in the year of o' Lord
Chrifte one thoufand fix hundreth & of the Raigne of o' Soũaigne Lady Elizabeth
the Queen's ma^{tie} y^t now is the xliij by John Golder, Richard Auften Nicholas
Squire & John Caftell the writer hereof all of Eaftry.

Imprimis his Girdle his purfe & reddy money   .   .   .   iiij^{li}

Itẽ his apparel one Saten doblett One filke rafh doblett wth filũ buttons
    One fuftian doblett One payer of velvett breeches three payer
    of broadcloth breeches Two clokes One cloth gowne[†] Two
    hatts lyned wth velvett Two cloth Jerkins Three Devonfhiere &
    cotten night weftcotes Two payer of Jerfey ftockings & fower
    payer of cloth ftockings Two ryding hoodes fix fhirts eight
    bandes[†]   x

"Itẽ in the litle chamber whear he died called the middle chamber
    One joynde ftanding bedd One fether bedd one bowlfter one
    payer of blancketts One rugg covertledd five curtens wth curten
    rodds One Truckle bedd One cheft One liuery cubberd One
    chayer wth other lumber there prized at   .   .   .   iiij x

"Itẽ in the beft chamber called the great chamber One fayer ftanding
    Bedfteddle one fether bedd one blanckett one covertleed five fey
    curtaines & curtaine rodds one Truckle bedftedle wth a quilt bedd

---

* Richard Boteler, of Eaftry, Gent., whofe will was proved 27 Ap., 1601, wills to
be buried in Eaftry Church, as does alfo Katherine Boteler his widow, whofe will
proved 29 July, 1617. William Boteler, of Rochefter, will proved 11 May, 1615, in
London.

† In former days the *gown* and *bands* were no mark of an ecclefiaftic, for the
gown was worn by every one, from the rank of fovereign to that of tradesman, as the
outer garment ; gradations in rank being marked by the material of which the gown
was made, and the way in which it was "faced" or trimmed.

One payer of millen [?] fuſtian underclothes two cheſtes one table
ᵗʰ a carpett thereon half a dowſon of high joynd ſtooles fower
low joynd cuſhian ſtooles two chayers One court cubberd One
joynd box One payer of ſtanding cob yrons Three window curtaines ᵗʰ the hanging about the chamber prized at . . xˡⁱ

Ite in the chambᵣ ouᵣ the litle Hall one ſtanding bedſteddle one fether
bedd theron a payer of blancketts one Covertleed five curtaines
of cloth one truckle bedſtedle one flockbedd one payre of
blancketts and one covertleed thereon one cypres cheſt one joynd
box ᵗʰ hangings to the ſaid chamber prized at . . . iijˡⁱ

Ite in the maydes chamber one bourded beddſteddle ᵗʰ a flock bedd
theron one covertleed one blanckett one cheſt two childrens
cradles ᵗʰ other lumber ther . . . . . xxˢ

Ite in the litle chamber one ſtanding beddſtedle one fether bedd a
payer of blancketts one Covertleede one Court cubberd one
truckle beddſtedle prized at . . . . . iijˡⁱ

It in Jonathan Botelers chambᵣ fower cheſtes ᵗʰ certain furniture for
the warrs viz two corſletts one Jack two muſketts fur One
Horſemans piec fur one caſe of daggs two caliuᵣˢ fur ᵗʰ ſwords
and daggers prized at . . . . . iiijˡⁱ

It in the great parloᵣ One table half a dowſin of high joind ſtooles
fower cuſhion ſtooles one court cubberd one chayer two table
carpetts Two cubberd carpetts halfe a dowſin of cuſhions fower
window cuſhions viz. two of ſilke and ſiluᵣ and two of ſilke only
one payer of cob irons or brand yrons prized at . . iiijˡⁱ

Ite in the lower chamber behinde the entrie one ſtanding beddſtedle
one fetherbedd a payer of blancketts two covertleeds one cubberd ᵗʰ other Lumber ther prized at . . . . iiijˡⁱ x

Ite in the folkes chambᵣ three boarded bedſteddles Two flock bedds
one mattreſs ᵗʰ covertleeds and blancketts furniſhed prized at . xlˢ

Ite in the chambᵣ ouᵣ the buntting houſe two boarded beddſtedles, one
flock bed one blanckett one undercloth and one covertleed
prized at . . . . xxˢ

Ite in the litle Hall one Table fower joyned ſtooles and one payer of
cobbyrons prized at . . . . . . xiijˢ iiijᵈ

Ite in the great hall Two tables one cubberd one fourme a payer of

cob yrons a payer of yron rackes one Jack to turn a ſpitt ᵗʰᵂ other
lumber ther prized at . . . . . xlˢ

Ite in the Buttry of the beſt pewter one dowſin of platters one dowſin
of Pewter diſhes one dowſin of fruite diſhes, one dowſin of
plates, half a dowſin of porrindgers half a dowſin of ſawcers
two baſens and an ewer fower pewter candleſtickes two douſin
of wearing pewter five chamber potts . . . . iijˡⁱ xiijˢ iiijᵈ

Ite in the ſaid Buttry one cheſt one payer cubberd ᵗʰᵂ other lumber
ther prized at . . . . . . vjˢ viijᵈ

Ite in the Kitchin ſeaven braſs kettells thre braſs potts one braſs pann
a warming pann two chafing diſhes fower ſtuppuetts five braſs
candleſticks five ſpitts two greedyrons one Trivett ᵗʰᵂ other lumber
ther prized at . . . . . . iiijˡⁱ

Ite in the mylke houſe A Bryne ſtock a table two dowſin of bowles
and Truggs three milk keelers two charnes a Muſtard quearne ᵗʰᵂ
other lumber ther prized at . . . . xxˢ

Ite in the buntting houſe one Bunting hutch Two kneding ſhowles a
a meale tubb ᵗʰᵂ other lumber ther prized at . . vjˢ viijᵈ

Ite in the cheeſe howſe One cheeſe preſſe ᵗʰᵂ his furniture two payer of
Ripps five payells ᵗʰᵂ other lumber prized at . . xiijˢ iiijᵈ

Ite in the Brewhowſe Two great brueng tonnes one Corleſatt Two
furnaces fower Tubbs ᵗʰᵂ other lumber ther prized at . vˡⁱ

Ite in the well howſe 8 Bucketts and two roppes ᵗʰᵂ other lumber ther
prized at . . . . vjˢ viijᵈ

Ite in the Wheat loft iij quarters of Wheat five quarters of Otes . vjˡⁱ xˢ

Ite forty payer of ſheetes twelve table clothes ix dowſin of table napkins viij payer of pillow coates ſix payer of pillowes One dowſin
of hand towells prized at . . . . . xxˡⁱ

Item in his ſtuddy diũs and ſundry books prized at . . xlˢ

Ite one ſilũ and gilt ſalt one ſilũ peell gilt cupp and one ſilũ cupp
prized at . . . . vˡⁱ

Ite xiiij horſe beaſts one wagon and wagon harneſſe three plowes three
courts ſower harrowes ᵗʰᵂ all furniture belonging prized at . liˡⁱ

Ite one couple of working bullocks prized at . . . vjˡⁱ

Ite vij kine iij towyering beaſts and fower twelve monthings priſed at xxiijˡⁱ xiijˢ iiijᵈ

Ite vj ſcore old weathers ewes and young ſheep priſed at . . xxxvjˡ

It xxij hoggs prized at . . . . . . vj^{li} xiij^s iiij^d

Ite xviij^{teene} hennes capons and cocks xvij Duckes and drakes five Geefe and ganders prized at . . . . . xx^s

Ite xx^{tie} quarters of Wheat by eftimaē in the Barne to threfh prized at xlvj^{li}

Ite Hey fodwar and otes in the Barnes and upp ftable prized at . x^{li}

Ite lxx acres of wheat fowen in the fields prifyed at . . cxl^{li}

Ite xxxvij acres of Tares and Peafe prifzed at . . . xxxvij^{li}

Ite xij acres of Oates prized at xx^s the acre . . . xij^{li}

Ite certain wood in wope [?] felled th/w all ftuff and lumber before forgotten by the prizers prized at . . . . iij^{li}

Su^m Totle ccccc^{li}   x^s

" A treue Invētory of the goods and Chattels of M^{ris.} Katherin Buttler Gentell woman of Eaftry late deceafed made & prized the xixth of January and in the year of our Lord Chrift one thoufand fyx hundreth and feauenteene by Thomas Whytfeld, Thomas Hugbon, and Alexander Mockett.

Imprimis her Purfe and girdell . . . . . v^{li}

Item all her weareinge apparell . . . . . xvij^{li}

Item in the Greate Hall two tables one Cup boorde one forme a payer of Cobirons a payer of Iron rackes one Jacke to turne fpytt th/w other lumber . . . . xl^s

Item the greate Parler one greate table & halfe a duzen of high Joyned ftooles, two Cufhen ftooles one Courte Cubbard one greate chayer one fquare table two table Carpets two Cubbard carpets halfe one duzen of cufhens fowre window cufhens one payer of cobirons one fire fhovell one payer of tongs & one payer of bellowes . . . . v^{li}

Item in the littell Hall one table to joyned ftooles . . . xij^s

Item in the Kitchen two tables one dreffer borde one brafs pann one warmeing pann one Chaffinge difh, two gridirons one fire fhovell one payer of bellowes one payer of tongs one fire forke of Iron, fower fpytts feaven Kettells fowr brafs potts three brafs ftupens one payer of potthangers fyxe brafs candellfticks th/w other lumber v^{li}

Item in the Buttery two Baffons one Eward fyx pewter Candellfticks fower dozen and a halfe of pewter platters greate & fmall five pewter plates three dozen & a halfe of fmall pewter, fower porringers of pewter one Voyder of pewter one dozen and a

halfe of weareing pewter one dozen of fpoones thre falts one
pewter pott & viij Chamber potts   .   .   .   . v^li xiij^s

Item in the fame Buttery beforefayd one Chift one heare Cubard three
driping panns one frying pann ^th_w other lumber .   .   . xxvij^s

Item in the Milke houfs one brineftocke two dozen of trugs ix bowles
three milke keelers one Charne & one table   .   .   . xx^s

Item in the Buntingehoufs one boultinge ^th_w one Kneadinge trofe & one
meale tub   v

Item in the Cheafe houfs one Cheafeprefs ^th_w his ffurniture one payer
of ripps five payles and one fope boule   .   .   . xx^s

Item in the Brewhoufs two brewinge tonns one Coole backe two for-
niffes fower tubes ^th_w other lumber   .   .   . vj^li xiiij^s

Item in the fame Wellhoufs two bucketts one rope one water ftocke . xx^s

Item in the Laderhoufs one brineftock one table ^th_w other lumber   . vj^s viij^d

Item in the great chamber on ftandinge beadfteadell one featherbead
one blankett one coverlyd five faye curtaynes ^th_w foe many roods
of Iron two pillows and one boulefter one truckell beadftedle ^th_w
a quilt bead one payer of millan* [?] fuftian under clothes two
Chiftes one table ^th_w one carpett halfe a dozen of high joyned
ftooles fower low joyned cuffhen ftooles two chayers one court
cubbard one joyned box one payer of Cobbiarns three window
curtaynes and one window cufhen   .   .   .   . xij^li

Item in the midell Chamber one ftandinge beadfteadell one featherbead one boulfter one payer of Blanketts one coverlyd one
truckellbead one Chift one flocke bead ^th_w a blankett a coverlyd
& boulfter & a prefs   .   .   .   .   .   . vj^li xiij^s

Item in the Chamber over the littell Hall one ftandinge beadfteadell
one feather bead one payer of blanketts one coverlyd five curtaynes of claoth one truckell bead one fypers† Chift one box ^th_w
cartayne hanginges about the chamber   .   .   . v^li xiij^s

Item in the Maydes chamber two borded beadfteadells one old featherbead one boulfter one blankett two Chiftes & one cradell   . liij^s iiij^d

Item in the buckeinge chamber one playne beadfteadle ^th_w a featherbead
and one boulfter one payer of blanketts one coverlyd ^th_w curtaynes

* What is this word "millan?" does it mean Milan ?

† "Sypers" = "cypres," *ante*, for cyprefs.

to the bead two Chiftes and one Courte Cubbard . . iiij^li xiij^s

Item in the Chamber wheare Mr. Buttlers lyeth one ftandinge beadfteadle ᵗʰʷ a feather bead one boulfter one pillow one payer of
blanketts one Coverlyd ᵗʰʷ curtaynes & roods to the bead be-
longeinge one Courte Cubbard two Chiftes ᵗʰʷ certayne furniture
for the warrs . . . . . . x^li

Item in the lower Chamber one ftandinge beadfteadle ᵗʰʷ a flock bead
one boulfter a payer blanketts and one truckell bead . . xxvj^s viij^d

Item in the greate Chamber xxi payer of Sheets fyx payer of pil-
lowbes fyx cubbard claothes one large fheete to cover the bead
xij table claothes, table napkins xij dozen viij towells . . xx^li

Item in the fame greate Chamber one duble falte of fylver to fylver
bowles one dozen of fylver fpoones . . . . ix^li x^s

Item in the buckinge chamber five payer of fheetes one payer coverlyd two pillowes xvj payer of fheets ordinaryly goeinge about
the Houfs feaven table claothes one dozen of Napkins x towells
and fyx pillow coots . . . . . xj^li v^s

Item in the Servants Chamber fower borded beadfteadles ᵗʰʷ fower
flocke beads fower boulfters fower coverlyds and fower
blanketts . . . . iiij^li

Item in the Chamber behinde the Chymney two beadfteadles ᵗʰʷ two
flocke beads to boulfters to coverlyds to blanketts one old cubbard and an old paynted claoth . . . . liij^s

Item in the Chamber over the great Hall one payer of Stowcards one
payer of wollen cards two wollen whiles two linen whiles one
oaft cloath ᵗʰʷ other lumber . . . . xxiij^s

Item in the littell clofett two payer of fcales ᵗʰ the wayghts belonging.
to them an old payer of tables tenn cufhens ᵗʰʷ other lumber . xl^s

Item in the fyller five hodgfheads fower barrells to put beire in and one
virkin . . . . . . xx^s

Item in the Studdye divers bookes . . . . xl^s

Item in the Kytchen loft one fery one bufhell one mould to make can-
dell mould one bridell a fadell a pillan & pillian claoth ᵗʰʷ all
other ftuff & lumber before gotten by the prizers . . xl^s

The mar'k of Thomas Whyttfield.
  Thomas Hugbone.
  Alexander Mockett.   Sm Cxlix^li xiiij^s ix^d

It may be interesting to compare the following inventory of the effects of a poor widow, in the neighbouring town of Sandwich, taken only three years before the first of the foregoing, with those of the gentry of our parish, given above. I am indebted to the kindness of the Rev. H. M. Maugham, late curate in charge of S. Peter's, for permission to make this extract from the vestry books of that parish :—

" The Goodes of fravnecis walker a wydow in the paryfhe of S^t. Peters was Prayfeyd the xviijth daye of Julye A^o. dom 1597 by Chryftoffer Clarke myghell Allyxander Samwell hooke and Thomas Godffrye.

ffirfte one littyll olde table of ij bordes . . .	. iiij^d
one olde littill fforme	. viij^d
one bafket beade [bed]	. xx^d
one olde Coverlet—xx^d the childe had it to wrape it in.	
one lyttyll olde Defke	. iiij^d
vj ftone potes and crockes	. vj^d
ij woodden Dyfheis iij wodden platters iiij olde Trenchers .	. iiij^d
one Olde Hamper	. ij
one olde wyckear chere—ij^d the chylde had yt.	
Twoo lyttyll old Tobes j olde peale j peare of olde bellos .	. iij^d

Sū . iiij^s—j^d "

The fummation 4s. 1d. probably reprefents the money value of the goods actually *fold*, the others being given to " the child " here mentioned.

Extracts from Wills

Proved in the Confiftory Court of Canterbury (taken from the *Boteler M.S.S.*, vol. A.) :—

1451. In the firft volume of Wills regiftered in the Archbifhop's Court at Canterbury (folio 52), is recorded the will of Wm. Bryan, of

Canterbury, in which he directs his Feoffees to fell his Tenement
in Eaftry with its appurtenances, formerly belonging to Adam
Carpenter, immediately after his Death, and with the money
arifing therefrom to provide a Chaplain to fay maffes in Eaftry Church
for the fpace of one year for the health of his foul, &c., &c. The
Priefts to have ten marks (= 13s. 4d. x 10 = £6 10s. 4d. which
x 12, on account of the difference in value of money, would
bring it to £78 of our prefent money) for his ftipend. The refidue
of the money arifing from the fale he directs to be applied to the
reparation of Eaftry Church. He gives to Margaret, his wife, his
tenement in Eaftry called Stapinbreghe, with all the lands and
appurtenances for the term of 5 years, and after the expiration of
the fame directs his Feoffees to fell the eftate, and with the money
arifing from the fame to provide a Prieft to celebrate in Eaftry
Church religious rites for his foul, the fouls of his anceftors, and
all the faithful deceafed for the fpace of two years, for which he is
to receive xx marks. From the money likewife arifing from the
fale he bequeaths to the repairs of Eaftry Church 40s. (this would
be equivalent in value to about £24 of our money). Alfo that a
Prieft fhall be provided to celebrate in S. Andrew's Church, Canterbury, for the fpace of three years, to have ten marks each year
for his ftipend, but not to be allowed to celebrate anywhere elfe
during that term; gives alfo to his wife Margaret £20 from the
fame money. Gives alfo from the fame to the Church of Faverfham, 13s. 4d.—to the Church of Worth, 13s. 4d.—to the Church
of Chiflet, 13s. 4d.—to the Church of Woodnefborough, 13s. 4d.
—to the reparation of the road leading from Eaftry to Sandwich
x marks. The refidue of the money he gives to his wife Mar-

garet, to whom likewife he bequeaths all his Lands and Tenements
in the Parifh of Chiflet to her and her heirs for ever.

> Dated at Canterbury, 6 Oct., 1451.

1464. William Sutton to be buried in Eaftry Church.

> Will proved, 12 Sep., 1464.

1484. Richard Atchurch, of Eaftry—wife Agnes—fons Thomas and
John—daughter Alice. To his fon John his tenement fometyme
called Brooke Place wth one acre of land at Wendefton [Venfon]
called Brookeaker in the faid Parifh. Wendefton in ye Lordfhip
of Mafter Langeleygh. Dated 4 Sep. 1484.

1487 Extract from the will of Johannes Broker de Eaftry, given in
Arch. Cant. vol. vi., p. 289: "Corpus meum fepeliend' in
cimiterio beati Marie de Eaftrie. Lego Alicie uxori mee. Joh'i
Broker filio meo. Alicie uxori mee et Thome at Welle quos
facio executores etc."

1487. Dns.* Wm. Craller "pencionarius Ecclie poch de Eftrie" directs to
be buried in ye Chancel of E. Church—Thos. Afhow ppetual
Vicar of ye faid Church.

> Will dated 14 March, 1487. Proved 9 June, 1488.

1489. Thos. Frynne of Walton in Eaftry to be buried in Eaftry Church.

> Will proved 27 Oct., 1489.

1492. Thomas Oore of Eaftry directs his body to be buried in Eaftry
Church near his father.

> Will dated 31 Jany., 1491. Proved 21 May, 1492.

1497. Peter Darby of Eaftry—to be buried in the body of Eaftry Church
"before y^e Autar of St. John the Baptift"—to wife Julian his place

---

* Dns. = Dominus, *i.e.*, "Sir," the ufual title of parifh priefts in thofe days.

called Godderds in Parifh of Eaftry—his place in Eaftry towards
the Butts call'd the nether place wth all lands belonging—Place
called Woohope at Heronden—all thefe to her for life—remainder
of all the aforefaid Preĩnes to fon Thos. and his heirs for ever.

Dated 16 Octob. 1496. Proved 26 May, 1497.

1497. John Frynne fenr. of Walton—to be buried in Body of Eaftry
Church.

1499. Thos. Elware of Eaftry—to Roger Frynne his executor his Tenement at Selvefton [Selfon] wth all the lands belonging which he
late bought of Harry Baxe fenr. to faid Roger his Heirs and
affigns for ever on condition he pays yearly to Churchwardens of
Eaftry 3*s*. 4*d*. towards the repairs of ye faid Church.

Dated 5th Aug. 1499. Proved 2nd Decr. following.

1504. Julian Rogers of Eaftry—to be buried in the faid Church near her
late Hufband Peter Darby.

1507. Will. Andrew of Eaftry—mentions our Lady's Chapel in Eaftry
Churchyard. Dated 25 Nov. 1507.

Mem. In another will, of prior date, mention is made of our Lady's
Chapel in Eaftry *Church.*

1507. John Whitefelde of Eaftry—to be buried in the Church—mentions Mafter Thos. Afhe Vicar of Eaftry.

Dated 21 Jany., 1507.

1524. Jane Afchowe of St. Bartholomew's near Sandwich—to be buried
in the Chancel of Eaftry Church near her deceafed uncle Sr.
Thos. Afchowe—wills a ftone to be laid upon her faid uncle.

1529. Wm. Paramour of Eaftry—to be buried in the Churchyard there
—wife Catherine daur. Conftance—fons Saffery [Sapphire], Robert,
Henry, and Thomas—Witnefs M. Robert Cooper Doctor of
Mufick. Will dated Octr. 24, 1529.

I I

1532. John Owre of Eaftry—to be buried in Eaftree Church.

1540. Willm. Benger of Herenden in Eaftry—wife Joan—Sons Wm. and Oliver.

1541. Willm. Owre of Eaftry wills, &c., to be buried in the Aisle of Eaftry Church where his father and mother John and Eliz. lie— wife Joan—fons Richard, William, John, Thos., Alexandr. and Stephen—Brother Thos. Hamond of Nonnington—devifes Lands in Eaftry Woodh. Word Sholden and Deale—to fon Richard prin- cipal Meffuage in which he dwelt wth the lands, &c., in Eaftry and Woodnefbro' called Gore, and alfo his Lands called Statten- borough in Worde and other Lands in thofe Parifhes and in Shol- den and Deale.—Gives his Meffuage called Siflifton [Selvefton or Selfon] wth all its Lands & Appurts. in Eaftry to fon Willm. & his Heirs for ever.—Wills his Meff: or Place called Syllefton wth its Lands and Apps. in Eaftry and Woodnefbro' to Son John (wch he lately purchafed of Thos. Mayhewe of Lincolnfhire Efqre.)

Proved 15 Dec. 1541.

1543. Richd. Champyon Prieft and Prebendary of Canty. (of Chr. Ch.) Wills, &c., *inter alia*—to Niece Margery Champion his Stuff at Eaftry—fpeaks of his Parifh of Eaftry.

Proved 20 June, 1543.

1551. Chriftopher Nevynfon of Adefham Dr. of Civil Law—born at Wederell in Cumberland—wife Ann—Son Thos.—Daur. Jane— Uncle Richard—Cozens Alexr. and John (Brothers)—cozn. Ste- phen of Cambridge A.M.—Brothers Rogers, John and Richard —Cozns. James & Thomas—To Servt. Robt. Stamp Leafe of Henford after his mother Monings death; to Son Thos. his leafe of Hedcorn Parfonage, Leafes of ye Parfonage of Adefham and Chapel of Staple, his Leafe of Keyt Marfh parcel of the Manor of Wingham Barton, his Leafe of Parfonage of Goldftanton, his Leafe of Bonington, his Leafe of Parfonage of Goodneftone,

his Leafe of Parfonage of Nonington & his Leafe of the Portion of Well in ye Parifh of Adefham   his Leafe of the Manor Place at Wingham & of the Lands belonging to it— and of the Scite of the Manor of Eaftry wth the Lands belonging to it—his Leafe of the Manor of Ratlynge—the Marfh in Wingham Valley—his Leafe of the Lands belonging to St. Stephens Chapel in New Romney in Romney Marfh belonging to Magd: College in Oxford—his Leafe of the Scite of the Manor of Tenham & of the Lands belonging — Wills to Brother John Nevyfon his Leafe of Tyknes [Tickenfhurft] in Northbourn—to his brother Richd. his Leafe of Mayo in Heron & to his Brother Roger & to Umphrey & Roland his Sons his Leafe of Maifon Dieu Broke in Romney Marfh in Parifh of Rokinge..—Alfo to fon Thos. garden at Sandwich, 2 acres of Land at Stelling & all the Tythes of Nonington & the late Chapel Wemingfwold and the Parifh of Goodneftone near Wingham.

Pr. 12 Sep. 1551. Jno. Orgraver a witnefs.

1553. Willm. Wollet of Eftrye—wife Alice—to his son Robt. all his Lands in Romney Marfh, &c. &c. Pro: 9 June—5th Edw. VI.

1566. John Paramour of Eaftry—his wife—fon John, Drs. Willmill & Martha.   Pr. Mar. 1566.

1568. Thos. Whitfield the Elder of Eftry—Dr. Elizabeth wife of Henry Pyfinge—Dr. Phillippa—Dr. Barborough—Son Wm.—wife Alys —to Son John his Meff: at Selfton wherein he then dwelt with the lands in fee of Adefham, Lands in Streetinge, &c.—to fon Marke his Tenement called Nether Knowle in Eaftry Street and other lands.   Pr. 22 Nov., 1568.

1574. Chriſtian Goddard of Eaſtry, widow of Oliver Goddard wills, &c. to her Cozen Jno. Fynche of Feverſham and Elizth. his wife all her Lands in the Town and Port of Sandwich and her Marſh Land in Romney and Walland Marſhes for Life, Remainder to their 3 daurs. Mary, Frances and Martha all in Tail general remainder to Anthy. and William Sons of ſaid John and Elizth. and their Heirs for ever. She wills to the Churchwardens of Eaſtry and their ſucceſſors one Tenement wᵗʰ a Garden and appurtenances in Eaſtry aforeſaid over againſt the vicarage to the uſe of the Poor people there for ever. To the ſaid Churchwardens likewiſe one other Tenement and a Garden in Eaſtry Street to hold to the uſe of the Clark of Eaſtry for ever ſo that the ſame Clark for the time being do teach and inſtruct in Learning one of the pooreſt Mens children of the Pariſh being a Man child from time to time for ever. She wills to Anne Fynche widow the late wife of Thos. Manwood of Sandwch. deceaſed all her Lands and Tenements unbequeathed in Eaſtry, Ham, and Worth, and her heirs for ever, dying without Iſſue remainder to Anthy. and Wm. Fynche aforeſaid for ever. Pr. 11 March, 1574.

1580. Peter Lenniter Vicar of Eaſtry wills to be buried in Chancel of ſd. Church. Pr. 11th Feb., 1580.

1580. Henry Boteler, of Hardenden, Gent. Wills his Body to be buried in Eaſtry Church—to repair of the Church 10s.—to the Poor of Eaſtry 20s. many other Legacies &c.—Wife Elizth.—Son Richd. —Urſula Green his Siſter's Daughter—Sibell Symes and Dorothy Web his Wife's Siſters—Siſter Elizth. Lee wife of Jno. Lee jurat of Sandw.—Siſter Margt. Salſtanſtol Wife of Jno. Saltl.—Sarah their Dr. and Elizth. Green another Dr.—Directs his Perſonals to be inventoried by Mr. Thos. Boys Mr. Vincent Boys & Mr. Thos. Nevynſon—His new built Houſe at Harnden—To Son Richd. all the Lands &c. which he had by his 1ſt wife mother of ſd. Richd. in St. Clements Sandwh. and in Eaſtry[*] and other eſtates in Sandwh.—to him likewiſe in Tail male the Manſion Houſe at Hardenden and Lands belonging in Eaſtry and Northbn.—Remainder to ſon Wm. remainder to ſon John—to ſaid Richd. Barn, Dovehouſe, Lands, &c. in Word wᵗʰ like remainders—to Son Wmˑ and Male iſſue Houſe & Manor of Poulton in Woodneſbro' alſo his new Houſe in St. Marys Sandwh., alſo 14 ã in Woodh. on north ſide of the cauſey [cauſeway]. To Son John and male iſſue Houſe, &c., and Lands at Hacklinge in Word : alſo ſeveral Houſes in Sandh. particularly principal meſſuage in Strand Street : alſo 9 ã of Land on Sth. ſide the cauſey Woodh.—to ſon Willm. a Houſe at Sandh. occupied by his Brother Jno. Saltanſtole—to ſon Richd. two ſmall pieces of Paſture on Sth. ſide the cauſey.

Pr. 4 Aug., 1580.

1585. Richd. Auſten of Eaſtry Yeoman wills to be bur. in Eaſtry Church Dr. Mary—Dr. Margt. wife of Jno. Dod—Dr. Elizth. married—ſon John—wife Alice—his Houſe at Harnden—Jno. Hilde of Den Cᵗ.—to ſon Vincent (his Exor.) his Tents. and Lands in Quyledge of Harnden in fee of Adiſham—ſon Jno.—to ſon Richard his Lands at Tykenhurſt in Northbourne but wᵗʰ this condition that they ſhall be Vincent's provided he pays Richd. £100 for them.

Pr. 17 July, 1585.

1591. Saphire Paramour of Stattenborow, Yeoman, to be buried in yᵉ Ch. Yard—to the Poor of Eaſtry 40s.—to the Churchwardens

---

[*] This refers to the farm at the corner of the Mill Lane.

Poors Fund 40s.—Son in law Walter Nower—wife Jone Exr.—
witnesses Saml. Nichols Vicar, Wm. Paramr.   Pr. 1591.

1593. Thomas Appleton of Eastry yeoman—gives £5 for the perpetual
benefit of the Poor of Eastry to be either laid out in Lands or the
Interest in Cloaths &c. to be bestowed at the discretion of 6 of
the principal Inhabitants, the Profits to be received yearly by the
Church Wardens—bequeaths in the same manner £5 to Wood-
nesbro'—£5 to Goodnestone and £5 to Mynster. He wills to
Thos. eldest son of his brother John, for 10 years, his Possession
for divers Years to come in certain Lands call'd Hardiles in Parish
Woodnesboro', he paying to the Queen 3s. 4d. annually and the
sd. yearly sums of £5 at the terms stated in his will. Mentions
his two Daurs.—Whereas he was indebted to Danl. Wollet
Gent. £430 for a Purchase, wills that said Thos. and John
Appleton shall satisfy him for it by sufficient securities so as to
procure his full release, in consideration of which he gives to said
Thos. and his Heirs for ever his Lease of Manor and Parsonage
of Woodnesbo' and all his goods and furniture in said Manor and
Parsonage House, all Corn, &c., in the Barnes Granarys, &c., &c.
                         Pr. 13 Nov., 1593.

1601. Richd. Boteler of Eastry Gent. to be buried in Eastry Church—
Daurs. Elizth. and Katharine—2nd son Henry—Matthew 3rd
Son—Thos. 4th son—Richard youngest son—to poor of Eastry
40s.—wife Catharine Exr.—To eldest son Jonathan all the lands
he purchased of Vincent Austen in Eastry or elsewhere—also 9
acres of Marsh Land in Woodnesborough that came to him by
the death of Brother Jno.—also his house at Chilham—also certain Houses in Sandwich that came to him by his Brother John's
death—also his now Dwelling House Lands &c. in Eastry [He-

ronden] and Northbourn in fee, alſo Houſe Lands Barn and Stables in Eaſtry Street [yᵉ corner farm in yᵉ Street, now in the occupation of Mr. W. Pittock]—To ſon Henry 12 acres of Garden Land in St. Clements, Sandwich—to his ſons Mathw. Thos. and Richd. Houſes in Sandwich and Lands near them.   Pr. 27 Ap. 1601.

1607.   John Whitfeild of Eaſtry yeoman—Daughter Elizth. wife of John Mantill—Sons Richd. Michael, John, Andrew—Daurs. Margt. Alice, Kath., Dorothy, Fortune and Elizabeth—wife Amy—Son Thos. Exor—to ſon Andrew a tenement in Eaſtry Street—to ſon Michl. 2 ā nearly of Brook Land at Hacklinge and the Old Orchard of ½ an acre lying at Eaſtry at Selſtone againſt the Street gate of his (the Teſtators) Dwelling Houſe—to Son Thos. his dwelling Houſe or Mancyon at Selſton wᵗʰ the Lands &c. unbequeathed in Eaſtry in the fee of Adiſham, and all lands in Streeting and Woodh. and 14 acres of Marſh Land in Word call'd Butler's Marſhe—wife to have her living and dwelling in the Parlor at the South Hedd of the Houſe and chamber over the ſame wᵗʰ ſundry allowances, &c.   Pr. 1607.

1607.   Chriſtopher Fynche of Faverſham (inter alia) wills to ſon Thos. his tenement or Meſſ. called Copers wᵗʰ its Lands and Appurtenances in Eaſtry—to his 3 ſons Thos. Richd. and Mark one Tenemt. or Meſſ: Barnes Buildings and Apps. and 42 ā in Eaſtry and Ham, and a Tenemt. or Parcel of Land in the Occ. of Sr. Roger Nevinſon Knt. and another Tenemt. or Parcel of Land in Eaſtry for ever—his wife Margt.—his lands at a place in Eaſtry call'd Butts.   1607.

1611.   Nicholas Squier of Eaſtry Yeoman, to be bur. in Eaſtry Church —4 Daurs. 2 Sons.   Pr. 3 Feb., 1611.

1613.   Jane Appleton of Eaſtry Widow—Dr. Mary wife of Thos. Kingſ-

ford—Dr. Bettris [Beatrice] wife of Nichs. Towne—fons John
and Thos. Hild—to fon John Hild her tent. and Lands in Eaftry
or Word near a place called Felderland, remainder to fon Wm.,
remainder to fon Thos.—wills her Tent. in Eaftry Street to Elizth.
Appleton her Daur.—her other lands in Eaftry.

Pr. Octr. 1613.

1616. Willm. Man of Canterbury Efqre. (inter alia) wills 19 ā. in Eaftry
which he purchafed of Sr. Peter Manwood.

Pr. 17 May, 1616.

1617. Katherine Boteler of Eaftry widow wills &c. to be buried in
Eaftry Church near the grave of her deceafed Hufband Richd.
Boteler—youngeft fon Thos.—God-daughter Katherine Rigden
daur. of Richd. Rigden of Chilham and Elizth. his wife, daughter
to Teftatrix. God-daur. Katherine Whitfield one of the Daurs.
of Thos. Whitfield of Eaftry and Katherine his wife the daur.
likewife of the Teftx.—Brothers Henry and Peter Hawker—fifter
Mildred Steele widow—Jane Idley widow—to Ch. Wardens of
Eaftry 50s. to remain in a Stock for the ufe of the poor—to the
Poor of the faid Parifh 50s. likewife Eldeft fon Jonathan Exor.

Pr. 29 July 1617.

Chronological Table of Events.

	A.D.
Murder of Ethelbert and Etheldred at Eaſtry Court	665
Palace and Manor at Eaſtry given to Chriſt Church, Canterbury	978
Thomas à Becket concealed at Eaſtry Court	1164
A Survey of Lands in Eaſtry Hundred made for repair of banks	1289
Bounds of Pariſh ſought out, in conſequence of diſpute	1356
The Vicarage of Eaſtry conſtituted and endowed	1367
Henry VI. granted a yearly Fair and Weekly Market at Eaſtry	1450
Pariſh Regiſters firſt ordered to be kept	1538
The Eaſtry Regiſters were commenced	1559
Eaſtry Regiſters newly copied out by order of Convocation	1598
Survey made of the Rectorial property by order of Parliament	1650
The Veſtry of S. Mary, Sandwich reaſſerted their right to Puttockſdown	1676
The Roof of the Nave rebuilt, the "pitch" being lowered	1687
Diſpute between Mr. Creſſener and the Pariſhioners	1708
Communion Plate given to the Church by Vicar Creſſener	1718
The foundations of the old Chapel of Shrinkling diſcovered	1784
The Vicarage rebuilt by Mr. Randolph	1821
The Chapelry of Worth ſeparated from Eaſtry	1854
The Pariſh of Worth conſtituted a Vicarage	1867
The Roof of the Nave of the Church reſtored	1869
Buttſole pond cleared out after long drought	1870

Index.

𝔉𝔦𝔫𝔦𝔰.

S. & J. BRAWN, PRINTERS, 13, GATE STREET, HIGH HOLBORN.

www.ingramcontent.com/pod-product-compliance
Lightning Source LLC
Chambersburg PA
CBHW020051030726
47498CB00006B/1729